BRASS & GLASS

THE CASK OF CRANGLIMMERING

DAWN VOGEL

RAZORGIRL
PRESS

Published by Razorgirl Press.

First U.S. Edition: March 2017

To Jeremy, Nate, Torrey, Dietrich, and Sarah, who understand exactly why this book had to be about airship pirates.

CHAPTER ONE

THE DECK OF *The Silent Monsoon* pitched, and Svetlana clung to the polished brass wheel of the airship. She turned to look at the pilot with her good eye, not daring to release the wheel long enough to adjust her monocular. "Dammit, Jo, will you please keep this boat level?"

"Trying, Cap'n. Talk to your mechanic about the stabilizers." Jo's speech came out in bursts, punctuated with grunts. She struggled to maintain the position of the altitude controls, her muscles taut and knuckles showing bone-white through her tan skin.

"Captain, we're near enough to run out the ship-to-ship. Err, I think." The ship's doctor, Annette, stood near the speaking tube, the length of hollow brass that allowed conversation between two airships. Air rushed through the telescoped metal tube, creating a high-pitched whistling that grated on Svetlana's nerves. Outside of the windscreen, the bulk of a second airship hovered perilously close. Chrome detailing gleamed across its dark teak hull. The bright blue and white flags marked it as one of Heliopolis's Port Authority vessels.

"You think?" Jo asked.

"Yes, I think," Annette spat back, her dark brown eyes flashing. "I can't be certain, seeing as this isn't exactly part of my job. Perhaps if our communications officer hadn't gone and gotten himself arrested, and if you hadn't abandoned him to that fate, he could be more certain if we were near enough."

Svetlana shook her head. "Holler at them if you want, but I don't think they're too interested in talking. And I just want to get Athos back. Are we close enough to net him?"

Jo looked out the windscreen. "I'm not sure we can get that close without ramming them."

"Well, that is an option."

The windscreen fogged as the airship passed through a cloud bank. From somewhere in the distance came a familiar war cry, followed by a muffled thump outside of the bridge.

"Or perhaps he'll just find his way over here on his own." Svetlana spun the directional wheel to swing *The Silent Monsoon* away from the Port Authority airship. Three additional thumps followed in rapid succession before Svetlana's ship maneuvered away.

"Boarded?" Annette asked. She looked toward the altitude controls. Svetlana turned to follow her gaze. Jo had vanished from the bridge, the controls she had been manning locked into position.

"Apparently," Svetlana said, beckoning Annette to the directional wheel. "Hold this course, unless—." A pained wail interrupted the rest of her orders. Svetlana cursed under her breath and broke into a run toward the aft deck.

Sounds of pummeling and Athos' sharp intakes of breath kept Svetlana's pace quick. As soon as she rounded the corner to where the fight was taking place, a loud voice boomed. "That's enough, Henry. Captain Tereshchenko, we're just here for a social visit."

Svetlana surveyed the scene. Three uniformed men, wearing the insignia of the Heliopolis Port Authority, surrounded Athos. Athos' head hung forward, spilling a mass of blond and brown curls across his face. His white shirt was torn and caked with dirt.

Even if Athos had not been possessed of a charming personality, his physical appearance would still have earned him hordes of admirers. His skin was the fine pale copper of a new small coin, and his hair was in tight curls, worn past his shoulders. He was tall without being imposing and muscular without being bulky. Svetlana, on the other hand, knew him too well to be swayed by his good looks. After she'd inadvertently rescued him from a bar fight when they were in the Air Fleet Academy together, the two had become fast friends. Even years later, he was still getting into trouble, and she was still bailing him out.

One bravo held Athos' thick arms behind his back, while a second bravo stood in front of him, fist at the ready. A third man, tan with hair the color of old straw, and with corporal's bars decorating his uniform, leaned against the railing of the deck, examining his fingernails.

"I didn't know social visits usually came with beatings, Corporal Richards." Svetlana slowed her pace and approached with a slight swagger in her step, stopping nearer to him than social niceties dictated and crossing one arm over her chest while she adjusted her monocular with the other. Richards changed from being a shapeless blur to a human-shaped blur. She shifted her head to peer at him with her left eye. Richards towered over Svetlana, but she glared up at him all the same. "What's the occasion?"

Richards took a half step back and gestured to Athos with a smirk. "Tucker here ... I'm sorry, Tucker, I don't know your rank around here. What is it? Drunkard Tucker?"

Athos looked up from under his curls and glared at Richards. His eyes were crystalline blue with a glassy sheen that wasn't normally there. A shiner had begun to blossom around his right eye, and dried blood left dark trails through his mustache and goatee. "Sod off," he slurred.

"Commander Tucker," Svetlana said, from between clenched teeth.

"Oh, so you're still keeping to the Air Fleet command structure? How cute." Richards smirked. His breath hung foul between them, bitterly scented by some pungent tea.

"The Air Fleet took their command structure from the sailing ships of the old days. Why wouldn't we use it?"

"Not here to bicker. As I said, just a social call. I'd like to talk about an exchange. My men found Tucker in the city center. What were the charges, Henry?"

Henry, the bravo in front of Athos, bald with skin the color of a fish's belly, answered. "Drunk and disorderly. Consorting with known prostitutes. Oh, and assaulting an officer of the law."

Svetlana smirked. "Yes, that sounds just like Athos. And what exactly do you propose to exchange him for?"

"Well, it's said that you're harboring a wanted fugitive. One Josephine Dean?"

"Jo Dean, the infamous pirate?" Svetlana gasped, feigning an upper class accent. "Oh my, I can't possibly imagine that horrible woman being here. Why, I'd just need a big strong corporal like you to protect me from her!"

"Then perhaps we'll have a look around for her."

"Suit yourself. But I don't think you'll find her."

"Of course not. Somehow she always seems to bugger off when the law's at hand. So I suppose we'll just have to see what else you might have in your hold." He started to turn away, toward her blind side, and Svetlana shifted to keep him in her sights. "Say, you didn't happen to take on liquor as a part of your cargo today, did you?"

"What ship doesn't take on liquor at every port?" she asked with a laugh, gesturing at Athos. "Guess he was just holding his share in his gut, huh?"

"Oh no, I doubt it. We're looking for a very specific cask. One for rarified tastes. The sort of thing you don't just pick up at the usual suppliers."

"'Fraid not, Corporal Richards. We're all square. You can review our cargo manifest at the Port Authority."

"Shame. If you had that cask, we'd clear out of here and have the charges against Tucker dropped. No questions asked."

Richards' eyelid trembled when he spoke. The bravo holding Athos licked his lips. The bald one, Henry, stared straight ahead, but a bead of sweat slid down his nose, despite the crisp winter air.

"I'm thinking it's worth a bit more than that to you. Do I sense someone offering a reward for this liquor?"

Richards' face slid into a sly smile. "I've heard that there might be."

Athos caught Svetlana's good eye and mouthed a single word. "Mill."

"Ten percent," Svetlana said.

Richards blinked and turned back to her.

"And Athos, of course," she said.

"Alright, fair enough. Ten percent, and we release Tucker. No charges."

Svetlana looked over Richards with her good eye. His hands shook, though he kept them clenched at his sides to try to hide it. "What's in the cask?" she asked.

In a whisper, with the reverence used when speaking of the Skyfather, he said, "Cranglimmering."

Svetlana's hand flew up and covered her mouth in an ineffectual attempt to hide her shock. She chewed at her finger for half a second before she responded. "How long does the offer stand?"

"Bring it back before it's uncorked, and we'll call it good. Ten percent of the reward. After it's uncorked—" He shrugged. "Well, it's not worth squat to us then."

Svetlana nodded, and Richards responded in kind. As soon as Richards turned around, his man released his grip on Athos' arms. Athos crumpled to the deck in a tangle of limbs. Henry blew on a small chrome whistle, and the Port Authority ship, which had continued to keep pace with *The Silent Monsoon*, maneuvered alongside for the officers to board. Only after Richards had left the ship did Athos prop himself up, his arms shaking.

Annette rushed to his side, her long legs folding beneath her as she crouched. Dark hair pulled back into a messy bun and sleeves rolled up to her elbows, she pulled up Athos' chin. "Drugged?" she asked.

"Yeah. Was drinkin' tea at Abelone's. Vision got all fuzzy, and then I started gettin' punched."

Annette looked back at Svetlana. For a moment, Annette's true age showed in her eyes. They were so dark brown that they looked black, the same color as her hair. Her deep coppery brown skin made them look even darker. The skin around her eyes creased with worry. "And they say there's no honor among thieves. I think the blame is misplaced."

"No, no honor here either. But now we've got something to look for. Where's Indy?" Before she turned around, Indigo, the ship's mechanic, was at her right elbow. He was a growing teenage boy, all flailing long limbs and bones nearly jutting through his pale freckled skin. His bones had been that close to the surface a year previous, when Svetlana and her crew found him, but in that year, she swore that all of his limbs had doubled in length, shooting him up to her own height, with imminent threats of surpassing her any day now.

His hair, the source of his nickname, made him easy to spot. The unusual color was common among the people of his homeland, in differing shades normally reserved for flowers and birds in warm climates. The few who left that tropical place often went by the color of their hair as a nickname. Svetlana had heard his real name uttered once, a multi-syllabic thing that was far too long for everyday use.

"Dammit, boy, how do you do that?"

Indigo shrugged, a small smile on his lips. "Magic, I guess." His eyes, almost the same shade as his hair, twinkled as his gaze played across Svetlana's monocular. He always approached Svetlana on her blind side.

Svetlana sighed. "Did we sustain any damages you can't fix in flight?"

The boy shook his head, his wavy hair flopping in every direction. "Not even a scratch."

"Nice flying, all. Annette, take Athos below. I'll join you when I'm sure that our visitors are on their way."

Of all the parts of *The Silent Monsoon*, the mess was the one that felt most like home to Svetlana, especially when her crew was all there.

Svetlana heard cries of pain as she approached. Sunlight streamed through the high windows that ringed the room and illuminated the worn oak table that Athos clutched as Annette prodded the swollen parts of his face. The odor of camphor hit Svetlana like a wall, but she continued into the dining area.

Indigo sat on the counter of the kitchen proper, tinkering with a pair of goggles and ignoring everything around him. Jo lounged in a chair, feet propped up on the table in front of her. The pilot had added a dark salmon colored scarf wound around her neck and shoulders, her chestnut hair mussed where the scarf had been moments before. She prided herself on her long locks, which grew thick to her waist, but which she never bound up, even when she was hard at work. Her vanity had gotten her in trouble in her youth, but now at least she knew to cover her hair when the authorities came calling.

"Not bad, Captain," Jo said, clapping slowly. "Didn't give me up, got Athos back, and got us a job. Not bad at all for what should have just been a lazy stop in Heliopolis."

"No such thing as a lazy stop for us," Svetlana replied evenly, tugging at the straps that held her monocular to her blind eye and letting the entire contraption slip down around her neck.

The monocular was a curious device of brass and glass, held to Svetlana's head with leather straps and assorted buckles. She had been born blind in her right eye, and failed to qualify as an Air Fleet pilot because of it. One of the Fleet's doctors had handed her the monocular at dinner one evening. It didn't give her the vision she longed for, but it made her aware of shapes and movement to her right. Svetlana had decided that she liked how it looked more than how it functioned, and wore it until the brass rubbed her skin raw. The warm air inside the mess felt better on her face than the cold air outdoors. She relished the moments when she felt comfortable not wearing the monocular.

"So Richards has taken to waylaying and beating senior officers so he can negotiate for Jo?" Annette asked. "Does that seem risky to anyone else?"

"Maybe he's just finally appreciating what I'm worth," Jo replied, arms crossed over her chest. She turned to Svetlana. "But I have a better question. Why're we working for Richards now?"

"If we were really working for Richards, do you actually think I would have settled for ten percent?" Svetlana climbed onto one of the chairs and perched on the back, hunching so her hair draped over her bad eye like a veil. Though her crew had seen her right eye plenty of times, she always wore her jet black hair short and choppy, and parted on the left so that the bulk of it fell over her right eye when she removed the monocular. "No, of course I wouldn't. But now we know two things. One, there's a cask of Cranglimmering that someone's lost track of. Two, someone's willing to pay a million Quinpence to get it back." She paused, chewing at her lip. "Now, if I'm reading this right, the person who lost track of the Cask isn't the same one who's offering a mill for it. Athos, I don't suppose you heard anything while you were out getting yourself arrested?"

"Not exactly, no. But the 'known prostitutes' I was allegedly consorting with were my elderly aunts. Auntie Riza said that there have been an awful lot of airships with hastily thrown together flags in Heliopolis recently. She was absolutely appalled by how often the stripe widths were mismatched."

"Seamstresses," Annette scoffed. "Will nothing make them happy?"

"Well, now Auntie Cady said that there was one thing they were looking forward to. The Mayor was throwing an engagement party for his daughter, Hortence. The invitations were sent and all. And then the family printed a retraction in the paper. Scandalous!"

Jo pounded her fist on the table, green eyes flashing. "Athos, would you please, for the love of all that is unholy and wrong in this world, just speak plainly, once?"

"Just as soon as you start earning your keep, Jo Dean. Who is flying this thing when you have to hide from the authorities, by the by? Deck was pitchin' something fierce when I came on board."

"It's handled," Svetlana said, climbing down from her chair and leaning over the table. "And I'd appreciate it if the two of you would keep your little spats out of my meeting, am I clear?"

Athos and Jo both nodded and looked away from one another. "Sorry, Cap'n," Athos muttered. "Anyway, that's what I know."

"Hmmm," Svetlana mused. "So that makes it the Bartram Cask that's gone missing, then?"

Annette nodded and headed into the kitchen. "I'm impressed, Svetlana. All these years, right under your nose, and you never once thought to steal it?"

Svetlana laughed. "It's never been worth a million Quinpence before. I figured it for a couple thousand, maybe. And it's not exactly pocket-sized." Her expression shifted to a frown as she considered just how near she had been to such a treasure. "I'm also a little surprised they were storing it on Heliopolis. I thought the Bartrams had land somewhere."

Indigo raised his hand. Svetlana arched an eyebrow. "What's Crang ... Crang ..." he began.

"Cranglimmering," Jo finished for him. "Well, boy, it's something that you'll learn to appreciate when you're older. But let's just say that if you ever do get a taste of it, you'll never be able to drink your watered-down grog with a happy feeling in your heart again."

"It is, if the stories are to be believed, one of the finest whiskeys ever made." Annette rummaged around the kitchen as she spoke, putting a pot on the stove. The smell of camphor was soon covered up by the earthy burning peat. "Seven casks, to be aged seventy years. Course, a few of the owners got antsy and opened theirs after twenty. Still was a mighty fine whiskey, even unfinished. And the number of the remaining casks of Cranglimmering can be counted on one hand."

Athos jerked his head up. "There was one other thing. One of Richards' bully boys, Tom, the one who was holding me, said something about a promotion. But then Richards hushed him up right quick."

"Interesting. You don't suppose it's all just a ruse to draw me and Jo out? Or to catch us red-handed with the Cranglimmering once we've found it?"

"Could be," Athos agreed. "Wouldn't put it past Richards, at any rate. But it's worth looking into, don't you think?"

Svetlana nodded. "Jo, get your stupid hat and whatever other disguise you need. We need more information." Athos started to protest, but Svetlana shut him down with a look. "Athos, your pretty face isn't going anywhere. You're too obvious right now."

"I'm not the one with an official bounty on my head."

"True," Jo said as she wound the scarf over her hair. "But unlike you, we don't need to be the center of attention."

Athos started to rise from his chair. Svetlana placed her small hand on his chest. "Enough. Stay here and let Annette get you all patched up. Ship is yours till I'm back."

"So, Captain," Jo called back over her shoulder. "What's our brilliant plan today?"

"First part of the plan involves you not calling me Captain so loudly. Second part involves you slowing down so I can keep up, and we can have this conversation at a more civilized volume."

Jo paused and allowed Svetlana to catch up to her. Svetlana had covered her head with a black shawl that hung low enough in the front to obscure both her eyes. It rendered the monocular useless, so she had replaced that with a plain black eyepatch. The rest of her clothes were black as well, in sharp contrast with Jo's outfit of clashing colors. The pilot wore her dark salmon scarf pulled up over her hair, another scarf in pale blue covering the lower half of her face, a loose white blouse, and a skirt in a riot of greens, browns, and oranges.

"Well, sneaking's right out, so I guess we go begging near the Mayor's house," Svetlana said.

"You couldn't have told me sneaking was the plan before we left?"

"Didn't honestly have much of a plan, other than getting out here." Svetlana did not want to have this conversation on the crowded, noisy streets of Heliopolis. But Jo seemed bound and determined to push the point until they did. "You've got to ease up on Athos. Your bickering is driving a wedge into the crew."

Jo threw her hands up into the air. "Really? You dragged me out here in this ridiculous outfit to tell me to ease up on Athos? Tell you what. Tell him to stop with the lying and the 'aunties,' and I'll ease up."

Svetlana shook her head. "Josephine, I warned you when I brought you on board. Athos has always been a flirt. Hell, when we were at the Academy, he took me on a date and went home with our waitress. You told me you didn't care. But clearly, you do."

"Whatever," Jo spat back. "We get this cask and the mill, and I won't care anymore."

"Suit yourself." Svetlana looked away and spotted an old washerwoman hunched over her basket. "Hang on. There's a plan. Grandmother, where does your load go?"

The old woman looked up at Svetlana and stared at her for several long moments. "Home with me."

"We'll carry it there for you, if you'll let us borrow it for a while. You can wait for us in the tea house up the way." Svetlana flipped a full Quinpence gold coin to the woman.

The woman's hand darted up to catch the coin, faster than most people of advanced age could be expected to react. Svetlana looked at her more closely, suspecting some sort of trickery or a trap. But when the woman bit the coin, her teeth stained brown from decades of tea drinking, Svetlana was reassured that she was just a washerwoman. The woman nodded, and Svetlana walked over and hefted the laundry basket. "Skyfather's blessings, Grandmother. We'll be back in an hour."

Svetlana and Jo climbed staircase after staircase to reach higher ground, where the Mayor's estate overlooked the entire city. As they got nearer to the walled home, Svetlana's smuggler instincts kicked in. She looked for places where the wall might be easier to bypass, for entrances that could accommodate something the size of the Cask. Aside from the main entrance, barred with an ornate iron gate, and the back entrance, wide open, but guarded, she could see no other adequate passages through the wall.

She squinted as she looked skyward. An air approach was possible, but it would be in plain sight the entire time. It would be impossible to avoid attention, yet the thief must have done just that for there to have been nothing in the papers about the Cask.

"This place is a fortress," Jo muttered, echoing Svetlana's thoughts.

"Just keep your head down and act like you belong here. I want to get inside and speak to some of the staff."

Jo nodded and Svetlana led the way to the back entrance. A pair of guards blocked her way.

"Come to pick up the washing, sirs," she murmured.

"Washing's already been picked up." One of the guards stepped closer and poked at the basket. "That's it right there, even."

Svetlana cursed under her breath. The second guard raised a whistle to his lips, but before he even blew it, Svetlana heard Jo's running footfalls behind her. As she turned to follow Jo, Svetlana saw the pilot brought up short by a member of the City Watch.

"Problem?" The watchwoman called out to the Mayor's guards.

"Forgive us," Svetlana called out. "Just a mistake, we don't want any trouble."

The watchwoman disregarded Svetlana's response and continued to look to the guards. "No real problem, Lieutenant," the guard who had poked the basket called back.

Jo jutted out one hip and placed her hand on it. Even without seeing Jo's face, Svetlana could envision the expression on it. She tossed a quick mental prayer skyward, in the hopes that Jo would hold her tongue. But even the Skyfather himself could not hope to control Jo's mouth. "See, no problem, *Lieutenant*." The sarcasm dripped from the last word. "May I pass?"

Svetlana scurried to Jo's side. "Forgive my assistant, she forgets her place."

The watchwoman studied Jo's face, and then turned her scrutiny to Svetlana. "You look familiar."

Jo shrank back at that and fumbled at her scarves. "Oh, no, people just say that about me a lot. I have a common face."

Footsteps approached Svetlana's blind side. One of the guards spoke. "These women said they were coming to collect our laundry, but the washerwoman's already come and gone. They've got her basket."

The watchwoman arched an eyebrow. Jo trembled beside Svetlana, and Svetlana reached out her hand to try to calm her pilot. As her fingertips brushed Jo's arm, Jo bolted. "Shit," Svetlana said.

Jo had already ducked into an alley by the time the watchwoman called out, "Stop!" Svetlana considered chucking the laundry basket at the watchwoman and guard, and then following Jo's lead, but she felt a pang of guilt at failing to return the old woman's livelihood. She tightened her grip on the basket and swung it in a wide arc. The guard and the watchwoman both leapt back, out of its path, and Svetlana used the extra breathing room to run in the direction Jo had gone.

Jo was almost a block away by the time Svetlana reached the alley. "Wait for me," she hissed, hoping that Jo could hear her over the growing hubbub behind them. Jo glanced back over her shoulder and visibly relaxed, though she only slowed her pace a bit. Before too long, she disappeared into a darkened area. Svetlana hurried to catch up, ducking behind discarded furniture and garbage in the alley when she could.

She reached the doorway just as Jo backed out of the building, hands held in front of her. A slender black tube was pressed against the center of Jo's chest, wielded like a pistol by a freckled girl with stubby pigtails in a brilliant sunshine orange color. Svetlana placed one hand in front of Jo's chest and used the other to tear off her own scarf. "Deliah?"

The pigtailed girl cocked her head to one side. Her lips, stained bluish from some sort of berries, moved silently for a moment. "Indigo's captain," she finally replied.

"Svetlana."

Deliah smiled. "Yes, Svetlana. Indigo's captain." She glanced at Jo, eyes narrowed. "Friend?"

Jo pulled her scarves down and smiled at the girl. "Josephine. I'm Indy's pilot."

Deliah frowned for a moment, but then smiled at both of the women. "Come in. Be quiet. No Watch allowed here."

Svetlana nodded and followed the girl into the darkness. Once Jo had reentered the building, the door slammed behind them. Svetlana spun around, and Deliah stood behind them, a small flame at the end of the black tube.

"A flame stick? You were threatening Jo with a flame stick?" Svetlana asked. "What were you planning to do, light a campfire for her?"

The girl smiled her impish grin and shrugged. In the flickering light, she looked downright demonic.

Svetlana had dealt with the urchins of Heliopolis before and knew that Deliah was one of the few who could be trusted, even if her choice in weaponry was suspect. "Since you're here, I need to hire you for two tasks."

Deliah nodded. "I can do things for you today."

Svetlana held out the laundry basket. "Take this to the grandmother at Hala's Tea House."

The girl accepted the basket and turned to leave.

"Wait, do that last!"

Deliah cocked her head to the side as she turned back around. "Yes. Then paid first?"

Svetlana nodded and fished around in her purse, producing three silver coins.

Deliah smiled. "What's next?"

"We need information. Someone took a very large box from the big house at the top of the platform."

"Yes." Deliah smiled. "Very clever. Do clever things during Lift. The Watch doesn't walk during Lift."

Svetlana sighed. Heliopolis was a platform city that owed its lofty location to the power of a geyser. Engines along the underside of the platform ran on the hydrothermic energy. But the geyser erupted four times a day, and even the most efficient engines had difficulty keeping a platform the size of Heliopolis elevated for a full six hours. So the platform descended slowly, only to be buoyed back up at Lift—the time when the geyser refilled the hydrothermic cells. Being out and about when scalding hot water pushed

Heliopolis back up into the sky was simply not done—warning bells rang throughout Heliopolis to encourage the citizens to take shelter during each geyser eruption.

"Well, that does cut down on the number of people who might have spotted a ship," Svetlana murmured. "Do you know where the box went?"

"Yes."

Svetlana waited for Deliah to say more, but the girl only grinned. "Okay, where did it go?"

"Far away."

Jo sighed. "This is worse than talking to Indy," she muttered.

Hushing Jo with a glare, Svetlana turned back to Deliah. "Which far away?"

"It's not there anymore," Deliah replied with a frown. "What you need to find is with Mirage. He will take it to Rrusadon."

"Mirage? The box is on *Calypso's Price*?"

Deliah laughed. "Oh yes. Many boxes. And one big one."

Svetlana smiled at Jo. "That wasn't so hard, now was it?"

Jo frowned. "Yeah, not hard at all."

As she handed Deliah the silver coins, Svetlana watched the girl put them away, waiting to see if her small hand would snake out for additional payment.

Her hand still in the pocket where she had placed the money, Deliah asked, "Now take the laundry to Grandmother at Hala's Tea House?"

"Yes, good."

"Tell Indigo that I said hello," Deliah whispered shyly as she slipped out the door and into the alley.

CHAPTER TWO

LUSH FOLIAGE SPILLED over the edges of the platform that held Rrusadon aloft. Its purpose was to camouflage the steel honeycomb matrix and geyser receptors beneath the pleasure platform, but its current status was interfering with Svetlana's line of sight. Finally, she put down her spyglass. "Stupid plants. How am I supposed to see *Calypso's Price*?"

"The boys should be back soon," Annette said. "They'll have noticed if she's here. I just hope our information is right. If they don't have the Cranglimmering, this is going to be a wasted trip."

Indigo poked his head in the door. "Athos is going to a party. Big one."

Jo rolled her eyes and tugged on Indigo's hair a little rougher than the boy was prepared for. "Of course he is. I told you to bring him back with you, Indy. What happened?"

The boy shifted his gaze downward. "Lost him."

"What sort of party?" Svetlana asked.

"New mayor." Indigo fished around in his pockets and came up with a slip of paper. "Larson Kavisoli."

"Kavisoli?" Jo asked, snatching the paper from Indigo and verifying its contents. "But that puts another crime family in the Republican Senate—"

"And assuming that their track record holds, it'll give the Trade Coalition another vote," Svetlana finished. Her brow creased. "But that's not even close to a majority. I'm failing to see the connection here. I mean sure, it's great news for the crime families and the Trade Coalition. But I don't think it's Cranglimmering great. Cranglimmering great would be ... a Kavisoli in command of the Air Fleet or something."

"So they're inappropriate drinkers?" Jo asked.

"No. There's something more going on here. I need visual," Svetlana said.

"I'm coming with." Jo scrambled to cram her bare feet back into her boots.

"Oh?" Svetlana asked.

"Indy couldn't get Athos to come back, so someone's got to retrieve him. If something funny is going on, we may have to get out of here in a hurry."

"All of that is true. But I'm thinking we don't want to cause a big scene in the middle of a party. I'll find Athos and bring him back."

"You can't go by yourself," Jo said. She spun and glared at Indigo. "Ship's policy. No man left behind. You're not supposed to leave Athos out on his own."

"He told me it would be okay with the captain," Indigo said, his voice suddenly sulky and sounding much more like the young boy that the crew sometimes forgot he was.

"Lesson one? Athos lies," Jo snapped.

"Enough," Svetlana said. "Indy, Jo is right. If you leave the ship, stay with whoever you're with. It's safer that way. Jo, you're staying on the ship with Indy. I'll take Annette with me."

"Me?" Annette looked surprised to be brought into the conversation. "I'm perfectly happy staying here."

"Indy's already been out, and he doesn't blend well. And I need Jo onboard to be able to get the ship moving fast if we need an escape. Jo, take us up to the north end and wait for us there."

Jo saluted, though her expression was far less reverent. "Aye, Cap'n. Don't have too much fun at that party."

Svetlana grimaced. "No worries there."

Walking across Rrusadon coated Svetlana and Annette with a fine layer of sweat and grime. The temperature on Rrusadon, like most of the outlying parts of the Republic, was easily twenty degrees higher than it had been in Heliopolis. Far beneath the pleasure platform, the sea roiled. Svetlana didn't know the timing on the geyser that provided the necessary energy to lift the city above the seas but speculated that it must be a frequent eruption that kept such a large city aloft. Even the heavy jungle foliage could not completely dissipate the sulfurous odor that lingered on all of the geyser-powered platforms.

On reaching the populated portion of Rrusadon, Svetlana's heart sank. Any hopes they had of blending in with the citizens of Rrusadon crumbled when she saw the fringes of Larson Kavisoli's inauguration party.

"Was that a stuffed peacock attached to that woman's hat?" Annette whispered as she tried to wipe the dirt from her face. She cleared one swath of flesh just to have fresh sweat spring up where her handkerchief had been.

Svetlana batted away some sort of flying insect that buzzed near her face. "Yeah, I think so."

Annette looked down at her plain dungarees and work shirt, spotted with damp patches. "So, pass ourselves off as party staff?"

"Doubtful. I think that peacock woman *was* party staff." The flat, cleared area where the party was taking place had decorative spires, studded with windows, marking the corners of the courtyard and providing structure from which strings of paper lanterns were hung. Though it was still daytime, Svetlana could picture how it would look in the evening, as the party continued after the inauguration. One end of the courtyard stretched beyond the towers and into the manicured edges of what she suspected was to become the mayoral estate, also filled with milling party guests. And beyond that, the docking area was spotted with airships of every size and shape. "Let's see if we can't get up in one of those towers and get a better view," she suggested. "Might be a little bit of a breeze up there, too."

Annette nodded in agreement. The two women stuck to the edges of the crowd and made their way to the nearest of the spires. When they reached the highest level, Annette pulled on a pair of goggles Indigo had modified and scanned the party. After a few minutes, she started muttering. "No, no, no. That's not right. It's too small to be the Cranglimmering."

"Too small?" Svetlana looked in the direction where Annette's head pointed. A large crate caught her attention. "That thing is the size of a sofa!"

"The shape is wrong. The Cranglimmering wouldn't fit in a rectangular box with those dimensions. Let me try Indy's new x-ray setting." Annette made an adjustment on her goggles. An unusual blue light flickered across the surface of the lenses and she gasped.

"What? What is it?" Svetlana asked. "Tell me Indy didn't just fry your eyeballs!"

"Find Athos. Now." Annette's voice trembled on the last word.

"Annette, I'm getting the distinct impression that finding Athos is the least of my worries right now. Tell me what you saw."

"It's a bomb."

Svetlana felt dizzy as her mind raced to make sense of the situation. "We need to get back to the ship," she told Annette after a long moment. "We can use the tow cables."

Annette shook her head. "Tow cable. The starboard tow cable snapped off after that run out of Gresch. We've only got the one. We need ... we're going to have to ram it off the edge."

"There're too many buildings around it. We won't be able to get close enough. What if we defuse it?"

Annette bit her lip as she thought. "We'd have to get back to the ship and get Jo back here to do it. We might not have enough time. Maybe *Calypso's Price* has someone?"

In the distance, an airship rose into Svetlana's line of sight. The black and green stripe pattern on the balloon was distinctive. "Or maybe they just dropped it and ran. Full inflation, full engines. *Calypso's* up, up, and away."

Annette cursed, but a loud thump that shook the entire tower covered what she said. The women looked at each other before running for the stairs. Halfway down, they heard a voice drifting up.

"Are you sure your shoulder is alright?" The speaker was a breathy young woman.

"I'll be fine," Athos replied. "Just didn't realize they left these things wide open for anyone to walk into."

"They don't," Svetlana called down. "Athos Tucker, tell your friend goodbye now. We've got work to do."

Svetlana and Annette reached the lower floor of the tower in time to catch a fleeting glimpse of a barely clad woman whose exposed skin had been covered in spirals of gold paint. "Another aunt?" Annette asked.

"Cousin," Athos said with a smile.

"You must be related to half the world," Svetlana said dismissively.

Annette chuckled.

"Amusing as this may be, we don't have time for cousins. There's a bomb in the box that's supposed to hold the Cranglimmering. Jo's got the ship at the north dock. Let's go."

Athos hesitated. "Wait, and just let the bomb blow?"

Annette looked at Svetlana. "But all those people—"

Svetlana sighed. "We may not have a choice. We don't have the ability to get it out of there. We don't know how long we've got to defuse it, so we could get Jo there only to have it blow her up along with everyone else. I'm open to alternatives, if there are any to be had."

Athos shook his head. "I think we might have time. The inauguration ceremony is in about three hours. If I were going to bomb something like this, I'd have it blow right when Kavisoli is up there in front of those guests. The bigger problem is that any attempts to defuse it are going to have to be in front of all of his guests. I don't think he'll take too kindly to bringing Jo Dean in when there's Air Fleet here."

"Air Fleet?" Svetlana asked, her voice shaking. "Who?"

"Bobby, actually." Athos smiled. "He sends his love."

"Bobby Beauregard?" Annette asked, laughing.

"The one and only."

Svetlana grinned, as a plan began to unfold in her mind. "And the *Himmelgnade*?"

"At the south dock."

Svetlana's grin shifted to a full-fledged smile. "Brilliant! Annette, head back to the ship and get Jo to move her to the south end. Athos and I need to go talk to Bobby."

"You've got it," Annette replied. "And give him my love as well."

"You know, Sveta, you really do need to dress for these things," Athos said, scrutinizing Svetlana's attire. She was dressed as she often was, in simple black pants, white oversized blouse, and slim-fitting black jacket with red trim. "We've got to get you into a dress."

"No thank you. I'd rather be able to move if I need to." But Svetlana was acutely aware of the eyes of the partygoers on her, and she did feel underdressed. Even the male attendees had far more elaborate outfits than she, and the female partygoers' attire, though it ranged the spectrum in terms of style, was all the very peak of what was fashionable throughout the Republic. While Athos' own clothing—a simple blue blouse that brought out his eyes and snug-fitting trousers tucked into his high boots—paled in comparison to the rest of the crowd, he wore it in such a way that he fit in.

Athos shrugged. "Suit yourself. I saw Bobby over by the food when I was here earlier."

Looking in that direction, the press of bodies at the party was thick. "I don't see him." She turned back to Athos, who had moved away and was talking to a young man in an Air Fleet uniform. Svetlana's years in the Fleet prompted her to check his rank insignia before she approached. He wore the single bar of an ensign, and she relaxed.

"Yes," Athos was saying as she got within earshot. "Vice Admiral Beauregard. We're old friends."

From the closer vantage point, Svetlana could read the ensign's name plate—Hayes. She had hoped for something a bit more exotic, perhaps a name she recognized. "Tell him Sveta Tereshchenko needs to speak with him, urgently."

"Uh, yes, ma'am," Ensign Hayes stammered. "It's only just that I don't know where the Vice Admiral is, at the moment. I'm not part of the *Himmelgnade's* crew."

Svetlana looked over the ensign's shoulder, toward the south dock. The bold navy and red Republican flag flew from half a dozen ships. But as Svetlana looked around the party, Air Fleet uniforms were not in great profusion. She turned to Athos. "Show of force, you think?"

Athos shook his head. "Larson Kavisoli has a lot of highly placed friends." He turned to the ensign. "What ship are you on, then?"

"The *Stoessel*, sir."

Svetlana and Athos looked at each other. "And whose ship is that?" Svetlana asked.

"Captain Fisher, ma'am."

"Athos, what happened to the good old days of the Air Fleet, when we knew everyone, and captains had good, memorable names?"

"That's why I quit, actually," Athos quipped. "Nobody could have respected a Captain Tucker."

With a chuckle, Svetlana asked, "Ensign, do you know where we could find Captain Fisher?"

"I suppose she's at the Officers' Club, ma'am."

Svetlana looked at Athos. "Officers' Club, here? Those Kavisoli sure move quickly."

"Oh, that's what's going on in the big tent!" Athos exclaimed. Ensign Hayes nodded. "Thanks, chum. You've been a great help. We'll put in a good word with the Vice Admiral for you."

Athos snagged Svetlana's arm and leaned in to whisper. "The big tent just off the docks. It's where all of the cream of the crop is spending their time. We are going to need to get you something different to wear if we're going in there."

"No, we're not," Svetlana said. "We're going in just like we are."

Athos paused midstep. When Svetlana turned to face him, he arched an eyebrow. "Is this one of your plans that I get to know about, or do I just get to try to keep up?"

"Try to keep up," Svetlana said with a grin.

"Lovely," Athos muttered as Svetlana marched toward the large tent.

Two lieutenants stood to either side of the narrow entrance to the tent. Svetlana stopped in front of them and saluted, her gaze sliding across their name plates. "Palmer. Bridges." Though she said no more than their names, she said it with practiced authority, learned from years of watching her superiors and commanding her own subordinates in the Air Fleet.

Both of the young men straightened to attention and saluted back. "Ma'am," Lieutenant Palmer responded.

"At ease, gents. Is the Vice Admiral in?"

Lieutenant Bridges shot a glance at Palmer. "Pardon me, ma'am, you are?"

Svetlana sighed and turned to Athos. "No respect from this younger set." Turning back to the lieutenants, she gave them a tight smile. "The answer to your question, Lieutenant Bridges, is so high above your pay grade that your head would spin if I told you just how high."

Lieutenant Bridges straightened and glared down at Svetlana. "With all due respect, ma'am, we're here in the name of the security of the Republic. Now I'll either need—"

Svetlana stepped in front of Lieutenant Bridges, focusing her gaze solely on him. The young man tensed as she enunciated each word. "Lieutenant. We are here in the name of the security of the Republic, the Air Fleet, and the nascent City-State of Rrusadon. You will let us in to see Vice Admiral Beauregard."

Athos tugged at Svetlana's sleeve, and she turned toward the tent entrance. An older man, white-haired, with a heavily lined face, stood between the open flaps, smiling. Though his advanced age showed in his hair and face, he stood ramrod straight, unstooped by the years. "So good to see you, Sveta."

"Bobby!" Svetlana exclaimed, stretching her arms out to hug him. The two young lieutenants moved away from the entrance to allow her access to the tent and the Vice Admiral.

Bobby embraced Svetlana, and she felt the vibration of his deep voice through her entire body. "Tucker, why does she still put up with you?"

"I'm useful." Athos smirked. "Good to see you, Bobby."

Svetlana pulled herself away from her former mentor. "We need to talk. Immediately." With a glance at the lieutenants, she added, "Preferably in private?"

Bobby looked at Svetlana, and then looked around. "It's a ten-minute walk back to my office on the *Himmelgnade*. Or we can find a quiet spot inside?"

Svetlana nodded and followed Bobby into the tent, Athos close behind her.

Inside was a chaotic clash of color, sound, and aroma. The party outside had been festive, but here the elite rubbed cuffs with the officers of the Air Fleet and the Kavisoli family. Music poured out of some corners, while laughter and chatter wove in and out of the melodies. Fragrant floral arrangements warred with heavily spiced dishes that Svetlana could not identify. Even the colors of the clothing here appeared more overwhelming, and the elaborate dresses looked as though they may have required the combined efforts of dressmakers and architects to attain the shapes they had. "Okay, now I feel shabby," Svetlana whispered to Athos.

"I'll save the 'I told you so' for another time."

Bobby led Svetlana and Athos to a ring of three chairs, set off to the side of the tent, and tucked behind a bank of the lush green plant life that grew on every portion of Rrusadon, cutting off Svetlana's opportunity to fire back at Athos.

"Will this do?" he asked, gesturing to the chairs.

Svetlana nodded as she sat down. The men joined her, and she leaned into the center of the circle. "There's a massive box outside that holds a bomb."

Bobby sat upright and his gaze darted around the area. Then he leaned closer to Svetlana. "Sveta, tell me honestly. Did you plant the bomb?"

"What? No! Of course not! Do you really think I would have done such a thing?"

Bobby shook his head, but said, "I had to ask. I hear rumors about you from time to time, and I worry about what you've gotten yourself into."

"You know me better than that," she snapped, leaning back and crossing her arms over her chest.

"I'm sorry, Sveta. I had to be sure that I knew where you stood. Please, start at the beginning?"

She huffed out a sigh at his apology, but shook her head. "Bobby, I'm not sure how much time we have. We think the bomb is probably rigged to blow when the inauguration begins, but we don't know that for certain. We need you to get it out of here. *The Silent Monsoon* can't manage that."

"Alright. Which box?"

"The one that looks like it could hold a sofa. It's supposed to be the Cranglimmering," Svetlana said.

Bobby stiffened. "What? Who would send their Cranglimmering to the Kavisolis?"

"Allegedly, it's the Bartram Cask. It was stolen ... I don't know when, actually. Recently, I guess. We were told it had been brought here." Svetlana frowned. "Well, sort of told. Bobby, I'm not liking this."

"Likewise," he said, rising from his chair, and nodding to someone across the crowded room. "I'll have it taken care of. Tucker, would you care to come with me to assist?"

Athos looked at Svetlana. "Why not Sveta?"

"Mayor Kavisoli would like to have a word with you, Captain Tereshchenko," said a woman's voice, smooth as silk and barely above a whisper, but still audible over the hubbub of the tent. Svetlana's head jerked up and followed the sound of the voice. The woman standing nearby was tall and slender, dressed in what looked like scraps left over from making someone else's dress. Her skin was olive, decorated with gold paint like the woman Athos had been with in the observation tower. "If you'd like to freshen up a bit, I can show you to the powder room at the Mayor's estate."

Mouth agape, Svetlana rose and looked at Bobby. His expression gave her no indication as to why the soon-to-be inaugurated mayor wanted to speak with her, or how he even knew that she was on Rrusadon.

Bobby simply nodded at her. "The mayor should be informed of this. We'll take care of the box."

Svetlana was not fond of waiting for anyone, but waiting for Mayor Kavisoli, in his ostentatiously decorated parlor, after his serving girl had attempted to paint Svetlana's face with glittery gold powder, pushed her tolerance to the limit. Heading back to *The Silent Monsoon* was an option, but as she rose, she realized that the view from the parlor window was directly into the heart of the outdoor party. The *Himmelgnade* hovered high above the party, tow cables lowering on either side of the box containing the bomb. Air Fleet men on either side of the box attached the cables, and soon the *Himmelgnade* was whisking the box far from the hundreds of assembled guests.

"Captain Tereshchenko," said a low voice behind her. "I understand I have you to thank for ... well, quite a bit, actually."

Tall, dark, and handsome were the first three words that came to mind as Svetlana regarded the speaker. His olive skin matched that of the serving girl, and his face was framed by slicked back dark brown hair and a narrow goatee. He wore a simple purple shirt, open at the collar and at his wrists, untucked over simple black slacks.

"You're Larson Kavisoli?" Svetlana blurted. Her face flushed as she realized he must have been preparing for the inauguration ceremony and was half-dressed. "You're, ah, much younger than I expected."

"Yes, well, you're much prettier than I expected," he replied, flashing brilliant white teeth as he smiled. "I thought all you ship captains were supposed to be used up old hags."

Svetlana stammered for a moment before she could form coherent words. "Your serving girl said you wished to speak with me."

"Serving girl," he laughed, a rich, warm sound that put her at ease. "So genteel. But yes, you're correct. When I heard that the famous Captain Tereshchenko had come to Rrusadon, I felt it only appropriate that we meet. I understand that you and your crew are quite skilled at evading authorities." He paused and frowned. "Only now I wonder if that is more due to skill or to personal connections."

"If you believe me to be famous, then surely you know my background. Yes, I was Air Fleet. And yes, I still have friends there. That's all. But as a matter of courtesy, we don't like to call what we do 'evading authorities.' That makes it sound like smuggling." She grinned and waggled her eyebrows.

"But of course. Forgive my unfamiliarity with the proper terminology. Perhaps you can educate me further on that topic at a later date. Because it seems I have something more pressing to discuss with you at the moment."

"Oh?" This man was not at all what Svetlana expected from a Kavisoli. He was charming, verging on flirtatious, and well educated, not the boorish rowdy she had been told the Kavisolis all were. And he danced from topic to topic with alarming speed.

"I understand you discovered a bomb that may have been planted to disrupt my inauguration."

"Oh, that. Yes. Annette discovered it, really."

He moved closer to her, and Svetlana caught a whiff of a pleasant woody scent, mixed with the faintest floral note. "Well, then perhaps I should be thanking Annette instead."

"Yes," Svetlana said. She took a deep breath to steady herself, but found that doing so disoriented her more. Whatever it was that made him smell as he did was intoxicating. She bit her lip, annoyed that she was getting flustered from talking to this man. "I don't suppose you happened to get a card with that gift, did you?"

"Card? Mmm, yes, actually." He moved away to one of the gilt-edged bookcases and tugged on a book. The bookcase to his left slid out and to the side, revealing a narrow doorway. "Step into my office?" Without watching to see if she followed him, he ducked through the opening. Svetlana hesitated, but then followed. The top of the doorway grazed her hair as she stepped through.

Kavisoli's office was stark, particularly compared with the parlor. A large desk dominated most of the space, but it was unadorned dark teak. A fountain bubbled at one end of the room, and the motion of the water kept the room cooler than it might otherwise have been. Svetlana jumped when the door slid closed behind her. Kavisoli looked up from the papers on his desk. "I'm glad you made it through before it closed, Captain."

"Svetlana," she said, her voice coming out much thicker and throatier than she had anticipated.

"Call me Lar," he replied. "All of my friends do." He lifted a piece of paper from the desk. "Here it is. 'Regards, Jonas Kean.'"

Hand outstretched, Svetlana frowned and approached the desk. Lar handed her the paper and shrugged. The writing on it was simple printing, all in capital letters, over a faint watermark. "Is there more light available?" she asked.

"Shield your eye." Lar seemed to notice her monocular for the first time. "What is that device?"

"Nothing of use at the moment." As Svetlana shielded her good eye, Lar twisted a knob, allowing the gas jets around the room to brighten.

Svetlana held the paper up to the light and looked for the watermark again. "It's from a shop back home."

Moving beside her to examine the paper, Lar asked, "Where is home, Svetlana?"

"Ah, not really home. Heliopolis. It's where we sail out of."

"Heliopolis." He paused a moment, brow furrowed. "I don't recall having offended anyone in Heliopolis."

"Well, it's where you'd expect the paper to come from, if it were really coming along with the Cask."

"Cask?"

Svetlana looked up at Lar, surprised to see confusion now written across his face. "The Bartram Cask was stolen. We received information that it was brought here. We're trying to find it."

Lar smiled. "The Bartram Cask, indeed? What would such a cask fetch, were you to find it?"

With a laugh, she said, "My first mate tells me there's a reward offered for it. A mill. But I don't know why it'd be worth that much. It still needs to sit another twenty years before its time is right."

"Mmm, but there are some who would pay dearly for the right to be the one to open it." He paused. "The Kavisoli Cask has a much nicer ring to it, wouldn't you say?"

"You're interested?"

"Of course."

"I'll bear that in mind, then, should we come across it."

"Very good." His gaze slid up and down her body. "I will be pleased to see you again, especially if you can bring me such a delightful treat."

Unsure if Lar referred to the Cask or her, Svetlana nodded slowly. "I'll see if we can't track it down."

CHAPTER THREE

"SO WE'VE GOT a name, that none of us have heard before, and a piece of paper, and that's enough for us to go back to Heliopolis?" Jo asked, waving the note that had come with the bomb. She and Svetlana were hunched over the steering column, this time with Jo on the directional controls and Svetlana on the altitude controls. Svetlana preferred this setup, where Jo was on her good side and she didn't have to turn too far from what she was doing to look at her pilot.

"At the moment, yes. Heliopolis is where the real Cask was taken from, and we didn't get too far with that investigation," Svetlana said. "This note came from the Swan Stationers, so at least that's a lead on the bomb. And if Mirage is the one who transported it, odds are he took the crate on in Heliopolis as well. Sorry, Jo Dean. All roads lead to Heliopolis."

Jo pressed her lips together for a minute before speaking again. "You're not going to take Athos out with you, right?"

"Nope, he's staying on the ship. And I'm guessing you'd rather lie low for a bit too?"

"I think I'd better. Pretty soon, even my disguises are going to be wanted."

"Sooner or later, we're going to have to resort to something more drastic," Svetlana said. "Maybe a haircut?"

"Over my dead body," Jo said, hands flying to her waist-length chestnut hair.

"That's what I'm worried about, Jo. You're recognizable by it. And sooner or later, either it goes, or we're going to have to spend a long spell outside of Heliopolis, living on the fringes again. And I don't know about you, but I rather prefer having a full belly and steady work."

"I'll come up with something," Jo grumbled. She made a point of twisting her long hair until it coiled near the nape of her neck and sticking a pencil through it, keeping it out of Svetlana's reach.

Annette strode onto the bridge. "Indy said you needed me up here?"

"Just wanted to see how you felt about a little field trip to the stationers," Svetlana said, handing Annette the note that had been sent to Larson Kavisoli along with the bomb. The doctor examined the writing and held the paper up so that the light through the windows filtered through it.

"Swan's? Mmm, I wouldn't be opposed to a new journal, but you can pick one up for me just as easily. I'd be happy to wait this one out." She looked away from the paper and back at Svetlana. "You'll be making a stop at The Fist?"

Svetlana shrugged. "If I want to try and find Mirage, yes."

"Then I'm definitely not interested. You could take the boy."

"Indy? You want me to take Indy into The Fist?"

Annette nodded. "You want him to learn how to live this life, he's got to get out there and live it."

"He's a kid, Annette!"

"Ah," Jo interrupted, shaking a finger at Svetlana. "When we hired him, I used those exact same words. Or three out of the four, at least. And you told me that he knew what he was signing on for, and that he'd be treated just as if he were an adult member of the crew. He gets his share of grog, just like the rest of us."

Svetlana opened her mouth to retort but stopped herself and shook her head. "Alright, fine. You are, as always, adept at keeping track of which of my words you can use against me someday. I'll take Indy to The Fist."

Annette nodded. "I'll talk to him before you go, tell him to keep his mouth shut and eyes open. He'll probably be better at that than any of us were the first time we tried to go in there."

Svetlana chuckled, remembering the night she had first taken Annette into The Flying Fist, an apt name for a bar that catered to those allegedly in the shipping industry. More often than not, that translated to smugglers, pirates, and other scoundrels. Svetlana tried to keep herself and her crew in that first category, but it was a simple fact that the other two categories of patrons often had the sort of information that the crew of *The Silent Monsoon* needed.

"Alright," she replied. "Get him ready. Oh, and find him a hat that will keep his hair out of sight. Don't need every soul in Heliopolis knowing that we're out and about."

Somehow, The Flying Fist managed to be on the darkest and dingiest street in a generally clean Heliopolis. It was as though every bit of filth that was swept or washed from the city proper wound up here. Svetlana kept Indigo to her left, near enough that she could reach out and grab his shoulder at any moment, as they made their way down the street.

She repeated her litany of instructions to him as they walked, knowing that Annette had already been over the same ground but wanting to ensure the boy was well prepared. "Mouth closed, eyes and ears open. If I give an order, obey as though your life depends on it." *It just might*, she thought to herself.

When they reached the entrance to The Flying Fist, Svetlana pushed Indigo ahead of her. "Open the door, go in, move to the left. If you end up in my blind spot, you'd best get to my good side as fast as you can."

Indigo nodded, just barely. Svetlana found it odd to not see his normal vigorous nodding and bouncing blue hair. But blending in was essential here, as the stationer's had been a dead end. She had learned all about second sheets, and that everyone in Heliopolis who bought their stationery from Swan's had the exact same sort of paper in their homes or offices. And, to top it off, they had none of the journals that Annette had asked her to pick up in stock.

Indigo nudged the door open and leapt immediately to the left. Svetlana followed him in and slung an arm over his shoulders. Rum, sweat, and the coppery tang of blood all hung in the air. The Flying Fist was packed, and the crowd was raucous. She had to lean in close to make sure Indigo could hear her. "If you spot Mirage, let me know," she told the boy.

At the bar, she ordered two grogs and paid with small coins, having left everything but those on the ship. As it was, she had to fight off the grubby hands of urchins that lingered near her purse even to pay for the drinks. When the bartender handed her two mugs, filled with the warm liquor, she handed one to Indigo and knocked the rims of their mugs together. "Cheers."

"I thought I saw Mirage upstairs," Indigo whispered. Svetlana glanced up, toward the balcony. There were voices singing somewhere above, but she couldn't pick out any that sounded like a bassoon.

"Let's try up, then. Better than down."

Svetlana and Indigo made their way toward the rickety staircase that connected the balcony to the lower level, but Indigo stopped abruptly when a topless young woman, her ochre skin splotched with pink welts, moved into his path. She gave him a gap-toothed smile, hand on her hip and thrusting her chest forward. "Looking for something to do, sailor?"

"Not really," Svetlana answered.

That earned her a scornful look from the woman. "Didn't ask you, love!"

Her left hand on Indigo's shoulder, Svetlana crossed her right hand to her left hip. She hadn't brought a knife, but the woman couldn't see that with Indigo between them.

"Alright, alright," the woman said, backing away. She flipped her matted dark hair over her shoulder and went in search of another target.

Svetlana nudged Indigo forward, and they climbed the rest of the stairs unaccosted. When they reached the top, an older woman, skin the color of aged leather, blocked their way. "That one doesn't want to spend time with my daughter?"

Pulling Indigo closer to her, Svetlana glowered at the woman. "That one is with me."

The woman squinted at Svetlana, but her gaze fixed on Svetlana's good eye, and she stepped back. "Oh, the golden-eyed princess of the Air Fleet."

"What did you say?" Svetlana asked, moving Indigo behind her.

Backing farther away, the woman shook her head. "I didn't mean nothin' by it. I just heard of an Air Fleet lady officer with one golden eye. But I must be mistaken. No lady officer would grace us with her presence here."

Svetlana looked around to see if anyone was paying attention to the old woman. There was enough going on in The Fist that she doubted anyone had heard the woman's words unless they were paying close attention to her, or possibly if they were already watching Svetlana or Indigo. "That's right. She wouldn't deign to set foot in this cesspool. Now get out of my sight."

Svetlana turned around to move Indigo back into her line of sight. Her heart leapt into her throat when she realized the boy was no longer behind her.

Rushing to the edge of the balcony, she scanned the crowd on the floor below, looking for Indigo's wavy blue hair, but the boy looked like any of the other ruffians here in the hat she had made him wear. She started to move down the stairs, hoping to find him outside, when a deep bass voice called her name.

Still hoping to spot the boy, she paused for a moment before turning. Something that looked like Deliah's bright pigtails bobbed in the crowd, and Svetlana sent a silent prayer that it was the urchin girl, come to rescue Indigo from The Flying Fist. Then she turned and smiled at Mirage. "We need to talk."

Svetlana sat opposite Mirage in a dimly lit booth near the back of the balcony in The Flying Fist. He looked awful. His beard was thick and dark, but it made his cheeks look sunken and gaunt. His dirty blond hair hung limp around his face. When he leaned back in the booth, it blocked what little light there was and obscured all but his silvery-grey eyes, which glowed with fervor. "What do you need to know?"

"Jonas Kean."

Mirage leaned forward and the smell of rum, tinged with something strange and bitter, wafted toward Svetlana. Her nose twitched as he spoke. "What of him?"

"You delivered cargo to Rrusadon—one large crate. Jonas Kean's name was on that cargo. I need to find him."

"Rrusadon, yes. I've just come back from there."

"Yes, I know that. Did you come back to Heliopolis for payment from Jonas Kean?"

Mirage spread his arms wide on the table. "Svetlana. You know that all roads lead back to Heliopolis. Always."

"Did Kean tell you what was in the box you transported for him?"

"Does it matter?" Mirage raised his eyebrow, smiling. "He offered a handsome price for the transport." He paused, a frown creasing his brow.

Svetlana didn't allow him time to finish his thought. "Mirage, it was a bomb. You had a gods-be-cursed bomb in the hold of your ship, and you didn't even know it. What would have happened if you hadn't made it to Rrusadon in time, huh? I'll tell you what. You'd be dead."

Mirage straightened up, moving his entire body into the shadows of the booth, and hiding even his eyes from Svetlana's gaze. When he spoke again, his voice was so quiet that Svetlana had to strain to make out the rumblings. "I didn't know."

Svetlana let out a slow breath. It made sense that he hadn't known. If the price was right, most airship captains would take on a cargo without asking too many questions. She was guilty of it herself, though she'd never transported a bomb before, to the best of her knowledge. "Hasn't anyone from Air Fleet been to speak with you?" she asked.

"I don't know. I haven't been on the ship since we got back. Kean still owes me the second half of his payment. I was going to try to win some money so I could pay my crew."

"Point me in his direction, and I'll make him pay."

Mirage shook his head, the ratty ends of his hair shaking back and forth in the light. "No good. I'd have to look to the Sky Wardens for recompense now."

"Sky Wardens?" Svetlana's brow furrowed. That was an organization she had never heard of. "Who are they?"

"You know them," Mirage whispered. His face lunged out from the shadows in the booth, grey eyes pleading with her. "Beware the ghost ship, Svetlana."

"What? Is that where the Sky Wardens are?"

"The ship that comes in the night. Crewed by ghosts. She'll take your soul and bind you to her."

"Mirage, what have you been drinking? You're talking nonsense. No one has seen a ghost ship for years."

He shook his head, his eyes burning with renewed fervor. "She's real. She is," he insisted, pounding his fist on the table.

Svetlana crossed her arms over her chest. "What's she called, then?"

"Can't say. Many names." Mirage looked around wildly, then focused on Svetlana. "I need food," he slurred. He slumped forward in his seat, head bouncing as it smacked against the table.

"Sweet Skyfather," Svetlana muttered under her breath as she rose from her seat. Looking around for any of Mirage's crew, she spotted the curly auburn hair of his boatswain at a nearby table. "Maggie?"

Maggie looked up, worried at first, but her face softened as she spotted Svetlana. A spiderweb of scars criss-crossed her face, marring all but her warm, brown eyes. "He passed out?"

"Out cold."

"Good, he's easier to carry that way."

"What's wrong with him?"

"He's decided that if he mixes ether with his rum, he'll get closer to understanding the mysteries of Aether. I tried to tell him that the spelling's not even the same, but you know how he gets when he thinks up a new way to seek enlightenment."

"Not first hand, thank the Skyfather." Svetlana helped Maggie hoist Mirage out of the booth. The other woman slung Mirage over her shoulders like a sack. Her arms were strong from years of hefting cargo, but when Mirage's shirt fell away from his torso, Svetlana could see his ribs jutting out. Now that he was fully in the light, it was more apparent just how far gone her fellow captain was. "Is he going to be alright?"

"Should be," Maggie grunted, adjusting Mirage's body for balance. "It hasn't killed him yet, and we ran out of ether yesterday. Doc says she won't buy no more until she's sure she can keep it from the Cap'n. So either he'll kick the habit, or there'll be a whole lot of screaming." She paused. "Probably both, in all actuality."

Svetlana nodded. "Take care, Maggie. He's ... he's not right in the head."

"I know." She laughed. "Probably none of us are in this life."

Svetlana nodded again. "Say, Maggie, you don't know anything about the cargo you dropped at Rrusadon, do you? The big box, from Jonas Kean?"

Maggie's eyes narrowed. "What'd Mirage tell you?"

"Not much. That Kean reneged on the second payment."

"That he did. Soon as I find him, he an' I are gonna have words. Only the sort of words you find at the end of a knife." She smiled bitterly, the narrow white scars across her lips reminding Svetlana how well Maggie knew her way around a knife blade.

"Find him? I take it that means he's cut and run?"

"I don't know. I never met him. This one was all Mirage." Maggie frowned. "That ain't normal, either, come to think of it. He usually has me handle it all, but he insisted on handling this one personally."

"You know it was a bomb?"

Maggie's face went as pale as her scars. "Son of a whore." She slung Mirage off of her shoulders and dropped him back in the booth, knocking his head off of the bench. "For that, you can sleep this off here, sir." She spat out the final word.

"He didn't know," Svetlana said. "Or at least he claims not to have known."

"That bomb. The one you found on Rrusadon. We were carrying that?"

Svetlana frowned. "Wait, you knew there was a bomb, but not that you were carrying it?"

"Well yeah. It's—*you're*—all over the papers since last night, Cap'n. Savior of Rrusadon."

"Ugh," Svetlana muttered. "This is going to make my life an abyss."

Indigo was waiting for Svetlana near the gangplank of *The Silent Monsoon*, his hair wild in the breeze. "Are you alright?" she asked, running the final steps to the ship.

"Fine. Saw Deliah. Got information."

Svetlana smiled. "And what did you think of The Flying Fist?"

The boy screwed up his nose. "Stinks."

"Yes, it does." Clapping a hand on Indigo's shoulder, she walked with him to the mess.

Athos, Annette, and Jo were assembled around the table, playing cards. From the looks of the piles of small coins in front of each of them, Athos was trouncing the women.

Jo looked up when Svetlana and Indigo walked in. "Oh, thank the Skyfather. You said we'd play five hands or till they're back. Give me my money back, Athos."

Athos laughed as he split up the coins. "Suit yourself. You could have made a comeback."

Annette looked at Svetlana. "So, what do we have now?"

"No journal. Sorry. They were out of stock. And apparently the paper was common. Could have come from nearly any home or business in Heliopolis."

"What about Mirage?" Athos asked. "Did that old flake know anything?"

Svetlana shook her head and pulled out a chair. "He wouldn't tell me who Kean was, but Kean reneged on the second payment. Mirage claimed he didn't know it was a bomb. I talked to Maggie, too, and she didn't know what they were carrying either." Looking at Annette, she asked, "How much long term damage would drinking ether do to a person?"

Annette blanched. "How long, and how much?"

"I don't know. Long enough to make him crazy? -er? Crazier. He's mixing it with his rum, but I don't know how much. He started going on about a ghost ship and then passed out."

"Is that really all you got from him?" Jo asked. "What a waste."

"Uh, he said something about the Sky Wardens. Ever heard of them?"

Jo and Annette shook their heads. Indigo looked puzzled, but Athos nodded. "It's an old legend about the defenders of the Skyfather. They're like knights, like the one on the Port Authority logo."

Svetlana cocked her head to the side. "What did he say? Something about going to them for recompense?"

"That wouldn't be within the Port Authority's jurisdiction, I don't think," Athos said. "Assuming it was a privately transacted agreement, he'd need to go to the magistrates to get recompense."

"Unless Kean's got some sort of ties to the Port Authority," Jo suggested.

"Indy, what'd you get?" Svetlana asked.

"Deliah and her friends have been couriering." He frowned. "Carrying stuff. Getting paid. They took a lot of stuff to an apartment in Dogtown."

"What sort of stuff?" Svetlana prodded him in the arm.

"Metal stuff. Maybe bomb stuff." Indigo shrugged. "Lots of pieces. Deliah thinks bomb stuff though."

"Richards has an apartment in Dogtown," Jo muttered.

Athos looked at her. "How in the abyss would you know that, Jo Dean?"

Jo reddened. "It's important to know where the people who want you locked up live. If I know where he lives, I can figure his route back and forth to Headquarters and avoid it."

"Hmm," Athos said. "It's also important to know where someone lives if you're making some sort of arrangements with them to keep them off your case and maybe pestering other people instead."

Jo glared at him. "Are you suggesting that I've been making deals with Richards? I'd sooner cut off my hair."

"Okay, enough of that," Svetlana said, rising and moving between Athos and Jo. "Nobody on this ship is dealing with Richards, above or below the table."

"No?" Jo asked. "So we're not looking for the Cranglimmering for him?"

"Not at this point," Svetlana replied.

"Is there anyone else who lives in Dogtown that we might want to put on our suspect list, or are we going straight for Richards?" Annette asked.

Svetlana hesitated. "Athos, you're sure the Bartram Cask actually went missing, right?"

"Yes. Well, mostly. The retraction that my aunties told me about didn't mention the Cask, but it's what the scuttlebutt is saying."

"Jo and I went to the Bartram Estate. There's only one way out of that place for something the size of the Cask." Svetlana pointed one finger toward the ceiling. "Up. Don't you think someone would have seen it, maybe gotten a few photographs for the papers? It seems like the kind of thing the reporters would be all over. Speaking of, has anyone seen the paper today?"

The rest of the crew shook their heads.

"Apparently I'm front page news, what with the bomb and all."

"Bobby?" Annette asked, arching one eyebrow.

"Likely," Athos agreed with a wink. "I'm kind of surprised he didn't have his legion of secretaries there with the paperwork to give Sveta her commission back then and there."

"He knows I wouldn't take it," Svetlana growled. Athos looked down at the table, the mirth drained from his eyes. "Anyway, neither here nor there, and we need here right now."

"Okay, so let's say the Bartram Cask was airlifted out of the Mayor's estate," Jo said. "Maybe they reported it to the Port Authority but kept it out of the papers? Which would explain how Richards heard about it before any of us did. Perfect set up for putting together a bomb, and then sending us after it."

Annette shook her head. "You really don't like that man, do you?"

"Nope," Jo replied. She turned to Svetlana. "How about we go check out his apartment for left over bomb bits? If we find them, then he's our guy. If not, we figure out who else might be of a mind to blow us up."

Svetlana shook her head. "I don't know that we were the target, Jo. I think Lar ... Kavisoli was the target."

"Not just Kavisoli," Athos said. He held up his hand and ticked off fingers. "Kavisoli himself, his family, the upper crust from at least twelve other republics, oh, and six flagships of the Air Fleet. We were just icing on the cake." He frowned. "Really insignificant icing."

"Air Fleet should be looking into this," Svetlana said. "Not us."

"Are they not?" Annette asked.

"Maybe, maybe not. They hadn't spoken with Mirage yet. But he'd been out drinking ether-laced rum all day, I guess."

"Should we check in with the local Air Fleet, see if our clues plus their clues get us any further?" Annette shrugged. "You and I could probably just walk in there, no questions asked."

"Maybe so," Svetlana said, deep in thought. "One way or another, something isn't quite adding up."

CHAPTER FOUR

ANNETTE SHOOK HER head as she walked out of the Heliopolis Port Authority headquarters. She hurried across the street to where Svetlana sat at the Ghesna Tea House, on the patio, despite the crispness in the air. At the sight of the doctor, Svetlana flagged down the waitress for another cup, which arrived as soon as Annette sat down.

"They say he's on special assignment, and he's not available to comment on my case." Annette shrugged as she buttoned up the front of her coat. "They offered to find me another officer who could help me."

"How'd you handle the case number?"

"I didn't," Annette admitted. "When they asked, I knocked over a jar of pens and then ran out in the confusion."

Svetlana laughed at the thought of the graceful doctor feigning clumsiness. "Good thinking. I knew you'd be fine on your own in there. Tea?"

"Maybe," Annette muttered, nodding past Svetlana. Svetlana turned. A handful of people walked in either direction, but she soon spotted what

Annette was pointing out. Richards' bully boys, Tom and Henry, were approaching the headquarters building.

"Got a plan?" Svetlana asked.

Annette leaned back in her chair and shrugged. "Come to think of it, I will have that cup of tea. And then I'll sit here and have a nice rest while you work your magic, Cap'n."

Svetlana grimaced, but then shrugged. "Suit yourself. You can pay the bill then." Vaulting over the waist-high railing that surrounded the patio seating of the tea house, she laughed as she ran.

As she neared the two men, she called out their names. They stopped and looked at her. "I'm looking for Richards."

Henry glanced at Tom. "He's on special assignment this week."

"So I've heard. Is it about the Cask?" Svetlana asked, twisting one of the lens rings on her monocular. The lens didn't do much to improve her vision, but she knew it would make her blind eye show through the lens, an effect some had called "creepy."

"Not at liberty to say," Henry replied, rubbing a hand across his shiny head.

Svetlana shook her head and pursed her lips. Both of them looked nervous to her, but that wasn't telling her anything she didn't already suspect. "Well, is there any way to get in contact with him? I have some information he's going to want to hear."

Tom opened his mouth, but Henry interrupted before the other man could say a word. "You could give us the information, and we can pass it along. I imagine you're not staying long in town, what with the whole shipping business and all."

Svetlana paused and frowned, as though she were thinking it over. "I don't know. I mean, what—" Gesturing at the insignia that they wore on their lapels, she asked, "What rank are you two, anyhow? I can't just be giving this information to some lowly ... half-corporals?"

"There's not a rank called half-corporals," Tom replied. "We're privates."

Turning to favor Tom with a smile, she said, "Thank you, Tom. Very informative." Svetlana looked back at Henry. "Definitely information above your pay grade. Unless you want to exchange information with me. You know, tit for tat." She bit the inside of her lip to keep from laughing.

"We don't deal with pirates," Henry spat back.

"I'm not a pirate. I'm an independent shipping contractor. I solemnly swear that I have never stolen the cargo of another ship and sold it for profit." She held her left hand aloft while she swore the oath that all in the shipping industry took, but held the thumb and pointer finger of her right hand in a small circle behind her back as she did, silently asking the Skyfather's forgiveness for her blatant falsehood.

"Swear all you like, we're not going to tell you where Richards went," Henry grumbled.

Svetlana grinned. "Went. Fabulous. Thank you, Henry, now we're getting somewhere. Went implies he's off platform." Covering a feigned gasp, she continued. "Oh, but that means he doesn't have jurisdiction, wherever he's gone to. Heliopolis Port Authority only has jurisdiction here on Heliopolis. Shall I go on?"

Henry shrugged. "Suit yourself. We haven't told you anything."

Svetlana studied the two men. Tom had begun shifting his weight from one foot to the next, giving away just how nervous he was. Henry stared at a point over Svetlana's right shoulder, which worried her. Aside from rubbing his bald head, he had shown few signs of anxiety over Svetlana's line of questioning.

She glanced to her left, catching only a glimpse of the wrought-iron fence of the tea house patio. Frustrated, Svetlana spun and looked behind her. A few people were out and about, and none of them looked particularly threatening. But now she was feeling paranoid.

"Alright, fine," she spat, as she turned back to Tom and Henry. "Tell Richards I said hello, and he knows where to find me if he deigns to speak with me." Turning on her heel, she hurried back to the tea house.

Annette arched one eyebrow as Svetlana climbed back over the patio fence. "Decided you'd finish your tea after all?"

"Richards is off platform, but that's all I got," Svetlana grumbled as she picked up her cup to drain it.

"Well, at least that means Jo shouldn't get caught if she somehow happens to find herself in Dogtown today with nothing better to do."

Svetlana frowned. "You think she's going to?"

"Does the sea scald flesh off a person in less than a minute?" Annette quipped back.

"Yeah. Then I guess we'd best go see who's holding down the local Fleet garrison and find out who's working on the bomb investigation."

The Air Fleet owned an enormous swath of land in the lower portion of Heliopolis with plenty of docking space. It was one of the few places in the lower portion of the city that was generally safe to wander, day or night. As the noon bells signaling the midday Lift had not yet rung, the area outside of the main entrance to the garrison was thronged with passersby. And where there were passersby, there were merchants hawking their wares.

Svetlana stopped in front of a newspaper boy and flipped him a small coin. The boy nodded in appreciation as he caught the coin, and handed Svetlana the paper. As she walked away, she scanned the front page and shook her head. "Remind me to find out where they keep the originals of the cadet pictures so I can burn mine?"

Annette leaned in as they walked toward the entrance of the Air Fleet garrison to see a much younger Svetlana. "Look at you, all fresh faced and innocent!" She laughed, and Svetlana grimaced. "Well, at least it's good press this time."

"Yeah, I suppose." Svetlana scanned the article. "Now we just have to watch out for all of the people who didn't want to see Rrusadon join the Republic, who are going to blame me when things go pear-shaped."

"If you're lucky, they'll have forgotten all about you by then. Fame is so fleeting."

"Hope so," Svetlana muttered as she paused in front of the doors to the main garrison building.

Annette reached past her to pull the door open. "After you, Captain."

Svetlana shook her head but preceded Annette in. A single young, dark-haired ensign manned the ostentatious teak desk. His eyes grew wide as soon as he saw her, his gaze flickering down to something in front of him and then back up. He started to tremble. Annette didn't seem to have noticed the young ensign's reaction. She had, as always, made a beeline for the Memorial of Fallen Comrades just beyond the doors.

Svetlana's curiosity got the better of her and she approached the young man. "Ensign." She glanced down at his name plate as she stepped up to the desk. "Barbarkovian. Oh."

"You're her, aren't you? The Butcher of Barkovia?"

Svetlana lowered her head and pinched the skin between her eyebrows. Her voice wavered when she spoke. "I didn't know the Fleet was taking cadets from Barkovia."

"They're not. I mean, there's no one there to join the Air Fleet. My father was traveling when you ... when the massacre happened."

"Look, we're not going to get anywhere until I get this out. I. Did. Not. Massacre. Anyone." Her voice increased in volume with each word.

The ensign nodded, though he didn't look convinced. "Of course, ma'am." His gaze darted back down to the newspaper that was spread in front of him on the desk. "Er, Captain Tereshchenko."

Svetlana felt Annette hovering near her right elbow in an instant. "Problem, Captain?"

With a gesture to the ensign's name plate, Svetlana said, "Just a little misunderstanding of history."

Annette breathed in sharply. "Shall I handle this, Captain?"

"No. Thank you. Ensign, we'd like to speak to someone who's involved with the investigation on Rrusadon. Preferably someone not from or related to anyone from Barkovia?"

"I'm afraid I can't help you with that, ma'am. No one here is involved with that investigation. It's being handled locally."

"Locally?" Svetlana asked. "You mean to tell me that the Air Fleet is leaving this one to the Kavisoli authorities?"

"No, ma'am, not entirely, though Mayor Kavisoli's local law enforcement is heading the operation. Rrusadon is in Sector J, just outside of our present territory. I believe Captain Fisher is the officer in charge."

Svetlana turned to Annette and mouthed, "Sector J?" Annette shrugged in response. Turning back to Ensign Barbarkovian, Svetlana said, "Sorry, I guess it's been a while. I assumed Rrusadon was still under this garrison's jurisdiction. Captain Fisher, you said? Of the *Stoessel*?"

"Yes, ma'am."

"Thank you, Ensign. We won't take up any more of your time." With a terse salute, she turned to walk away.

"She won't take up any more of your time, but I will," Annette hissed. Svetlana froze as the doctor continued, torn between dragging Annette out of the office right then and there, and letting her finish.

They had never spoken outright about Annette's views on what happened at Barkovia, though Svetlana knew that the doctor didn't believe her responsible for the so-called massacre. It had been a battle for everyone involved, dubbed a massacre only after the fact by enemies of the Air Fleet. But the shadow of it still hung over Svetlana whenever she was recognized. Especially by the few remaining former Barkovians.

Annette continued before Svetlana could stop her. "Your so-called massacre happened because the Republic declared the Barkovians in a state of rebellion. Captain Tereshchenko did her duty to stop the rebellion and to stem the needless loss of life. And though my captain might not want to delve into the past, I will. Good men were killed that day. Maybe you lost your family, but I lost my husband. Just remember that. Good men. On both sides of the battle."

Svetlana let out the breath she hadn't realized she was holding when the ensign made no response other than a timid, "Condolences, ma'am."

"Likewise." A fist thunked down onto the desk. "Two sides. Thank you for your time."

Annette's footsteps behind her sent Svetlana scurrying for the door. When they were both outside, beyond the doors, she turned to face Annette. The lines around Annette's mouth were tight and hard, and the weight of the years showed in her tired eyes. "You didn't have to defend me—" Svetlana began.

"It's not just about you, Captain. It's about all of you. Mostly it's about Jack."

"Thanks all the same, Annette." Svetlana reached out and squeezed Annette's shoulder.

Annette placed her hand over Svetlana's and nodded solemnly. "So, back to Rrusadon?"

Svetlana considered their options for a long moment. "Not yet. I was thinking we'd start at the airwave office here and find out if Lar needs us there."

"Lar?" Annette asked, her mouth curving into a smile. "I didn't know you were on a nickname basis with the Mayor. Is he calling you Sveta?"

Realizing how familiar the name Lar had asked her to call him sounded outside of their single conversation, Svetlana shrugged. "Uh, no, I don't think so." She smiled, but shook her head. "He's pretty, but he might be a bit too respectable for my blood."

Annette laughed, and Svetlana saw the lines in her face relax. "Oh, please, he's a Kavisoli. If he's respectable, he's probably not really one of them. Go get him, Captain."

Svetlana chewed at the end of the pen she had borrowed from the airwave operator. Composing airwave messages was something of a science. The shorter the message, the more likely it would arrive intact. But too short, or too abbreviated, and your message might be misinterpreted. On the other hand, if you wrote a longer message, the cost could become exorbitant, and even paying a full Quinpence couldn't guarantee a flawless transmission.

Finally, she printed the simplest message she could. "*Info on Kean?*"

The airwave operator took Svetlana's message and keyed it in on the elaborate brass and glass device that allowed messages to be sent across vast distances far more quickly than they could be flown via airship. Svetlana longed for the day when such a device could be installed on her ship, but this one was easily the size of the entire bridge of *The Silent Monsoon*, and the price for a moveable device would have depleted most of the ship's income for an entire year.

A few minutes after he had sent her message, the operator brought Svetlana a small slip of paper containing a response from Larson Kavisoli. "*Rather you come here.*"

She dashed off a response. "*Can't. All roads Heliopolis.*"

Annette walked into the shop with two steaming hand-pies. Svetlana caught a whiff of savory spices that did their best to mask the bland flavor of the crust and the mixed vegetables inside the pie. Annette glanced at Svetlana's message to Kavisoli as she handed the captain one of the two pies. "Ah, the time honored tradition of using far fewer words than necessary to say absolutely nothing. How goes the conversation?"

"I'm just hoping he's got something we can use." Svetlana spoke more softly. "I know Jo is ready to jump if we have even an inkling that it's Richards, but I need more than an inkling for this one. This feels like it's way bigger than what we're seeing so far."

"Have we checked all the possibilities here?" Annette asked around a mouthful of her meal. "Are there any more leads we can follow, or should we see what we can find at Rrusadon?"

"We still have the address in Dogtown that Deliah gave Indy." Svetlana shrugged, pausing to blow on the pale crust of her hand-pie. "And really, odds are that we've checked there too, just you and I don't know about it yet."

The airwave operator brought Svetlana another slip of paper, this one longer than the previous response. "*Amateur assembly, mostly high grade parts. Watch engraved A. R.*"

Svetlana's eye widened as she recognized the initials. She handed the slip to Annette and turned to the operator. "Can you confirm the last two letters?"

The operator looked at the slip. "I'm absolutely certain of the A, without even looking at the backlog. There's no other letter that can get tripped in that quadrant of the board."

"I need absolute confirmation of this." She flipped the response slip over and wrote, "*A as in Aether, R as in Rope?*"

The operator took the new message and headed back to the machine.

"What's the A for?" Annette asked.

"Adrian. Adrian Richards."

"What?" Annette exclaimed. "Why in the abyss would he use his own watch for the timer? That's ... this reeks of a set up."

Svetlana frowned. "That's a good point. Do you remember if he was wearing his watch when he followed Athos on board?"

"I wasn't paying much attention to whether he was," Annette said. "He was leaving by the time I got out there. You got a much better look at him than I did."

"Honestly, I was busy being furious with him. And getting in his face about it." Svetlana sighed. "Doesn't much matter, though, if he's not on Heliopolis right now." Idly looking out the window, she tilted her head to the side, good eye growing wide, as she watched Richards stroll past the airwave station.

Her heart skipped a beat as he neared the door, but then resumed its rhythm when the door did not swing open. She reminded herself that the thin curtains in the office's windows that blocked out the early afternoon sun would have obscured her from his gaze, and she suspected that he wasn't looking for her.

"I'll be cursed. He's right here!" Svetlana said, rising to follow him. Before she made it to the door, she spotted a familiar black hat with a curving pink feather bobbing up and down. Amidst the other similarly adorned hats on the street, it didn't look out of place, at least until its wearer ducked behind a carriage outside the station.

Svetlana waited until she was sure Richards had gotten past the end of the block, then slipped the door open and hissed, "Jo Dean!"

Jo froze and looked around, her eyes wide. When she spotted Svetlana, she visibly relaxed. Jo raised one finger to her lips.

"Keep on him," Svetlana said softly. "I'm waiting for confirmation that he's our man."

Jo nodded, then looked down the street. "He's gone into the Key. I'll wait here till I see him come out."

Svetlana turned back to Annette. The doctor held a slip of paper up triumphantly. "Confirmed, Captain. And Lar left you a little note as well. Who would have thought that you could flirt across platforms in so few short words?"

As she took the paper from Annette and read it, Svetlana sighed. "*Yes. Now will you visit?*" Crumpling it into a small ball, she tucked it into her purse as she found the silver pence coins she needed to pay the operator.

"Will there be a response to the gentleman's question?" he asked as he counted the coins.

"Thank you, but no." Svetlana smiled. "I'd like to leave him hoping."

CHAPTER FIVE

SVETLANA THANKED THE Skyfather that the High Gate Key was a much nicer place than the Flying Fist. It only smelled like ale and spiced rum overlaying peaty smoke. A bit more crowded would have been ideal, but beggars couldn't be choosers. At any rate, she and Jo were in position, and she expected the rest of her crew any minute now.

Jo lurked in the darkness of the balcony, but Svetlana could see her from her position on the ground level, behind Richards. She gave her pilot a quick nod, which Jo returned before moving deeper into the shadows.

Svetlana's gaze went back to the clock. There was no way of knowing if Annette had made it back to *The Silent Monsoon*, and she was growing more anxious as each minute passed.

A whisper behind her made her jump. "Where in the abyss are they?" Jo asked.

"I don't know, but if you're down here when they do show up, then our plan is shot," Svetlana replied in a hiss.

"What if they're not coming? We should do this now and be done with it."

"Patience." Svetlana wasn't certain that her pilot was familiar with that concept. And to be honest with herself, the delayed arrival of her crew was trying her own patience.

Jo shook her head. "If you're not going to do it, I will."

Thrusting her arm out to stop Jo from approaching Richards, Svetlana glanced at the clock once more, and then said, "Alright. Get back a bit, at the very least." Jo obliged her, and Svetlana moved forward.

She pressed her revolver against the middle of Richards' back. "If I aim up," she whispered, reaching into Richards' holster and removing his six-shooter, "you'll be dead before you know what hit you. If I aim down, then I can just leave you here, bleeding like a stuck pig." She tossed Richards' gun in Jo's direction. "The good news for you is that I need you to talk. Shall we adjourn outside?" The bar around them had grown silent, though at least most of the patrons had the common decency to keep their eyes averted from the scene.

Richards shook his head. "I'd pegged all of you for goners as soon as you went after that damnfool cask. I'm not even going to ask how you pulled this one off, Tereshchenko. 'Savior of Rrusadon'?"

"I don't write the stories, I just star in them," Svetlana said with a sigh. "Apparently."

"What do you want? Do you want to know where the Cranglimmering is? I'll tell you."

"Mmm, tempting, but no. I can smell your desperation from a mile away. You'll just feed me some lie to get me off your back. I want to know who you're working for."

Richards laughed. "I work for the Port Authority."

"If I didn't need you still talking, there'd be a bullet in your guts," Svetlana snarled, poking Richards with the barrel of her gun to emphasize her words. "You might be clever, Richards, but you don't operate on this sort of scale. The Port Authority doesn't operate on this sort of scale. No, this has to come from higher up. Beyond Heliopolis."

Richards shrugged. "Well, you're entitled to your opinion, but I'm telling you the truth. I work for the Port Authority."

"Fine, you keep deluding yourself about that. The real truth is that you're just a means to an end." She laughed. "And you didn't even succeed! I gotta wonder which is going to be worse: going back to your real boss or ending up —"

The door to the Key swung open, and Svetlana paused in her taunting of Richards. She leaned to the left to peek around Richards' broad back. Annette and Athos stood framed in the doorway, backlit by the bright midday sun. "I told you she'd start without us," Annette said, shaking her head.

As Svetlana straightened back up, Richards spun and knocked Svetlana's revolver out of her hand. He kicked it away as soon as it hit the ground.

Svetlana swung at Richards' face, but he caught her small fist in his larger hand and tossed her backward. The top of the bar caught her in the small of the back and knocked the wind out of her as she fell to the floor.

Svetlana rolled to her side, catching quick glimpses of what was going on around her. Richards charged Annette, who was still in the doorway. Athos had moved to the side and drawn his gun, but Annette's hand hadn't gone near hers. Indigo was nowhere to be seen. In a blink, Richards had Annette, both her arms pinned behind her back, and held her between him and Svetlana.

Athos leveled his gun at Richards, and Svetlana heard the cocking of Jo's revolver behind her. Svetlana reached for her gun, but her hand spasmed as waves of pain shot up her back and into her arm. Richards' eyes darted between the two armed members of Svetlana's crew as he slid his hand down Annette's side, found her holster, and drew her gun. He turned it toward Annette and put the barrel against her temple.

"Drop 'em or she gets it," he boomed out. Athos lowered his gun, and Richards continued. "That's better. Now, Doctor Campbell and I are just going to take a nice little walk. Anyone makes any funny movements at all, and I will shoot her."

Svetlana lay on the floor, using every ounce of her willpower not to writhe in pain. "Fine," she spat out. "Let him go."

Richards smiled. "My momma always told me to find myself a doctor to take care of me." He backed toward the door of the bar, keeping Annette in front of him. His gaze checked Athos with a steely glare, and then darted back to Jo's position, before he stepped out onto the street. "Be seein' ya." The door swung shut behind him.

Jo bent to help Svetlana up from the floor. "Shouldn't we maybe stop him from taking Annette?"

"I'd love to," Svetlana gasped. "If I could move without wanting to scream."

Athos joined Jo and helped Svetlana to her feet. Svetlana bit down hard on her lip but couldn't muffle the sharp shout that escaped her throat when she put her weight down on her right foot. "Where's the boy?"

"Lookout," Athos replied, sliding under Svetlana's right arm. "He insisted, and who am I to get that boy to do anything he doesn't want to do? Seems he's had his fill of bars for a while."

"Good. Jo, go find Indy and get a bead on where Richards is taking Annette."

Jo nodded. She glanced over her shoulder at the bartender. "Give her a whiskey. Put it on Richards' tab."

The bartender made a noise of protest, and Jo leveled her gun at him, raising her eyebrows.

Svetlana heard something heavy and glass thunk down beside her on the bar. Jo smiled. "Much obliged." She turned and ran out the front door of the bar.

"Plan, Captain?" Athos asked.

"Whiskey first. Then—" She paused to gulp down the drink. "We follow."

Athos smirked. "We? You can barely stand. How do you plan on running?"

"I don't. Hail a cab."

Svetlana limped down the street, only Athos' arm, steady beneath her arms, keeping her from crumpling to her knees. No cabs were on the streets near the bar, and they hadn't seen a single aircab pass overhead, either.

"No fly zone in this neighborhood, I get," Athos grumbled. "But how are there no street cabs out in the middle of the afternoon?"

"I don't know, but Richards is getting a big lead on us," Svetlana grunted, trying to wriggle out of Athos' grasp. "Let go. You'll move faster without me."

"You need to walk it off, Cap'n. Otherwise your back's going to seize up."

"Fine, then let me walk it off without you holding me up."

Athos released his grasp on Svetlana and stepped away from her, watching as she reestablished her balance without his support. The first steps she took unassisted were agonizing, but as she continued, the pain settled into a dull ache in her lower back. "Alright, I need my doctor back, and the sooner the better. Where are Jo and Indy?"

Athos peered down the street. "I think I see Jo down the way." He set off at a brisk pace.

Svetlana tried to keep up, but anything faster than a casual stroll wracked her body with new and interesting pains. Probing her back for the spot that had hit the bar, her fingers traced across an old scar. She laughed bitterly and shook her head. It seemed she had used up her good luck spotting Richards from the airwave office, and all the rest of the luck was his today.

Athos returned after several minutes, with Jo following behind him. "Indy's tracked Richards back to Port Authority headquarters. He's keeping watch there in case Annette gets out."

Svetlana cursed under her breath. "I don't suppose there's a nice bathhouse anywhere near there where I can soak for a while, and just let the three of you keep track of Richards and Annette?"

"Plenty for gents, but not a one you can go in, Cap'n," Athos answered. "You'd have to get clear to the other side of Heliopolis for a halfway decent bathhouse for ladies."

Svetlana sighed heavily. "I'm in no shape to walk clear to the other side of town." Looking around at the shops nearby, she grinned through the pain. "Gods be good, I just had the worst idea in a long history of really bad ideas.

Athos, do you still have your cadet uniform?"

Athos' eyes grew wide. "Oh, no. No way."

"Look, I know it'll be a bit snug. But we can take them to that tailor—" Svetlana pointed to the small storefront. "—get me into some tight stays to keep my back immobile, and then just walk in to Port Authority headquarters like we own the place."

Athos shook his head. "Svetlana Mikhailovna Tereshchenko, you never fail to outdo yourself with ridiculous plans. Let me guess, we throw Bobby's name around like there's no tomorrow?"

Svetlana shrugged, with a wince. "If you've got a better plan, I'm all ears."

"If we can find where he's got her, we could break in," Jo suggested.

"Port Authority headquarters is enormous, Jo," Svetlana said. "All the windows are barred until you get up to the upper floors, and I'm in no shape for climbing. And even if I was, we'd just be picking some room at random. We could end up in the sergeant major's office just as easily as we could find Annette."

Athos nodded. "She's right, Jo. I like your plan better than Sveta's plan, I'll give you that. But we can't expect to sneak in either."

"Details," Jo grumbled. She looked at Athos. "So what do you have?"

"Nothing yet. Give me a minute to think of something better," Athos said.

Svetlana nodded and hushed Jo when the pilot began to speak up again. Athos stayed silent for a while. "Okay, alright. Storming the place not being a viable option, I guess we play dress up. One of these days, though, we're gonna wind up in scalding water because of you and your plans."

"You say that like we've ever had a plan that didn't get us into trouble."

"Trouble's one thing, Cap'n," Athos replied. "I'm talking about literal scalding water of the oceans. Mark my words. We'll be there too soon."

Athos tugged at his collar. "Can we make this quick? I think my jacket wants to strangle me for leaving it in the closet all these years."

"Quick and painless is my goal," Svetlana replied, studying Athos. "Can you actually reach the papers in your inside pocket?"

Athos raised his arm and tried to bend it. His sleeve went taut and he sighed. "I guess that means saluting is right out as well."

Chuckling, Svetlana reached into the pocket for him. "Then let's hope we don't spot any high ranking officers, or you'll be in trouble."

"It's not my fault the tailor ran out of fabric taking your coat out," he grumbled.

Glaring at him, Svetlana snapped, "Watch your tongue, Private."

Athos smirked. "Yes, Captain."

Svetlana turned and marched toward the gate outside of the Heliopolis Port Authority's headquarters building. A smile played across her lips for an instant, but she straightened her face as a guard spotted her and Athos approaching. The guard scrutinized them before saluting and standing aside.

"Not bad," Athos muttered when they were out of the guard's earshot. "Doubt it's all going to be that easy."

"It never is," Svetlana replied. She yanked open the front door and strode up to the desk. "We need to speak with Corporal Richards immediately."

The desk clerk, not even wearing rank insignia, looked from Svetlana to Athos at a dizzying speed. "Who ... what ... why?" he stammered.

Athos shook his head and handed the clerk the sheaf of papers. "Corporal Richards. Please find him. Immediately."

The clerk took the papers with trembling hands and unfolded them. He scanned the information, and he grew pale. "Vice Admiral Beauregard?"

"That's right," Svetlana said. "He's sent us to collect Corporal Richards and the woman he brought in with him earlier."

The clerk looked up at Svetlana. "Corporal Richards is on special assignment—"

"Yes, yes, we've heard that rigmarole. But seeing as we saw him in the city today, with our own eyes, and watched him abscond with the widow of a highly decorated former Air Fleet officer in front of multiple witnesses, we know he's here."

The clerk shook his head. "No, ma'am, he's not. He can't be. I've been at the desk for the past six hours, and he hasn't come in during that time."

Svetlana looked at Athos, who shrugged in response. She turned back and smiled at the clerk. "Will you excuse us a moment?" Pulling Athos aside, she whispered, "Indy saw him come in, right?"

"Indy and Jo both." He hesitated. "Well, they said they saw him go through the gate. I doubt either of them got close enough to see much beyond that." He sighed.

Svetlana nodded and returned to the clerk. Another man stood beside him, looking over the papers that Athos had carried in. Though Svetlana wasn't clear on Port Authority ranks, he had more bars on his uniform than Richards, so she assumed he outranked the corporal. The man looked up, one eyebrow arched. "Prisoner release?"

"That's what the paperwork indicates, sir," she said with a quick nod.

"Well, see, here's the thing about that, ma'am. This paperwork is a bit out of date."

"Is it?" She shrugged, but cold sweat prickled the back of her neck. "I'm afraid that's what we had on hand at Air Fleet headquarters. If you don't mind getting us the new forms, we'd be happy to take them back. Once we get our Air Fleet widow back, of course."

"Paperwork aside, ma'am, we haven't had anyone brought in to the prison today. It's a bit hard for us to release someone who's not here."

"No prisoners?" Svetlana looked at Athos. "Is there any way for you to verify that?"

"Of course." The more decorated officer picked up a log book from the desk and handed it to Svetlana opened to the present date. While the log showed several prisoners brought in on the previous day, the sheet for today was blank.

"It seems possible that the intelligence we received was inaccurate, sir," she replied. "We appreciate your confirmation of such." Turning to leave, she signaled Athos to do the same.

"Just a moment," the officer said. "Doctor Annette Campbell. Isn't she the doctor on *The Silent Monsoon*?"

Svetlana froze, glad that the stays under her uniform were already keeping her back stiff, so that her shoulders did not betray her newfound tension. Athos glanced back at her.

"Yes, I believe she is," Svetlana said, with the slightest stammer. She turned back to the desk and smiled at the officer. "And while you certainly didn't hear it from me, that's the precise reason why Vice Admiral Beauregard is interested in her whereabouts. It seems that ship's been popping up here and there in the news lately."

"Yes," he replied. "Especially that captain of hers. The woman with one golden eye."

Hesitating to calm herself so that her voice would not betray her, she turned to face him fully. "Funny, you're the third person I've talked to today who has thought I'm her." She shrugged. "I suppose I do fit the description."

He leaned back and scrutinized her. Sweat trickled down her neck and continued down her back. The heavy wool of the Air Fleet uniforms was ideal for airship wear, less practical anywhere else. But she kept her gaze level, staring at the officer's chest.

Finally he shook his head. "Nah, you can't be her. She's gotta be taller than you."

Svetlana barked out a nervous laugh, but smoothed it out into a vigorous chuckle. "You're right, sir. Also, she's not Air Fleet."

He nodded, and his gaze flicked down to the breast pocket of her jacket, where her name plate had once been. He frowned for a moment, but then handed Svetlana the papers. "Sorry we can't help you, Captain—"

"Walker. Thank you all the same." With a stiff smile, she followed Athos out the door.

Chapter Six

Svetlana started the winches to pull the gangplank back onto the ship. After checking the lines that tethered *The Silent Monsoon* to the dock, she headed down to the mess, still in her old uniform.

Athos had already stripped down to his undershirt by the time she arrived. "Captain, permission to burn that jacket and never speak of how ill it fit again?"

Svetlana smirked, but then her face slid back into a frown. "I think he recognized me."

"Possibly," Athos said. "Turning back around to face him might have helped with the confirmation." He ran a finger across the fabric of Svetlana's breast pocket. "The wool is compressed where your name plate was. 'Walker' doesn't take four inches of space."

Svetlana sighed and shrugged. "He didn't call me on it."

"What if he had? For all we know, he's reporting you to Air Fleet headquarters as we speak. Impersonating an officer isn't the sort of thing they'd be likely to overlook."

"Fine, I'll go talk to Bobby in the morning. We're going to need his help to find Annette anyway." She peeled off her jacket and tossed it across the back of a chair. "Still feels like Bobby owes her, after Jack. Now, you going to help me out of these stays?"

Athos rolled his eyes and tugged the back of Svetlana's shirt out from the waistband of her slacks. "How did your airwave chat with Kavisoli go? Any chance we could get some help from him?"

"I'm not sure what help he could offer. He's on Rrusadon, with no signs of wanting to leave there. Can't say that I blame him. I bet they've got plenty of bathhouses for fine upstanding women there."

"Wouldn't you like to find out?" Athos asked. Svetlana could hear the smirk in his words. He slid his hands up her back deftly, loosening the laces that kept her stays tight. With a brief twinge of pain, the pressure compressing her torso began to lessen.

"I thought I heard—" Jo trailed off as she walked through the door to the mess and surveyed the scene in front of her. After a moment's hesitation, she laughed. "Anyone other than you, Captain, and I might be a little jealous."

"Get over it, Jo," Athos snapped at her. "This is strictly ship business."

"I know," she spat back. She turned her attention to Svetlana. "So no luck on the doc?"

"No. Did you actually see Richards take her in the building?"

"Yes."

"The front door?"

Jo scoffed. "No, the side door."

Svetlana frowned. "Well, that explains one thing. But you'd think that officer would have realized if they had Annette locked up somewhere in the building."

"Sure, maybe. But it's a big building."

Athos tugged at Svetlana's corset, and it slid down past her hips.

She stepped out of it and kicked it to the side. "If you're going to burn your coat, take care of that while you're at it." Glancing at him and then at Jo, she continued. "We'll have to figure out where Annette is in the morning. Meantime, get some rest."

"Aye, Captain," Athos said with a quick nod.

Svetlana walked back to her cabin, one hand probing her back as she walked. The pain had subsided considerably, but she still felt it twinge when she twisted to the side. She stopped in the infirmary, which felt cold and sterile without the doctor bustling around inside. Svetlana had no idea what she should look for to help ease her pain. "Gods be cursed, Annette," she muttered under her breath. "I need you."

She stumbled over the threshold of her cabin and closed the door. A breeze slipped through the open windows, cutting through her thin blouse. Pulling off her eyepatch, she moved to the windows to close them.

Something white and wispy appeared out of the corner of her right eye. She turned to look in that direction with her good eye. The moonlight played across a heavy cloud bank, turning it into something that looked like a sailing ship from the old days, before the seas had boiled. "There's your ghost ship, Mirage. Nothing more than moonlight on clouds."

Svetlana slipped out of her blouse and tailored pants and into a worn shirt and a pair of loose slacks. She turned back the threadbare sheets on her bed, but rather than climbing beneath them, she sat on the edge of the bed. Her boots, discarded a moment ago, seemed to call to her.

She couldn't be certain that Annette was at Port Authority headquarters, and even if she was there, Svetlana had no idea where in the building the doctor might be held. While she could wake Athos or Jo to take them with her, Svetlana suspected that they might both be in one or the other's cabin at this point. And Indigo wouldn't be much help for an attempt to sneak in and break Annette out.

Athos had mentioned Kavisoli, but even if she was willing to ask for his help on this, she doubted the newly minted mayor had enough pull to get information out of the Heliopolis Port Authority from his home platform. And if he did have that sort of pull, it seemed like the sort of information he might have mentioned, since he knew the bomb had originated on Heliopolis.

Svetlana had heard that the Kavisoli played their cards close to their chests, but there was a distinct difference between that and withholding information from someone who was helping them investigate a threat against their new position of respectability.

Low, mournful bells signaled impending Lift. "I'm sorry, Annette," she muttered to herself. "We'll find you as soon as we can."

Svetlana stumbled into the mess in the morning and tried to peer through her squinted eye as she yawned. The cook stove had something nearing a boil atop it, and someone was bustling around in the kitchen. "Annette?" she ventured.

"No such luck," Athos answered. "Kettle's on. We should have tea soon."

"Make the stuff we got at Indy's village." She shook her head as she banged her shin against the leg of the mess table. "I'm going to need it."

"You too, eh?"

Svetlana twisted around to look at Athos, glad that her back seemed to be healing. "Kept trying to come up with a way to go get Annette. I almost came to get you about half a dozen times."

"Oh, yeah, umm, me too," Athos said, turning away to rummage through the heavy ceramic tea mugs. He almost looked like he was turning pink, but she'd rarely seen Athos get embarrassed by anything.

Svetlana chuckled as she put two and two together. "So you and Jo did make up, then?"

Athos spun back to face her, his eyes dark. But he looked at the doorway instead, and the stormy look passed. "Morning."

"Tea?" Jo asked.

"Soon enough."

"Good." Jo sat to Svetlana's left, and began combing out her long hair.

With the position Jo had taken, Svetlana couldn't keep her good eye on both Jo and Athos at the same time. She more than suspected that they had, in fact, shared a bed last night, a fact that neither of them wanted their captain to know about. But *The Silent Monsoon* was a small enough ship that secrets rarely stayed that way for long. Even without seeing both their faces at the same time, she'd know sooner or later what the current state of their on-again, off-again relationship was.

Athos spooned tea from a battered tin into a thin muslin bag, which he placed into the now boiling water on the stove. The kettle was little more than a spare pot with a snug-fitting lid, but it served its purpose. And all of them had gotten quite adept at pouring the steaming liquid from the pot into their mugs without spilling a drop.

Jo spoke again, drawing Svetlana's attention. "So, what's on the agenda today, Cap'n?"

Svetlana sighed. "I'm not sure. I should send a message to Bobby to see if he can pull some strings and locate Annette."

"That'll take too long," Jo said with a shake of her head.

"Well, we could go see him in person." She hesitated then rephrased her thoughts. "Or, rather, I could go to headquarters."

"Nope," Indigo said, dropping the morning newspaper on the table to Svetlana's right. By the time she turned to look at it, the boy had already clambered onto the counter between the kitchen and the mess and was spooning hefty scoops of sugar into one of the mugs that Athos had set out.

The headline on the newspaper, splotchy from the powdered sugar of Indigo's favorite morning treat, read "Suspects in Bar Brawl Sought" and was placed directly above photographs of Svetlana, Athos, and Jo. Svetlana shook her head. "One day you're a hero, the next you're wanted. Lovely."

Jo grabbed the paper and scanned the article. "Sweet Skyfather! It's naught but lies. Listen to this: 'The pictured suspects are said to have assaulted an officer of the Port Authority, who was making a routine arrest.'" Growling beneath her breath, she threw it back onto the table. "It doesn't even say a word about Annette."

Svetlana looked at the paper again. "And there's no byline. I don't even know who to complain to."

Athos carried steaming mugs to the table and placed them in front of Jo and Svetlana. A creamy cloud bloomed in Jo's cup, but Svetlana's was a deep brown. She picked it up and swallowed a gulp, ignoring the temperature as it scalded her tongue.

"So, change of plans, then?" Athos asked from across the top of his mug.

"Well, we could still try to go to Air Fleet headquarters, convince Bobby that this is all a set up. Surely, there'd be witnesses at the bar who could—" She trailed off. "But who am I kidding? Bobby might take me at my word. I think we're back to sending him a note and hoping."

Jo shrugged. "Sure, he might believe you. But honestly, if someone is serious about arresting you or taking you in for questioning, why haven't they already come knocking?"

"That's a good point," Athos said. "Sure, Jo's an elusive criminal, but everyone knows where to find Captain Tereshchenko. Makes me think that headline's more of a scare tactic than anything else."

"To what end?" Svetlana asked. "Get me running scared? Anyone who knows me would realize I won't just take off without Annette."

Athos nodded. "But for all we know, Port Authority's just waiting for us to cut and run."

Laughing, Svetlana said, "Then they definitely don't know who they're dealing with. But all the more reason to stick around to find Annette before we deal with any of the other problems we've got on our plate."

"I still think we should just go to the Port Authority headquarters and find her ourselves," Jo said. "I can get off ship without anyone spotting me, easy."

"I'm sure you can. But we still haven't a clue where to start looking for her. I've never been past the front desk, and I don't believe any of the rest of you have either?"

Athos and Indigo shook their heads, but Jo tapped on the newspaper to get Svetlana's attention. "What if we use this? We go turn ourselves in for questioning. They'll take us back, maybe even to the same area where they're holding Annette."

"If they're holding Annette," Athos reminded her.

"Where else would she be?" Jo asked.

"Wait, wait," Svetlana said. "You think we should turn ourselves in, get locked up, and then get Annette out?"

Jo shrugged, tilting her head back and forth. "Okay, some of us turn ourselves in, and the rest of us break everyone out?"

"No. If you turn yourself in, I doubt they'd put you anywhere near Annette," Svetlana said. "Same with Athos. Maybe I'd get lucky and they'd put me near her. But if they know us, then they'll want us as far from each other as possible. And even if only one of us turns ourself in, then it's Indy and two of us trying to get the other two out." She shook her head, emphasizing her point. "It's not going to work."

"We could get a copy of the building plans in town," Athos suggested. "If we look it over, we could at least narrow down where they'd be likely to hold her."

"Or I could just tell you where the cells are." Annette's voice rang out from the doorway of the mess, and Svetlana leapt out of her chair to turn and face the doctor.

"You're back! Are you alright?" Rushing over and enveloping Annette in a bear hug, Svetlana pinned the doctor's arms to her sides.

Annette laughed. "I'm fine, yes. Could use a bit of breakfast. And maybe less squeezing my insides?"

Svetlana released her hold on Annette. Leaping down from the counter and into the kitchen, Indigo banged around through the pots and pans. When the din died down, Svetlana asked, "What happened?"

"Richards took me in through some sort of tunnel network," Annette said. "Service tunnels, I guess. He tossed me in a cell and then vanished for a while. When the morning crew came in, they were a bit perplexed as to how I had gotten myself locked up. I told them it was Richards, and they let me out of there, no questions asked. Even hired a cab to get me back to the ship."

Svetlana frowned. "That seems odd. Do you suppose you were followed?"

"Wouldn't surprise me if the cabbie went straight back and told them where she dropped me off. But I don't think they'd need that information.

They knew who I was." She paused. "I did hear one thing as I was going out. Something about Richards making a mess of things for the last time. Oh, and it seems you've seen that nonsense in the paper."

"Yeah, did you read it?" Jo asked.

"I did. And I've already seen a retraction."

"Of the lead story?" Athos asked, a smile playing across his lips. "Ooh, someone's going to be in trouble."

"Got something else, too," Annette said, fumbling through the many pockets on her jacket. "Indy's little pigtailed friend found me on my way back to the ship."

A clatter of pots and pans emanated from the kitchen, and the crew all turned to look. Indigo's face had turned a brilliant shade of pink, a startling contrast to his hair.

"What's wrong, Indy? Did you burn yourself?" Svetlana asked, hurrying toward the kitchen.

Indigo shook his head vigorously. "Pigtailed friend. Deliah?"

"That's her name," Annette said. "She wanted me to tell you that she hopes to see you soon and to give you this note."

Indigo slipped out of the kitchen and took the note from Annette, scurrying back just as quickly as he had emerged.

Turning to Svetlana and handing her a second note, Annette continued. "And she told me to tell my captain that she's sorry about the Rrusadon mistake, and that you need to seek out Bonebriar."

Svetlana's brow furrowed. "What in the abyss is a Bonebriar?"

CHAPTER SEVEN

"BONEBRIAR," ATHOS SAID, jabbing a finger at the map and shaking his head. "It's uninhabited, according to this. If I had to guess, I'd say it probably got too hot when the seas boiled."

Indigo leaned in close to the map, tracing a spiral out from the location Athos had found. His finger completed several rotations before it came across another island. "Nothing there either."

Annette closed a book and added it to the stack beside her. "That's five histories of the Republic with no reference to a place called Bonebriar."

"Alright, so a named, uninhabited island that's not in the history books. Sounds like another wild goose chase to me," Svetlana said. "How many more histories do we have to look at?"

"Just two," Annette said. "Oh, three. I've got one still in my cabin." A strange look crossed her face. "It's a rather old one. Maybe if Bonebriar is an abandoned place, it'll be in there." She left the bridge in a hurry.

Jo sat near the port window, turning the note that Deliah had given to

Annette over in her hands. "Svetlana, how closely did you read this note?"

"I just glanced at it, why?"

"The writing is strange, like there's something more to it than what it says. Hey, Indy, can I see the note that Deliah wrote to you?"

Indigo looked up from the map, eyes wide. "No. Secret stuff."

Jo rolled her eyes. "Indy, we all know that it's a secret note. I don't care about what it says, I just want to see her handwriting on your note."

Indigo drew his mouth in narrowly, corners turned down. It was a face he made when he wanted to say no but knew that doing so would do him no good. Fishing the note out of his pocket, he trudged across the bridge to hand it to Jo.

She took a moment to scan it before she went back to the note Deliah had written Svetlana. "There are numbers in her letters." Laying the note on the desk beside the map, Jo looked at Athos. "Can you still follow coordinates?"

"Who can't?" Athos scoffed.

Jo smirked and jerked her head toward the hallway outside the bridge. "Doc." Then she turned her attention to the paper. "Okay, so try 28 degrees, 57 minutes—"

"North or south?" Athos asked.

"Oh," Jo said, a frown crossing her face. "I guess we have to check all the possibilities."

Athos nodded. "Just for the record, the Bonebriar on this map is sitting real close to 29 degrees south."

"Promising." Jo squinted at the letter. "Svetlana, is this a 4 or a 9?"

Svetlana bent over the table to examine the strange handwriting. "Maybe a 7?"

Jo sighed. "Yeah, translating Deliah's secret code isn't an exact science." She looked at Athos. "What's the easterly on your Bonebriar?"

"About 177 or so."

Svetlana, Jo, and Athos all looked at each other. "What do you think, Captain?" Jo asked.

Svetlana frowned. "Not sure what to think. This is information from a girl who told us what we were looking for was on Rrusadon, and I'm pretty certain I wasn't looking for a bomb." She sighed. "But I'm not sure we've got any other leads."

Annette appeared in the doorway to the bridge. "You're not going to believe what I found." The book she held up in front of her was titled *Whiskeys of the World*.

"I like the sort of books you call history books, Doc," Athos said with a laugh.

Annette smiled. "It's a history of whiskeys, to be fair. But it mentions Bonebriar." She set the book down alongside the map. As she flipped through the pages, the sweet scent of old paper filled the bridge. "Seems it's the native habitat of one of the spices they used in the recipe for Cranglimmering. It's been successfully grown elsewhere since the Boiling. But at least this confirms that people lived there once."

"And Deliah's note had some coordinates that Jo was clever enough to find," Svetlana said. She glanced back at Jo and smiled. "I think we've got ourselves a course."

Looking around the bridge, Annette asked. "Anyone know where Indy went?"

Jo sighed. "He's probably sulking because I made him show me the love note that Deliah wrote him."

A flash of bright blue caught Svetlana's gaze. "He's on deck. Let's go."

Before she could give the command to cast off, Indigo ran onto the bridge, out of breath. "People watching the ship."

"What sort of people?" Svetlana asked.

"Some kids. Some grownups."

"Do any of them have uniforms on?" Jo asked, poised to slip out the back entrance of the bridge.

"No uniforms," Indigo said.

"Does it matter that we're being watched?" Athos asked. "I mean, let's be honest here. When do you suppose someone isn't watching us?"

"Yes, but who *is* watching us?" Jo asked. "That's what I'm concerned about."

"Well, let's list the possibilities," Annette suggested. "Port Authority's top of the list, of course, but who else might be interested in our comings and goings? Technically, several of you are still wanted for questioning by the local authorities, even if not officially, and Jo's probably got a number of bounty hunters hoping they can get a piece of her—"

"They wish," Jo scoffed. "Cap'n, you want me to go nab one of them for questioning?"

"No, Athos is right," Svetlana said. "We're always being watched. I'm not worried about who it is this time. They won't have any way to know where we're going, other than away from Heliopolis. And even if they did, who'd be crazy enough to follow us to the middle of nowhere?"

Svetlana stood at the prow of the airship, spyglass in hand. But rather than viewing the air around the ship, her gaze was trained on the waters below. The froth atop the overheated oceans roiled, with no sign of land in sight. She lowered the spyglass and looked at the bearing compass beside her. Without a reference point, the fancy device showed as much as her blind eye did.

"Captain?" Athos called out behind her, his voice barely carrying over the wind and sound of the propellers.

She turned back to face him, and he beckoned her closer. Sighing, she collapsed the spyglass and collected the bearing compass. He had stepped inside before she started back to the bridge. A hot blast of air hit her as she opened the door, giving her the sensation of pins and needles pricking at her frozen fingers and toes. She flexed her digits as she looked at Athos, who lingered at the door. "What is it?"

"Jo wanted me to get you in here." Athos shrugged.

Svetlana handed him the spyglass. "Then you can keep a lookout for this mysterious island." She approached the altitude controls, where Jo was tinkering, as Athos slipped back outside.

Jo looked up. "Has Indy said anything about the stabilizers since I complained about them?"

"No. It hasn't been a pressing matter. They worked fine on the way to Rrusadon and back."

"That they did." Compressing her lips into a fine line, she said, "But now they're ... twitchy."

"Twitchy?" Svetlana arched an eyebrow.

"I just keep feeling a dropping sensation, like—" She hesitated, searching for the right words. "Like the first Lift after you've been off platform for a few weeks."

Svetlana nodded her acknowledgement. The switch from platform engines to geyser-driven elevation during Lift rarely bothered her anymore, provided she wasn't trying to move around while it occurred, but she remembered her queasiness the first few weeks she had spent in a platform city. Then she shook her head. "I know what you're saying, but I haven't felt it."

"It's been tiny. Little gradual drops, not one big drop."

"What's the altimeter say?"

"No change."

"So maybe Indy's just making some adjustments to keep us flying on a more even keel?"

"Okay," Jo said. "But what would be *un*-evening our keel?"

The ship lurched, giving the sensation of having dropped several feet, and Svetlana looked at Jo. "Like that?"

"Just like. Only that's the biggest one so far."

Svetlana looked out the front windows of the bridge, to where Athos was keeping watch. He looked unfazed by the sudden change in elevation. She frowned. "Are we imagining it in here? Did Athos notice it before?"

Jo nodded, eyes wide. She slid back to the directional controls and looked at more gauges. "Compass is spinning like a top."

Svetlana lifted the bearing compass but felt the needle rotating in its housing. "Magnetic fields?"

"Maybe."

Moving to the map, where Athos had left a large magnifying glass on the location of Bonebriar, Svetlana looked for any notations left by previous aeronauts about this area.

Jo spoke up while Svetlana searched. "Captain, I recommend we drop down a bit. If we're gonna crash, I like our odds a whole lot better when there's not so much space between us and whatever we're going to hit."

Svetlana nodded hurriedly, just before she found the information she was looking for on the map. "Go down to about 500 feet. There are some high magnetics noted on the map." After checking the distance between the map notation and the island, she looked up at the clock. "We should be there soon, right?"

Jo checked the clock as she adjusted the altitude controls. "Yep. Within the hour."

"Not soon enough," Svetlana muttered.

Without warning, the ship surged forward and Jo yelped. Svetlana jumped to the altitude controls and took hold of them.

"We're speeding up," Jo said, her voice trembling. "I didn't do it."

Svetlana stomped on the floor to open the plate that covered the speaking tube to the engine room. "Indigo? What's happening?"

A moment passed before his response. "Going faster. Don't know why."

"Slow us down, Indy."

"Trying," he grunted.

Athos flung open the bridge door. "Captain, have you noticed that we seem to be on a collision course with the water?"

"Sure have," Svetlana said. "And we're trying to fix that. Either make yourself useful or get off the bridge."

"Where do you want me?" he asked.

Svetlana considered the options. She and Jo were capable of flying the ship—in fact, it was meant for no more than two pilots. There was no one to communicate with, and more or less no reason to add anyone else to the bridge. "Stay up front," she replied. To Indigo, she called out, "Send Annette topside."

Athos hurried back to the prow and resumed scanning the rapidly approaching water. Svetlana turned her attention back to Jo.

"It's no use," the pilot said, without prompting for a status report. "All of the gauges are going wild, and we're going down faster and steeper than we should be."

"Well, then I suppose we need to hope we hit something soft and not boiling." Looking out at the featureless blue of the skies around them, she said, "Just hope Athos remembers to get inside before we do."

Athos waved his arms frantically from outside the bridge, drawing Svetlana's attention. When she looked at him, he mouthed, "Land."

Her heart sank. So much for her first hope. "Because we needed another problem," Svetlana sighed. As she started to turn back to Jo, another flash of motion at the front of the ship caught her attention. She turned back in time to see a tentacle snake up toward one of the balloons that kept the ship aloft and stab into it. The blood drained from her face. "Skyfather save us."

"Jo, Jo, Jo, Jo, Jo," Svetlana chanted before realizing that her panic was stuck on a single word. "Up!"

"We can't. That's one bag out." The crunch of metal punctuated her explanation. "Frame's smashed."

Annette stumbled onto the bridge. "What in the abyss is happening?"

"Don't know yet." Svetlana stomped near the speaking tube to the engine room to get Indigo's attention. "Indy, get up here, now. Take the back stairs." Outside, Athos clung to the front of the ship and looked down.

"Athos, get in here!" Jo cried out before Svetlana could think to suggest the same. Athos looked up and back at the women, his mouth gaping open. Nodding, he turned to run just as another tentacle swept into sight. The tentacle was mottled greens and greys, speckled on one side with white flakes, but the flakes writhed and then straightened into some sort of feelers. The tentacle shot directly at Athos and coiled around him.

Svetlana screamed, dimly aware that her voice was not the only one. The tentacle lifted Athos off his feet and yanked him toward the edge of the ship, knocking his legs into the stout ironwood bulwark. Still clutching Athos, the tentacle slammed him against the bulwark twice more. Then it lifted him higher and pulled him off the ship and out of sight.

"What is that thing?" Annette asked.

"It looked like ... like a ... a kraken, from the days of sailing ships," Svetlana stammered.

One tentacle wriggled among the remaining balloons, while two more slithered across the deck. Annette rushed forward and slammed the door at the front of the bridge. "Hope that'll keep it out."

"If it gets one more balloon, we're down," Jo said, her voice eerily calm in the midst of the chaos. She barked out a sharp chuckle. "Though the instruments seem to have stabilized. We're at 100 feet."

The ship shuddered as something struck the hull, and Svetlana saw green outside the bridge. "We're above Bonebriar. Or some other island. We need to get back out over water."

"How am I supposed to do that if we don't have a lookout?"

Annette hurried to the starboard windows, then crossed the bridge to the port windows. "No good. I can't see the ground from here."

"You'll see it soon enough," Jo warned, swinging the wheel to the left as hard as she could. The ship pulled away from the tentacles.

Indigo scurried through a small panel in the back of the bridge, panting. "Trees. Trees all over."

Svetlana pulled back on the altitude controls. The ship lurched forward, but the prow didn't rise like she had hoped it would.

"I told you," Jo spat. "Forward balloon is out."

"Any extra elevation is better than none, Jo," Svetlana replied, continuing to tug on the controls.

A tentacle darted into Svetlana's view and wrapped around the cables that tethered the main balloon to the ship. Annette cranked open one of the windows, grabbed her pistol, leaned out, and took a shot. Her shot went several feet wide from the tentacle. She took a deep breath and fired again. This time, the bullet grazed across the tentacle, leaving a dark scorch mark across the murky grey surface.

"Hold on to something, Annette," Svetlana said. She locked the altitude controls and joined Jo on the steering wheel, adding her strength and weight to the attempt to turn the ship. Between the two women, they managed to turn the slow arcing course of the ship into a sharper turn.

The tentacle on the balloon cable scrambled for purchase. Svetlana heard a loud snap as the tentacle flailed backward, still wrapped around a chunk of the cable. The frayed end of the cable wavered in the wind for a moment before darting up, out of sight.

"Front main balloon cable out," she reported, even as her mind raced to consider the possible outcomes. The other two cables *could*, in theory, keep the main balloon in place, under ideal flying conditions. Today was anything but ideal.

Jo gestured out the port windows. "Beach. I'm going to try to land there."

The slender strip of blinding white sand wavered in Svetlana's vision. On its right, the ocean sent scalding waves crashing across it, sometimes obscuring it entirely. To its left, a vast expanse of green stretched out. Svetlana thought she saw more grey-green tentacles lashing out of the forest onto the beach. But as she ran an eye across the gauges, she nodded. "Yes. Land there."

"Aye" was Jo's only response. She reached behind Svetlana and unlocked the altitude controls.

Svetlana stayed where she was, pinned between Jo and the controls, unable to do much more than hold the steering wheel. Jo told Svetlana to release the wheel as the ship aligned with the beach strip.

Numbness crept over Svetlana, not just because of how tight her grip had been. The tentacle attacks had stopped. But she had no idea where Athos was or if he was even alive. It took all of her will to remain upright.

"We're going to feel this landing," Jo murmured.

Jo's words were an understatement. The impact of hard wood against a scoured beach was sharp, punctuated by splintering sounds. Svetlana hoped that it was the trees beside them rather than the ship beneath them that cracked. The ship slid along the sand. Friction slowed it to a stop just before the prow plunged into the roiling water.

As soon as the ship stopped, Svetlana collapsed against the steering column. Jo followed her down, and Annette and Indigo soon joined the crying heap on the floor of the bridge of *The Silent Monsoon*.

CHAPTER EIGHT

"WE'VE GOT TO find Athos," Svetlana said as she dried her eye.

"Any guess where we were when we lost him?" Annette asked, voice shaky.

"I'd say we were over the island. The air ... kraken ... thing didn't seem to attack us when we were over the water."

"So instead of falling into the ocean and being boiled alive, he might have fallen a hundred feet through tree cover, or maybe just been eaten by a monster," Jo said, pulling herself to her feet and dusting off her slacks. She looked out the windows of the bridge and shook her head.

Svetlana rose and surveyed what she could see of the ship. The smaller forward balloon covered most of the prow of the ship, fragments of its metal skeleton poking through the fabric. The front cable from the main balloon lay snaked across the deck and what remained of the forward balloon. "We need to check the ship for any other structural damage. But Athos first."

The air here was potent with the earthy scent of more growing things than even Rrusadon had hosted. Svetlana didn't recognize many of the tree species. She could pick out a dozen different sorts of leaves. Wood was always in demand on Heliopolis and many of the other platform cities that they traded between. "Athos first," she reminded herself. She could worry about cargo after they found her first mate. And after they fixed the ship.

As Svetlana helped Annette climb down from the ship, Jo stood, hands on hips, shaking her head. "The balloons are the main thing, but we're going to need to check the entire hull, so we're going to have to find some way to hoist her up to check the keel and strakes."

"If this place is uninhabited—" Svetlana began.

"Then it all gets a whole lot harder," Jo spat back. Then she shrugged. "We'd better get moving."

Calling up to the deck, Svetlana said, "Indy, stay with the ship, see what you can fix. We're going to look for Athos."

"I can't fix the balloons," Indigo said. "Just the controls, maybe."

"Then start there. But we can't go anywhere till we fix the ship, and we're going to need help for that."

Indigo nodded and went back inside the bridge.

"Pardon me, ma'am," a cultured voice behind Svetlana began. Her hand flew to her holster as she spun to locate the source of the voice before it said anything more.

Standing a few dozen yards away was something that looked like a man. He was a little too tall, and a bit broad around the chest and waistline. His face was covered with a filigree mask that made his eyes look overly large, with no discernible holes for mouth or nose. But his attire was impeccable, hardly the sort of thing that one expected to see on an island in the middle of nowhere.

Svetlana's hand still on her holster, she asked, "Who are you?"

"My name is Drassilis. I see that you have some sort of difficulty with your ship."

"You don't say," Jo muttered.

Svetlana shushed her with a quick gesture. "It's a pleasure to meet you, Mr. Drassilis. My name is Captain Svetlana Tereshchenko, of *The Silent*

Monsoon. As you say, she's in rough shape. This is our pilot, Jos ... ah, Jo, and our doctor, Annette Campbell. We're looking for another of our crew members. And for people who can help with the ship repairs."

Drassilis hesitated, his head cocked to the side. "My condolences on the loss of your crew member. I can, however, help with your ship. More accurately, I can take you to someone who will be able to enact the necessary repairs."

"You said condolences," Jo said. "Did you ... is he dead?"

Drassilis shifted his shoulders upward in a stiff shrug. "I do not know, Miss Josahjo. But as it appears that you have been crying, I have deduced that you believe them to be deceased."

"It's just Jo," she grumbled.

"My apologies, Miss Jo."

"He's automatic," Annette whispered, slipping past Svetlana and hurrying to Drassilis's side. She peered at the mask, but then recoiled.

"Automatic?" Svetlana asked. Her gaze swept over Drassilis's strange shape. The oversized body made sense for an automaton, as did his stiff movements and lack of an obvious way to breathe.

"We should be going," Drassilis said.

Svetlana cocked her head to the side as she noticed additional oddities about Drassilis. He did breathe but very slowly, and she wasn't sure she had seen his eyes blink. She walked forward until she was standing nearly nose to nose with him. Drassilis blinked then, two curved, articulated silver colored plates sliding down to cover his eyes. When they slid back up, his blue eyes continued to stare at Svetlana.

"Time is of the essence, Captain Tereshchenko. It is imperative that we cross the jungle in daylight so as to reach the city before nightfall. The jungle is unsafe at night."

Frowning, Svetlana asked, "Unsafe how?"

"All manner of beings inhabit this island. Many of them are quite unfriendly."

"Does that include you?" Svetlana asked.

"On the contrary. I hope to be your friend and guide to the person who can help repair your ship."

"Does this person have a ship hoist?" Jo asked.

"She does, in addition to other necessary equipment," Drassilis replied. "Now then. I need to return to the city. If you wish to accompany me, we must go now." Drassilis shifted his body upward with a whirring of gears. The lower half of his body rotated, followed by the upper half. Four small studded wheels beneath both of his feet rolled across the uneven terrain, each raising and lowering in turn to keep him stable.

Svetlana hesitated. She didn't want to trust this automaton who had showed up so soon after her ship had crashed. But without help, there was no way for them to ensure that the ship was ready to fly again. They were stuck here for the time being. She considered asking Drassilis if they had, in fact, found Bonebriar. With all of the difficulty the crew of *The Silent Monsoon* had had trying to locate the island, she wondered if she should mention the name of the place. Finally, she nodded to her waiting crew. "What choice do we have?"

Drassilis led the crew along a wide path that wound through the jungle. Despite the wildness around them, the path itself was smooth and level, criss-crossed with narrow wheel tracks. But Svetlana kept her eye on the trees. She hadn't seen the creature that had taken Athos since they had landed, but she had spotted places where it might have been earlier, judging by the splintered tree branches high above.

"Drassilis," she called out. "One of our crew was taken by some sort of ... well, it looked like a kraken, what with the tentacles and all, but it seemed to be flying or perhaps in the tops of the trees."

Drassilis rotated the upper half of his body to face Svetlana, though he continued to move forward. "What color was it, Captain Tereshchenko?"

"Grey, green, sort of swirled together."

"Ah, it sounds as though you have encountered the Arboreal Kraken."

"Arboreal," Svetlana repeated. "You've got to be kidding me. A kraken that lives in the trees?"

"Quite right, Captain. And though you may not believe it, it is but one of the unusual forms of life that inhabits this island. We must keep our pace quick if we are to evade some of the other creatures who make this their home."

"If the Arboreal Kraken took someone from our ship...," Jo started.

Drassilis somehow managed to open his absurdly large eyes even wider. "I'm terribly sorry, Miss Jo. The Arboreal Kraken is believed to be carnivorous. Though it does typically prefer to scavenge corpses."

"That's ... unusual." Jo paled as she spoke.

"I assure you, its dietary preference is a part of its entire life cycle. By consuming decomposing flesh, the Arboreal Kraken fills its digestive tract with gasses that allow it to fly short distances—"

"Thank you, Drassilis," Annette interrupted. "We get the picture." Turning to Svetlana, she whispered, "Can we change the subject? I've handled corpses, and I think he might even make me queasy."

Svetlana nodded stiffly. "Jo, could you come here a minute?"

Jo glanced back, eyes dark and teary. Pausing mid-step, she allowed Svetlana and Annette to catch up to her. "What?"

"Despite what the bucket of bolts says, I'm still hopeful that we can find Athos." Svetlana looked sidelong at Annette. "Maybe hurt but alive."

Jo shrugged. "It'd almost suit me if he's horribly maimed. I just want to know one way or the other." She stalked off.

"Do you believe that?" Annette asked quietly.

"Which part? That he's alive, or that she'd like for him to be maimed?"

Annette chuckled. "Well, I meant the first, but I'm guessing you have thoughts on the second as well."

Svetlana sighed. "Athos is damn hard to kill, I know that much. But against this Arboreal Kraken?" She shook her head. "I don't think that's the sort of death sentence he can charm his way out of."

"If anyone could, it'd be him," Annette said.

"As for Jo, I can't quite figure her out. One minute, she's jealous of his other women, and the next minute, she hates his guts and wants nothing to do with him. And then they make up, and act like it's all been peaches and roses for as long as they've known each other. If I hadn't seen her going through this for two or three years now, I might be worried. I think she's only happy when she's unhappy about something."

A low growl from behind her cut off anything more Svetlana might have said. The fine hairs on the back of her neck rose. Reaching out and grabbing Annette's hand, she pulled the doctor along. "Drassilis? You mentioned other creatures. What sort—?"

Drassilis turned his torso around to face Svetlana again. Before his eyes had a chance to grow wide, he shouted, "Drop!"

Svetlana's instincts took over. She tugged Annette down to the ground with her, throwing her body over Annette's. Rolling to her back, she still covered as much of Annette as she could. A nearly naked woman hovered above her, mid-leap. Svetlana raised her legs and kicked both feet into the woman's stomach as she fell. The woman exhaled sharply as the momentum knocked her back. Her breath reeked of spoiled meat.

Scrambling to her feet, Svetlana helped Annette up. And then she saw the group of naked people ringing the path around them. As she paused to look more closely, she noticed that they were all covered in a fine fur, some bearing stripes, others bearing spots. The range of colors of their fur was as vast as the range of human skin colors—some pale as Indigo, and others even darker than Annette. Unnaturally round eyes, with slitted pupils and no visible eyelids, stared at the crew. Their noses were broad and flat, and their ears lay flat to either side of their head.

From behind her, Drassilis growled and hissed.

"Drassilis? What are you doing?" Svetlana asked.

"My apologies, Captain, I am working as quickly as I can to forge an amicable situation."

The woman Svetlana had kicked had regained her feet, and stalked back and forth. She crouched lower to the ground as she went, until she was nearly on all fours. As she arched her back, Svetlana almost expected to see a tail swishing back and forth above her rear end. The other cat people surrounding the crew of *The Silent Monsoon* moved more subtly, their gazes glued to the humans. They appeared to be ignoring Drassilis's impassioned sounds.

Slowly, the cat woman moved closer to Svetlana. Svetlana spread her arms wide, trying to shield the rest of the crew. "We don't want any trouble," Svetlana said. "Drassilis, tell them that."

"I have," the automaton replied. "They have not yet responded to my overtures."

The cat woman who had tried to attack Svetlana and Annette stopped a few paces in front of Svetlana, and then rose up to her full height. She smirked, and then spoke in a low, throaty voice. "We hunger."

"We don't taste good," Svetlana said.

The cat woman sniffed the air, then stepped closer to Svetlana. Her tongue darted out and licked the tip of her flat nose, bringing with it a waft of decay. "No, smell bad. Taste bad too."

"Yes. We smell awful. And taste worse," Jo said

The cat woman hissed at Jo. "I only speak to this one." She pointed one slender finger at Svetlana, who could not fail to notice the sharp, curved nail on the end of the woman's finger. "You smell of that man."

Svetlana looked more closely at the cat woman. "What man?"

"Man who fell from trees."

"Where is he now?"

The cat woman shrugged. "We cared not. He smelled bad too." She paused, looking past Svetlana at Annette. "That one will do."

Svetlana shifted her stance to block the woman's line of sight. Though she was protective of every member of her crew, she and Annette went back almost as far as she and Athos. And she wasn't about to hand over the member of her crew best suited to help Athos, assuming they found him alive.

"No." Svetlana reached for her pistol, though she kept it in the holster.

The cat woman's gaze flickered downward, and she took a step back. "We hunger," she whined.

"Hunger somewhere else," Svetlana said.

The cat woman backed away slowly, winding from side to side and lowering her upper body back toward the earth. As she did, the other cat people crouched similarly and disappeared into the growing gloom. Soon, only the cat woman who had spoken with Svetlana was visible, and then she turned her head and bounded away.

Svetlana released a long sigh as she helped Annette to her feet. "Alright. Double time. Let's move."

The bits of sky that Svetlana could see were beginning to turn purple and pink when Drassilis spoke again. "We are here. Please, watch your step as there is a slope."

A warm orange glow backlit the automaton, who stood at what looked like the mouth of a cave. He shifted to the side, and Svetlana saw a ramp extending behind him, hewn from stone, but well-worn in the center.

"Where are we, then?"

"This is the city of Bonebriar."

Svetlana peered past Drassilis, her gaze tracing the ramp down. From this elevation, it was impossible to see anything more than a gradually descending slope and the surrounding rugged stone. It hardly looked like a place that would be hospitable to life, in stark contrast to the green forest they had passed through.

Annette spoke up. "Drassilis, before we came here, we weren't able to find much information about this place. It's real?"

"Quite real, Doctor Campbell. But please, follow me. The Felinus were but infants compared to the threats outside of the city after the sun has set."

Svetlana nodded, and the rest of her crew moved into the cave entrance. She paused as she neared Drassilis. "What about the ship? One of our crew is still onboard. Will he be in danger?"

"Is your ship seaworthy?"

Svetlana's jaw dropped at the mere thought of a ship on the boiling ocean. "No one has sailed the seas for more than a hundred years."

Drassilis tilted his head to the side. "High tide comes in the early morning hours. Your ship will be scoured by the tide. If she is seaworthy, then there will be no need for concern."

"And if she's not?"

"Then there *is* a need for concern."

Svetlana spun around and looked back at the jungle, now barely visible. The trees stood like silent sentinels, but beyond them, a low murmur of life hummed, punctuated with growls and the occasional scream. "We have to go back."

"We cannot go back, Captain Tereshchenko. It is far too dangerous."

"I'm not leaving Indy out there to be boiled. We should have brought him with us if that was a risk!"

Drassilis tapped an overly long finger against his mask near where a mouth should have been. "Would Indy recognize airwave signals?"

"What does that matter? We don't have a receiver on the ship."

Drassilis made a motion approximating a sigh. "That is not the question I asked."

"I don't know. Maybe. I don't know half of what's in that boy's brain."

"Then we will attempt to send him a message, warning him about the danger. It is the best we can do." He rotated both his upper and lower body as one, and began rolling down the ramp.

Svetlana shook her head and followed. Though she had no idea what she expected to find at Bonebriar, an automaton guide and a perilous forest had not been high on the list. It seemed as though Deliah had sent them on another wild goose chase. Svetlana hoped that things would prove otherwise when they reached this city of which Drassilis spoke.

As Svetlana and Drassilis rounded a curve, she saw Jo and Annette staring dumbfounded at something below. She approached them and followed their gaze.

Beneath them, spread out as far as the eye could see, was a city. The walls and ceiling of the cavern looked natural, but the buildings had been carved from stone, some of which was clearly not that of the cave. The orange light that emanated from the cave's mouth came from strings of glowing globes that hung above the city and illuminated the whole area as though it were daytime. They were still too high above the city to see the people, but Svetlana could see motion in the streets. It was like looking down on any major city from *The Silent Monsoon*.

"Bonebriar," Svetlana whispered. "Sweet Skyfather."

"The Skyfather is rarely invoked here, Captain Tereshchenko." Drassilis gestured up. "Few here have seen the sky."

"Wait, few here have seen the sky?" Jo repeated. "How do you plan to find someone who knows the first thing about airship repair, then?"

Drassilis turned to look at Jo, the orange light casting shadows across his filigree mask that almost made it look as though he were smiling. "I don't plan to find someone, Miss Jo. I plan to take you to the only one who can. Mother to us all." He bowed his head in reverence. "Come along, I don't want to keep her waiting."

CHAPTER NINE

THE PATH DRASSILIS led them on wound around the upper portions of the city, where there were few buildings. Those they did see looked to be long abandoned. The group walked in silence, in awe of this place, far beneath the surface of the earth. The air was comfortably warm, and the walls of the cave blocked out both the potent peat smell of the jungle and the sulfurous stench of the ocean.

When a cooler wind blew, Svetlana looked around for the source. As her gaze moved skyward, she saw the twinkle of starlight. The path leveled off to a flat plaza, and all around were more stone buildings, taller and grander than those on the floor of the cave.

Drassilis led them to a house that looked quite respectable, even by the standards of a place like Heliopolis or Rrusadon. The front door was at the same level as the street, as were all of the entrances to these buildings. In fact, Svetlana had not seen a single step since they had arrived on the island.

"Drassilis," she called out as he opened the front door. "Is everyone here an automaton?"

"Certainly not," a female voice replied from somewhere inside the house. "Are these our guests, Drassilis?"

"Yes, Mother." Drassilis moved to the side, allowing the crew to file in behind him. Svetlana detected a floral odor as soon as she crossed the threshold, sweet but not overpowering, though she could not put her finger on the exact scent.

A tall woman stood at the base of a spiral ramp with an ornate bannister encircling it. She had red hair and the pale white skin that typically accompanied such a color. The pink ruffled shirt she wore beneath her black jacket and skirt matched the circles of color on her cheeks. Her eyes were the clear blue color of the distant horizon.

Drassilis cleared his throat and introduced each of the crew members in turn, referring to the woman as Mother each time. Finally, he introduced her to the crew, saying, "And this is the Mother to us all, Doctor Vertiline Dowhty."

"Doctor Dowhty," Svetlana began.

"Please. Vertiline is perfectly acceptable."

"As you say. We're looking for—" Svetlana took a moment to compose her thoughts. "We're looking for quite a bit, actually. I suppose the most pressing matter is getting a message to the crew member we've left behind on our ship, on the beach. Drassilis suggested sending an airwave, but we have no receiving equipment on board our ship."

"Good, good," Vertiline replied. "Start with the smallest problem first. Tell me, Captain. Your ship, does she have any brass components?"

Svetlana frowned. "Of course. It's necessary for—"

Vertiline interrupted her. "Indeed. I have constructed a transmitter here that is capable of sending a message to any location with a sufficient quantity of brass. It will not be possible for your crew member to send a reply beyond a few taps, but you will find that we are not bound by the typical conventions of message length transmission from here."

As Vertiline spoke, Svetlana dug her hand into her pocket, finding her monocular. The majority of its construction was brass, and she didn't relish the thought of someone tapping an airwave message that would be transmitted to brass while she was wearing it. "What constitutes a sufficient quantity?"

Vertiline shrugged. "I have not had cause to test it extensively, but I am certain that an airship has quite enough."

Svetlana nodded, removing her hand from the monocular and her pocket. "We're also looking for one of our crew members who may have fallen to the island before we crashed. And Drassilis said that you could help us repair the damaged components of our ship." *And then there's the Cranglimmering,* Svetlana thought, gnawing at the inside of her lip to keep from bringing it up.

"I am sorry to hear about your crew member. We can send out search parties come morning. We will need to await the morning to examine your ship as well." Vertiline paused and stared at Svetlana. "But what was your ship doing so far off course? We see few airships in our skies. There is nothing near us for quite some distance."

Rubbing her hand over her mouth, Svetlana shot a warning glance at Jo. She trusted Annette to stay silent. "We received a tip that something we were looking for was in this area. Now that we've seen the city, it appears that the city itself might have been the thing in question." She lowered her voice, almost unconsciously. "You're not a part of the Republic."

Vertiline stiffened and arched one eyebrow. "I find it advisable not to talk politics on empty stomachs and a lack of sleep, Captain." She lingered on the final word. "Might I suggest that you and your crew sit down for a bit of dinner first, and then Drassilis can show you to my guest suite. I am afraid two of you will have to share a bed."

"That's fine," Svetlana replied, puzzling over Vertiline's sudden change in demeanor.

"Excellent. Then we shall talk more in the morning." She turned and ascended the ramp halfway. "Ah, the message for your crew member?"

"The tides," Svetlana replied. "We don't know if our ship is seaworthy, and Drassilis says the tides will scour the beach where the ship sits. I'll compose something at the dinner table, if that suits you."

"Very well," Vertiline said, and continued upward. "We shall speak further tomorrow."

Drassilis gestured to a darkened hallway. "Dinner then, and some paper. This way."

Annette caught Svetlana's elbow as she turned to follow. "Cap'n, I'd like to state for the record that there's something strange going on."

"Very astute," Svetlana murmured, her gaze following the course of the ramp that Vertiline had ascended. The woman was intriguing, to be certain, but there was also something about her that troubled Svetlana. "But the options seem to be go out into the jungle and die, or get some food and sleep. I'd prefer the latter."

"Just want you to keep it under advisement."

"Thank you, Annette. Consider me advised."

Daylight came early, and Svetlana woke when the sun crossed her face, despite not having gotten much sleep. With nothing else to wear, she'd slept in her clothes, and their heavy seams had left indentations all over her body. Annette was still curled up under the blankets on the bed she and Svetlana had shared. On the opposite side of the room, Jo was sprawled across the entire second bed.

When Svetlana rose, Annette stirred, but repositioned herself without waking. Svetlana pulled on her boots and scribbled a quick note to let Annette and Jo know where she had gone.

The scent of cooking meat and baking bread wafted up from the lower level of the house, and Svetlana followed it to the kitchen.

Vertiline was at the stove, dressed in the same clothes as she had worn the night before. The smell of flowers cut through the cooking aromas. It reminded Svetlana of something purple, but she still could not place the scent. Svetlana cleared her throat, and the woman looked up.

"Good morning," Vertiline said, smiling. "I am afraid I do not often have guests, so I hope you can make do with what I have."

"If you've got tea and food, I'm sure we'll be fine."

Vertiline nodded and gestured to the table. It was covered with brightly colored fruits, a platter of something that looked like sausage links, and a large pile of round flatbreads.

Svetlana looked at the bounty before her. "Where does all of this come from?"

"The meat is from a sort of pig that lives in the jungle."

"Not one like the cat ... Felinus, was it?"

"Oh no," Vertiline said with a laugh. "A far less bipedal sort of pig. The fruits grow there as well. We grow the grains in hothouses in the city below."

"It all looks wonderful. I hope we won't eat you out of house and home."

"I think that unlikely," Vertiline said.

Svetlana helped herself to a plate and took a seat at the table. "So, politics?"

Vertiline chuckled as she sat at the table across from Svetlana. "If you insist. No, we are not a part of the Republic. Long ago, this place was a city-state. But when the seas boiled, our foremothers objected to some of the policies of the High Council that bypassed the authority of the Republican Senate." She shrugged. "We withdrew from the Republic."

Svetlana frowned. "They just let you withdraw?"

"In theory, any city-state can withdraw. It is just not frequently done, because to withdraw from the Republic cuts a city off from trade, Republican assistance, exchange of ideas with other cities, and more. I believe that our foremothers had hoped that other cities might follow our lead, but they did not, and the Republic seemed to have no quarrel with our departure. I suppose, in the grand scheme of things, we are just a small island that produces an abundance of fruit and is plagued by a large number of hostile inhabitants. We are no great loss to the Republic."

"Bonebriar has been written out of the histories of the Republic."

Vertiline sighed. "That is the way of the Republic. Sometimes, if there is a city-state they cannot control, they choose to forget that place." She paused, gazing at Svetlana over the top of her teacup. The corners of her mouth turned up for a moment, but then fell again. "They do the same thing with people they cannot control."

Svetlana nodded. "I'm just glad we had coordinates, or we might never have found this place."

Vertiline arched an eyebrow. "Coordinates? Now why would someone give you coordinates to this place? Truthfully?"

Svetlana sighed softly as she scrambled for a good response. "Honestly, I'm not sure. We've been receiving some cryptic tips from an associate of ours in Heliopolis."

"Oh, Heliopolis? I had not realized that is where you were from! I lived there for a short while, when I was younger." Vertiline smiled, a genuine expression of happiness. "You must tell me all of the gossip while we fly back to your ship."

Svetlana winced at the word gossip. "Ah, sure. You said something about search parties to look for our missing crew member? We'll need to find him if you want gossip ... Wait, did you say fly back?"

"It is just a little gyrocopter," Vertiline said with a shrug. "But I have been looking for a chance to try it out. We can walk if you prefer."

"After running into those Felinus, flying sounds wonderful."

Svetlana sighed with relief when she saw *The Silent Monsoon*. Water lapped against the lower third of the hull, but the ship had neither gone out to sea nor sunk when the tide came in. Her home, such as it was, was intact. Indigo's blue hair was visible near the bridge as the gyrocopter's whirring blades brought Svetlana and Vertiline closer.

Vertiline circled the ship, frowning. "There is nowhere to land."

Svetlana scanned the ship and the water around it. A small spit of dry land lay about a hundred feet from the ship, but she didn't relish the thought of landing there and then having to cross even that small of a gap through the steaming seawater. She pointed to the spit anyway.

Vertiline laughed. "You have more faith in my ability to land this than I do, Captain."

Svetlana grinned. "I can land it." Vertiline raised an eyebrow, and Svetlana continued. "I've been watching how you fly this thing. Looks simple enough."

"Very well," Vertiline murmured. Releasing something beneath the steering column, Vertiline swung the entire mechanism in front of Svetlana's seat. She held on to the controls until Svetlana had gotten a good grip on them, and their hands brushed against each other several times in the process. Svetlana felt something like electricity pass between their skin but could not tell if it was a part of the gyrocopter or something more. Vertiline said, "Landings never have been my strong suit."

Svetlana tested the steering, verifying that she had gotten the gist of its workings from watching Vertiline fly. As soon as she was comfortable, she swooped the gyrocopter around in a wide arc and began her descent. She aimed for one end of the spit, not sure how far the gyrocopter might roll on the sand.

The gyrocopter shuddered as it approached the ground, and Svetlana gulped. The heat from the ocean was already making her sweat. After a tense moment, the vehicle's flight smoothed just in time for the wheels to contact the sand.

Svetlana grabbed for the brake, but Vertiline beat her to it. They shared a quick smile, and then Svetlana concentrated on the controls. She adjusted their path to compensate for the curve and slope of the spit, and the gyrocopter slid to a stop just at the far end of the sandbar.

Vertiline breathed. "If you're ever looking for a job, I would hire you to train my pilots in a heartbeat."

"You have pilots?"

"A few." Vertiline shrugged. "Far more who would like to be pilots, but we have few ships for them to fly. Of any size."

Svetlana looked down at the roiling water to the side of the spit. "Now we just need to find a way to get to the ship."

"I think that little blue-haired boy has found a solution," Vertiline said.

The gangplank winches were lowering what looked like a section of the deck into the water. Nearby, Indigo scaled down a rope. Atop the wooden platform sat a small boxy object that Svetlana couldn't identify. But as the raft reached the water, Indigo leapt from his rope to the platform, and Svetlana heard the whine of one of the small air pumps that they used to inflate the balloons after a long shore leave.

Indigo's raft moved across the water swiftly, and he cut the engine to slow down before he hit the sand spit. He grinned when he reached the gyrocopter. "Hi, Captain," he called out. "Hi, Captain's friend."

"Indigo, this is Dr. Vertiline Dowhty. Jo and Annette are on their way with a tow ship. She's going to see if she can fix our ship."

Svetlana and Vertiline boarded the raft, and Indigo moved the pump to the opposite side to power their way back to *The Silent Monsoon.* The heat from the water permeated the raft. *Well, at least it's better than swimming back,* Svetlana thought.

When they reached the ship, Indigo attached the winch cables to the platform. "We have to climb back up. The winches can't move the platform with all of us on it."

"Good thinking, Indy," Svetlana grunted as she shimmied up the rope. "Remind me to give you a bonus next time I've got some spare Quinpence just lying about."

"More money? Okay!" Indigo exclaimed.

The climbers came upon the deck at the bow, and Svetlana surveyed the wreckage, shaking her head. Vertiline joined her and drew in a sharp breath through her teeth.

"That bad, huh?" Svetlana asked.

"Oh well, I suppose it should not be too difficult to get you back up and running," Vertiline said, pointing as she continued. "The cable is easy enough to repair. The break is low enough that we can brace it with a static piece for a temporary fix. As for the forward balloon, that we will have to replace. My people may be able to salvage some of the components, so we should cut that one loose and take it back with us."

Svetlana nodded. "The hull?"

Indigo spoke up. "No damage on the inside. Didn't check the outside."

A loud whooping sound came from the stern of the ship. "No," Svetlana said. "How in the heavens—"

Indigo was already running full tilt in that direction. Looking at Vertiline, Svetlana gave her an apologetic smile and took off after him.

By the time she arrived, Athos was struggling to disentangle himself from Indigo. He grinned at Svetlana. "Little help here?"

Svetlana returned the smile but shook her head. "'Fraid not." She threw her arms around Athos' neck and shoulders and hugged him tightly. "Where in the abyss have you been?"

"That ... flying kraken thing dropped me. Straight into a tree. Lucky for me, it was straight into some sort of nest, so I didn't get too banged up. Soon as I could, I got out of there. But the ground didn't seem friendly either, so I've just been hanging out in the trees, keeping an eye on the ship. Didn't know you'd left Indigo behind, or I'd have come down sooner." He shrugged, as much as he could with Svetlana and Indigo attached to him. "Saw that gyrocopter land, and I knew there were only two pilots out there who'd try that sort of landing. And seeing as I adore the both of them, I figured it was safe to come aboard."

"Yeah, well, that other one's gonna be mighty angry and then mighty glad to see you. C'mon, we're waiting for Jo and Annette to come around with a tow ship."

Athos frowned. "Who else was on that gyrocopter with you, then? And where in the abyss are we?"

"Bonebriar, as it turns out. There's a city, Athos. An entire city, part underground, and part out on the far side of the island. That's Vertiline. She's helping us get back up on our feet." Svetlana paused and glared at Athos. "Don't try to get her in bed, alright?"

Athos grinned. "Me? Whatever would make you think I'd do something like that?" He paused and arched an eyebrow. "Why, you got designs on her?"

Svetlana shrugged. Vertiline had been becoming more interesting and less suspicious with each new topic of conversation, but she would hardly admit that to Athos. "Now why would you think that?" She paused. "Don't answer."

As they reached the bridge, Svetlana spotted Vertiline inside, frowning at the controls. She grabbed Athos' hand and pulled him into the bridge.

"Vertiline, this is Athos, our lost lamb."

Vertiline glanced up for the briefest moment before returning her attention to the gauges. "Captain, did you notice any problems with your instruments before you got here?"

"Yes, actually," Svetlana replied, moving to Vertiline's side. "The compasses went wild, and the altimeter was off as well."

Vertiline held her hands parallel to the floor, fingers splayed, and moved around the bridge. "There is some sort of signal." She winced then lowered herself on all fours and reached beneath the steering column. When she rose, she held a small chrome device, slightly smaller than the palm of her hand, and about as thick. She shook her head as she looked at it. "Captain, I believe you were sabotaged. I have never seen anything like this. May I take it back to my lab?"

Svetlana nodded. "Does this mean we were tracked here?"

"I will not know until I crack this open and look at it." Vertiline raised the device to her ear. "It is a weak signal, if there is one. Someone would have had to follow you physically, or be casting a sizable net to find this thing."

Svetlana nodded. "Athos, ship is yours. I want to get Vertiline back to her lab faster than that tow ship is going to go." She smiled and hugged him again. "I'm glad to have you back."

CHAPTER TEN

SVETLANA DUCKED TO get out of the way of one of Vertiline's repair crews on the deck of *The Silent Monsoon*. The men, women, and handful of automatons Vertiline had sent to work on the ship were everywhere. Heading below deck, Svetlana popped her head into Athos' room, the door standing wide open. He wasn't in his room, so she continued on to the mess, noticing that Jo's door stood open as well.

Annette sat at the table, flipping through a book and sipping tea. She looked up as Svetlana walked in. "How are things going?"

Svetlana shrugged. "I can't tell. The workers don't seem to understand me when I ask them questions. Or at least they don't give me answers. Vertiline is still working on that device, whatever it is. Where's everyone else?"

Annette frowned. "You didn't hear them?"

"Them who?"

"Athos and Jo, who else? They were screaming at the top of their lungs at each other ten or fifteen minutes ago."

Svetlana sighed. "No, I was trying to see Vertiline and being rebuffed by Drassilis. I'm guessing by the state of things, they've moved their fighting elsewhere?"

"From the sound of it, yes. Oh, and I suppose Indy's in the engine room. He took off in that direction when the fight started."

Svetlana sighed. "I wanted them to stay on board, so we can leave as soon as we're patched up. But I guess that didn't get through their thick skulls."

"To be fair, this is the first I've heard of it, Cap'n. I thought we had more to do yet," Annette replied.

"Like what?"

"Well, was it just me, or have you and Vertiline gotten a bit chummy?" Annette winked.

Svetlana licked her lips and shook her head. "Is it possible for me to hold a polite conversation with anyone and *not* have it be called 'chummy'? Dr. Dowhty is quite interesting, that's all."

"Interesting," Annette said. "Yes, I can see that. She's also smart, pretty, and a ginger. Which means I'm surprised that your clothes aren't flying off."

Svetlana shook her head. "I'm not that bad. These days. Anyway, like I said, we're leaving soon. And I'm not looking for some quick fling. Really, Annette. I'm not Athos, with a warm bed in every port."

"I will grant you that. How does he have time for them all?" Annette shook her head and held up a warning finger. "You know what, I don't actually want an answer to that question. So, instead, have we found out anything about the Cranglimmering here?"

Svetlana shook her head. "I'm beginning to think that Deliah isn't on the same page with us. She sent us to Rrusadon to find a bomb, and she sent us here to ... I don't know, find this place? Find out that it exists?"

Annette held up her book. The title was long rubbed off of the cover, but Svetlana thought she could see the shapes of letters that might spell out Bonebriar. "I borrowed this from Vertiline. It's from before they dropped off of the Republic's radar."

"No, they left," Svetlana murmured. "They renounced their membership in the Republic, or something along those lines." She frowned, trying to remember the words that Vertiline had used.

Annette cocked her head to the side. "Why would they do that?"

"Vertiline wasn't specific. She said it happened quite some time ago. There was something about the High Council overriding a vote of the Republican Senate."

"Hmmm. Vertiline's library is dated. There aren't many books that were published less than a hundred years ago. But I could try to see if I can find anything more about what happened."

Svetlana shook her head. "I don't see the point in it. When we get back to Heliopolis, we'll talk to Deliah and see if we can't get some straight answers out of her."

"Still, I wouldn't mind getting to read a few more of Vertiline's books," Annette said.

"Well, if you want to talk your way past Drassilis, be my guest."

Annette bit her lip. "No, I don't think so. There's something unsettling about him."

"The eyes. They're too big."

"No. I mean, they are, but that's not it. If you look closely at his mask, it almost seems like there's flesh underneath."

Svetlana recoiled at that suggestion, suddenly queasy. "So, not an automaton?"

"More like a hybrid," Annette said slowly. "Part man, part machine. It's not like anything I've ever seen before. Granted, there aren't a lot of automatons running around in any part of the Republic."

"Do you suppose that was why they left?"

"Anything's possible. I suppose there would be some in the Republic who would be opposed to so much of a mix of technology and humanity. Regardless, this whole place is just on the edge of being creepy."

"On the edge?" Svetlana laughed. She ticked off the list on her fingers. "Arboreal Kraken, Felinus, a hybrid automaton, and an underground city, and it's just on the edge? No, it's downright creepy. But I've gotta go out in it and round up my crew. If they come back while I'm out, tell them to stick around. Ship's yours."

Svetlana was not surprised to find that Bonebriar had a brothel. An older woman, who might have been quite beautiful in her younger days, sprawled in a plush chair near the entrance. Her hair had once been blonde, but it was now streaked through with silver. She dressed in what looked like underclothing, like many of the girls in brothels did, but with pencil and paper in hand and spectacles perched atop her head, she looked more like a secretary than a prostitute. As Svetlana approached, the woman looked up. "Lady or gent?"

"Oh, no. I'm not here for company. I'm looking for someone."

The woman chuckled. "That's what some people say when they <u>are</u> looking for company. Name's Gretchen."

"Captain Svetlana Tereshchenko. I'm looking for one of my crew, who might have found himself looking for company."

"Oh, so you're the one with the airship that's got most of our regulars too busy to stop in?" Gretchen laughed. "Well, can't complain too much, seeing as that means 'Mother To Us All' is lining their pockets with more spending money." She held up her hands and made air quotes around the title that Drassilis used with such respect. From the smirk that she gave as she did so, it seemed clear that Drassilis was far more reverent toward Vertiline than others were.

"What can I say," Svetlana said, smiling. "I'm happy to be good for business. But you haven't seen any young, dashing strangers today, have you?"

"Can't say that I have. A stranger would be something to talk about." Gretchen paused then shouted toward the interior of the brothel. "Molls? C'mere."

A few moments later, a younger woman with long, straight, jet black hair and ebony skin stepped out of a dark hallway, completely nude. "We got guests?" she asked, favoring Svetlana with a winning smile.

"This here's the airship captain. She just wants to know if any of her crew has stopped in."

Molls shrugged, somehow giving the simple motion a sinuous grace. "If they have, they haven't come to me."

Svetlana glanced around the sumptuously decorated sitting room. "If you don't mind my asking, how many ladies does a place like this employ?"

"Four ladies, two gents, and me," Gretchen replied. "But it's always me or Molls keeping an eye on the door. Since the old automaton we had broke down beyond fixing."

Svetlana was tempted to learn more about the automatons from Gretchen, who seemed to be happy to have someone to chat with. Molls had already vanished back into the hallway from which she had emerged, and Svetlana reminded herself that she needed to find Athos and Jo, not learn more about the local culture. She fished into her pocket and found a pence, which she handed to Gretchen. "I don't know what that buys in these parts, but I hope it makes talking to me worth your while."

"That it does, love. You come back any time you like, and I'll talk both your ears straight off if there's more where this came from."

"Thanks, Gretchen. If I've got some time later, I'd love to."

On leaving the brothel, Svetlana realized she had managed to lose track of the docks. Granted, *The Silent Monsoon* was the only large airship docked there at the moment, and with her balloons deflated, the ship was tough to spot from a distance.

Svetlana stood in a narrow alleyway, paved with cobbles, that ran behind some of the large stone houses. From this side, they all looked similar—two stories high, painted brick in shades ranging from tan through brown, with tidy little gardens flanking a rear entrance. She had walked the length of the alley twice, but now couldn't even determine how she had gotten onto it. She approached one of the houses, the back door of which stood slightly ajar. Svetlana frowned but nudged it the rest of the way open. "Hello?" she called out softly. "Anyone home?"

In the dim twilight that came through the windows at the back of the house, Svetlana saw that she was in a kitchen, similar to the one in Vertiline's house. The fire in the hearth had burned down to glowing embers. Svetlana's stomach rumbled, and she realized she hadn't stopped for dinner. She checked the pot above the fire, but the contents were long cold and had hardened to the consistency of rock.

A sliver of light led Svetlana to a door out of the kitchen, and behind it, a narrow staircase, the first she had seen since their arrival. She proceeded up, trading her eyepatch for her monocular as she went. Not for the first time, she considered the possibility of handing it over to Indigo to make some upgrades, but she never knew what sorts of features the boy might see fit to install for her.

When she reached the second story landing, dimly lit with gas lamps, she listened for footsteps. She called out again but received no response. The only sound nearby was a low buzzing from a door, beneath which no light shone.

Svetlana tested the doorknob, and the door swung open. On the other side, a strange purple glow suffused the room, marred only by streaks of bright white lightning. In the center of the room stood a large device, made up primarily of a series of vertical glass tubes. The buzzing electricity was centered on the device, but occasionally the lightning arced out toward a distant wall.

The wall caught Svetlana's attention. The rest of the room was constructed of white painted brick, but the far wall was made of wood. Svetlana approached it cautiously, watching where the lightning strikes most frequently hit. Seeing most of them hit the righthand side of the wall, she approached along the lefthand wall.

She passed in front of a row of windows and glanced out. The moon slid from behind a cloud, and Svetlana could see the sea stretching out far beyond. She frowned. The residence she had entered had houses nearby on either side. And the front and back of the edifice looked out onto the street and alley, respectively. That made the view she was seeing highly improbable. She considered for a moment if perhaps this house had been taller than the others, but as she looked down, she could see no rooftops. Vertigo washed over her, and she turned away from the window, just in time to smell flowers and look deep into a gas lamp's growing flame.

Vertiline smiled at Svetlana. "Hello, Captain. Looking for something?"

"I ... this is your house?" Svetlana stammered. "This is ... what is this?"

"Yes, this is my house. You will need to be a bit more specific on your second question."

Svetlana gestured to the windows behind her, refusing to turn even an inch, lest it bring back her vertigo from the improbably vista. "We're on the sea."

"Oh, yes. And also no." Vertiline paused, considering. "More yes than no, I suppose. All of the benefits of being on the sea, but with an address in the city. Quite delightful, really."

"How?"

"The application of advanced technologies, far beyond what is seen in the Republic. My own design."

"And then what is that?" Svetlana asked, pointing at the tube device.

"A probability engine. Again, my own conception."

The words Vertiline was saying were intelligible on their own, but Svetlana could make neither heads nor tails of them in conjunction with one another. "Probability ... what does it do?"

"Ah, it takes a set of data, and extrapolates for possibilities. Or probabilities, if you prefer." Vertiline gestured to the far wall.

Svetlana turned her head slowly, wishing that the windows were on her bad eye's side, where their view would remain blurry. But the details of the wooden wall consumed all of her focus, so much so that the windows soon faded to the background.

The wooden wall was made up of narrow slats, half of which had dark black etching across them. The other half were etched in a grey so pale it was nearly white. Taken together, the etchings created a map of the entire world. But Svetlana had spent more than half of her life flying above those land masses, and each of them looked slightly off.

She turned back to Vertiline. "I can see that it's a map, but it's not right."

"It is old," Vertiline replied. "It represents the way that the world looked more than five hundred years ago." She moved toward the probability engine and flipped a switch, so that the purple glow and lightning bolts stopped. "Take a closer look, if you like."

Svetlana approached the map. "What is it for?"

Vertiline sighed. "Alas, it is incomplete at the moment. But it is said to be a map that will locate the hoard of the last Emperor. Which is, of course, valuable beyond measure, but one particular piece of that hoard is more important than all the rest combined. The Gem of the Seas."

Svetlana frowned, turning to face Vertiline again. "The Gem of the Seas? That's a legend. Most people don't think it ever existed."

"Yet our seas did not always boil as they do now. And while I find it suspect that a magical gem could be the reason why that is the case, the scientist in me still believes it should be investigated."

"I suppose that's reasonable. Where did the map come from?"

Vertiline smiled. "About a dozen years ago, I had reason to attend a meeting in the Republican City. One of the Council showed me around their building, and I spotted part of a map on the wall. Like you, I was confused by the coastlines, and I asked about it. Have you ever heard of Cranglimmering?"

Svetlana arched an eyebrow. She had been waiting for the opportune moment to bring up the cask to Vertiline but hadn't found an excuse yet. "Of course, who hasn't?"

"This Councilor told me that the Republic had assembled the map from staves made of the first three opened Casks of Cranglimmering. He said that the four closed casks held the remaining staves. With all of them owned privately, the Republic had no good reason to demand that the Cranglimmering be uncasked before its time. But as they are uncasked, the rest of the map will be revealed.

"I committed the map to memory, and sketched it out when I returned home. Then I built it on the wall, the black lines representing what I had seen, and the white lines sketching out assumed land forms. The probability engine has been working for the past few years to verify my sketched lines and try to pinpoint the location of the Gem of the Seas."

"I doubt you've heard, but the Bartram Cask—"

"Mm, I have heard. Missing from Heliopolis, they say."

Svetlana hesitated before she spoke again. Vertiline had been helpful in getting *The Silent Monsoon* back up and running. Beyond that, Svetlana wasn't sure she had much reason to trust the scientist. But if what she said was true, it did at least explain why Deliah had sent them to Bonebriar, and it could be another piece of the puzzle in the theft of the Bartram Cask. The more pieces they had, the more likely they were to track down the cask. Besides which, there was something, Svetlana couldn't put a finger on it, that made her want to trust Vertiline. She took a deep breath. "We're trying to find it. That's why we came here, or rather, why I thought we came here."

"Indeed? Alas, the cask is not here." Vertiline smiled. "I wish that I could help you to recover it, but that is not among my abilities."

Svetlana smiled in return. "The sentiment is still appreciated. We'll find it sooner or later, I hope. But tell me more about this Gem of the Seas."

"If the legends are true, whoever holds it can control the seas. If it were found again, one could stop the boiling. In theory."

"So if the Republic finds the Bartram Cask, they'll have more than half of the map?"

"Yes." Vertiline agreed.

"And if you find it, you'll have more than half."

Vertiline smiled and nodded.

"But everyone is still missing the same parts."

"Unfortunately, yes."

"Why not just buy the rest of the casks and be done with it?"

"Anyone moving toward consolidation of the casks is likely to be noticed. I, personally, prefer to work from the shadows."

Svetlana walked toward Vertiline and the probability engine. "And this machine? Do you think it can find the treasure on its own?"

"I don't have the answer to that question yet. I think it is likely that with another set of staves, my machine could narrow down the location. But find it?" Vertiline shrugged, a smile tugging at the corners of her lips. "I am afraid I will not know that until the machine reaches its conclusion."

Svetlana shook her head. "This is all ... I don't know what to make of any of it." A terrible thought came to her. Vertiline had been so forthcoming with this information. Svetlana looked up suddenly. "Oh, please tell me this doesn't mean that you have to kill me now!"

Vertiline laughed. "Not at all. I was concerned when I realized someone was sneaking around in my probability engine room, but I believe that you and I might be able to come to some sort of arrangement for the procurement of some of the remaining casks."

Svetlana smiled. "Now you're talking. And if you only want what's outside, I think we could reach an easy agreement."

Vertiline spun around into the space between the probability engine and the map. The moonlight washed over her for a moment, just before a shadow fell, blotting out the brightness of her skin.

Vertiline turned to the windows, and sudden terror gripped her face. Before Svetlana could move, every window pane in the room shattered, raining a shower of glass over Vertiline.

Three men clambered through the window frames. Even with the gas lamps burning, the men were grey from head to toe, like figures bathed in that selfsame moonlight. They wore baggy shirts and trousers, high boots, and scarves across their heads, much like the attire Svetlana herself preferred, modeled after the pirates of old sailing ships.

One of the men seized Vertiline, pinning her arms down. Another grabbed her feet and lifted her, while the third began to wrap a length of rope around the scientist, his compatriots holding Vertiline still.

"Stop!" Svetlana shouted as she drew her pistol. The man tying the rope opened his mouth as though he were laughing, but no sound emerged.

Svetlana fired, but the bullet flew through the man and embedded itself in the map wall behind him. She blinked as she looked at him, but no wound blossomed through the grey of his garb.

"Swords!" Vertiline cried out. "Find a sword!" The man holding the upper half of her body shoved a rag into her mouth and held it firmly in place.

"I don't carry one!" Svetlana reached down to her boot. "Knife?" she asked, producing one.

Vertiline nodded, eyes filling with tears, and Svetlana rushed forward. She slashed at the man who was tying up Vertiline, but he ducked out of her way and grabbed her wrist.

Cold radiated from his grip and lanced up Svetlana's arm. Her hand trembled, and the knife slid from her grasp. The man shoved her away. She stumbled back, clutching her arm.

He bent to pick up her knife and tossed it out the window then he turned back to his knots. When he finished, the three men all grabbed hold of Vertiline, and one tugged the end of the rope that stretched out the window. He winked at Svetlana as the three pirates and Vertiline were yanked out of the room.

CHAPTER ELEVEN

SVETLANA RUSHED TO the window. A huge ship, outfitted for sailing, not flight, hovered outside the window. The sails were turned to carry the ship away from the building, and it was already farther from the window sill than Svetlana wanted to jump. A flash of pink stockings and black booted feet caught her eye, and then she saw nothing more of Vertiline.

Running back to the door, Svetlana bellowed, "Drassilis! Drassilis, where are you?"

Drassilis was halfway up the spiral ramp from the entry hall by the time Svetlana arrived. "Captain Tereshchenko? I didn't know you were still here."

"Not still here, I came back. Or, rather, I wound up here."

"How did you get in?"

"Through the back door and up a staircase." Svetlana frowned. There were no other stairs anywhere in Vertiline's house, presumably so that Drassilis could get around the entire place. The fact that she had found and climbed stairs made little sense.

If Drassilis could have made his filigree mask frown, Svetlana was certain he would have done so. "The staircase? Oh, dear." His gaze fixed on a point beyond Svetlana, and she turned to follow it. The hallway she had come from was gone.

Drassilis continued. "My apologies, Captain Tereshchenko. Mother must have left the back ways open again. I'll ask her to close them up from both sides."

"Back ways? What does that mean?"

"The back ways are a device that Mother created to give her more space to work. Either she or I can access them from this side of the house, but only she can use the staircase. How careless of her to leave it open." He shook his head. "Where might I find her?"

Svetlana frowned as she tried to put words to what she had seen. Could it have been the ghost ship that Mirage had warned her about? Taking a deep breath, she said, "If I hadn't seen it, I wouldn't believe it myself. Three men came in through the window. Bullets didn't hurt them. And they pulled Vertiline out of the map room, and onto a—" She shook her head. "A ghost ship. A ghost ship just hauled her out of the map room." Svetlana watched Drassilis's eyes closely as she spoke. They remained still when she said "map room," but widened when she said "ghost ship."

"I see," Drassilis said, his voice smooth. "Fortunately, we are prepared for such an eventuality."

"Prepared? Does that mean you were *expecting* her to be kidnapped?"

"When one is the Mother to us all, one must be prepared for any event that would keep one from one's natural role. Ghost ships were one such possibility. Mother thought it best to prepare even for things she had not seen with her own eyes."

"Wow, you guys think of everything," Svetlana said. "Okay, so what's the plan?"

Before Drassilis could answer, a loud thump shook the door to one of the nearby rooms.

Svetlana spun to face the door. "Who else is here?" she whispered.

"There should be no one else here, Captain." Drassilis tried to lower his voice, but only managed an approximation of whispering.

Svetlana drew her gun and leveled it at the door. "Count of three," she called out.

"Can you give us a moment to get dressed?" Athos' voice answered.

"Athos Benjamin Tucker, what in the abyss are you doing here?"

"Ah, long story." He paused. Thumping inside the room filled the silence. "No, actually, short story. I went out looking for information on your new doctor friend, ran into Jo, and she brought me here."

The door to the room swung open, revealing Jo buckling on her gun belt. "Cap'n," she said.

Svetlana blinked, and raised an eyebrow when Athos padded up behind Jo, barefoot. "And you found yourselves a room. Peachy." She sighed. "Well, the more the merrier, I guess. Drassilis, want to show us the preparation now?"

"Preparation?" Athos asked. "Did I hear you say something about a ghost ship?"

"Yep. Ran off with Vertiline."

Athos froze, confusion blanketing his face. "It's real? Like an actual ghostly ship, crewed by ghosts?"

"Near as I can tell."

"Okay." He let out a low whistle. "Was not expecting that. And it took the ginger?"

"Like I said."

"Great. Never dealt with a ghost ship before. So now what?"

Svetlana grinned. "Oh, there's a plan. Drassilis, lead the way. We'll talk while we walk. Er, roll."

Drassilis moved past Svetlana and approached the blank wall where the hallway had been. He touched what looked like a random spot, and three doorways opened. Swiveling his wheels, he headed for the farthest left doorway. Svetlana shook her head, but beckoned Athos and Jo to follow.

"Did he just—" Jo started.

"Uh-huh. 'Back ways,' he calls it."

Jo let out a long whistle, and then whispered, "Aetherwhere."

Svetlana shook her head. "Aetherwhere's just fairy tale nonsense, Jo. It's gotta be that she took advantage of unused space in her house or something."

"Svetlana, we're following an automaton into a space that didn't exist a minute ago, to a contingency plan that a *scientist* put in place in case she was kidnapped by a ghost ship? And you want to tell me Aetherwhere isn't real?"

Athos nodded. "I think she's got you there, Captain. I mean, I'm not saying I believe in any of this, but for right now, seeing is believing."

Svetlana shrugged. "All I know is that Vertiline was giving me some interesting information right before she vanished, so I'd like to find her and finish our conversation. Whether this is or isn't Aetherwhere, let's not take any chances. So Fairy Queen be blessed."

Athos and Jo repeated the blessing, and the three humans followed the automaton deeper into the back ways of Vertiline's house.

When they reached the top of the ramp, Drassilis was tinkering with an oversized cannon. Far overhead, Svetlana saw the ghost ship, moving slowly away from the rooftop. The breeze was cold, and Svetlana dared not let her eye wander. She focused on the ship. It was grey, much like the men who had taken Vertiline, all wispy and ephemeral.

Svetlana shivered, remembering how solid the man's grasp on her wrist had been. Absently rubbing a hand across where he had grabbed her, her wrist still felt colder than the rest of her arm.

She nearly asked Drassilis how the ghost ship had gotten to Vertiline but realized that she already knew the answer to her question. The ghost ship might have been able to access Vertiline because they *were* in Aetherwhere. Instead, she asked, "So, what's the contingency plan, Drassilis?"

"I am calculating the trajectory necessary to land you on the upper deck of the ship."

Jo pointed at the cannon, then the ship, and then back at the cannon. "You're going to put us in that cannon and shoot us at the ship?"

"Precisely, Miss Jo."

Jo cackled with glee in response.

Svetlana's eye widened at Jo's excitement about being fired out of a cannon. But a more practical concern crossed her mind. "Uh, Drassilis? It might not be solid."

"That is why you should each collect a parachute pack from the cabinet behind you."

Svetlana turned and caught a glimpse of Athos, wide-eyed, color draining from his face. The cabinet, gleaming white and strangely out of place on the rooftop, had one door ajar. Svetlana opened it the rest of the way and pulled down three packs.

Jo accepted hers and donned it quickly. "Me first, please. Let me get on there and find their bridge. I want to fly that ship."

Athos shook his head. "No. No way."

"Athos, what's the problem?" Svetlana asked. "You got grabbed off the ship by an Arboreal Kraken and dropped how far? And you're afraid to try it again with a controlled descent?"

"I've had more than enough of any sort of falling, thank you very much. You and Jo go get your girlfriend."

"She's not my girlfriend," Svetlana spat back, thrusting the pack at Athos.

"Then all the more reason for me to not want to stick my neck out for some woman whom I've just met."

"The fact remains that she needs our help."

"Why should we be the ones who help her? Let's stick Drassilis in the cannon and let him go get his 'Mother' back," Athos retorted.

Drassilis rotated his upper torso and stared at Athos. "My body is too large for the firing chamber."

"That's a design flaw, don't you think?" Athos asked. "Who was going to rescue her on a normal night, when we weren't here?"

"Her other children would come to her aid. If you do not wish to go, I can summon some of her children."

Svetlana shook her head. "No, we'll go. Jo and I will go."

Jo bit her lip. "Athos is right, Svetlana. We don't know her very well."

"You just wanted to fly that ship a minute ago!" Svetlana sputtered. "Okay, you want a good reason? She has solid information on the missing cask. Better than what Deliah's been giving us."

Athos stiffened, his face pulling into a grimace. "Truly?"

Svetlana nodded. "It's more than just what's in the cask, Athos. A whole lot more. Treasure beyond measure."

Athos mouthed the words to himself, puzzled. Then realization dawned in his eyes. "The Last Emperor's Hoard?"

Svetlana grinned and waggled her eyebrows. "You got it."

Jo gasped, and Athos took his pack from Svetlana. "Alright. How's about I bring up the rear. If I see you parachuting down, Jo Dean, I'll just meet you on the ground."

"Fair enough," Svetlana said. "Drassilis, how long do we need to wait between shots?"

Drassilis inclined his head to the side, gazing at each of the three humans in turn. "There is room enough for you and Miss Jo to go together, if you wish."

Svetlana shook her head. "I'd rather see if Jo can land on the ship before you send both of us. How long between shots?"

"One minute, then."

Svetlana grinned at Jo and Athos in turn. "Then let's do this!"

Svetlana tumbled as she landed on the deck of the ghost ship. The wooden planks were cold, though not as frigid as the man's grip had been. She scanned the area, looking for anyone who might have seen her arrival. Moonlight cut through most of the patchy fog on deck, but some shadowy corners remained. The ship had a musty smell that surprised her, as the attackers had borne no scent.

Remaining in a crouched position, she headed for the area of the ship that she suspected would take her below deck. The layout differed from that of *The Silent Monsoon*, but Svetlana had been on enough converted sailing ships to have a general sense of her surroundings. She found the stairs down on her second try.

From behind her, she heard a crash, and she spun to investigate, knife already in hand. Athos stood near the same spot she had landed, dusting himself off and shaking his head. "Never again," he murmured.

Svetlana beckoned him over. "Find the bridge. That's where Jo was going. Help her take it or hold it. I'm going after Vertiline."

Athos nodded and turned away. "Good luck."

"You too." As Athos walked away, Svetlana turned back to the poorly lit stairs and started down them. Her good eye took a moment to adapt to the darkness, and she used that opportunity to adjust the brass rings of her monocular. She was able to focus on her hand directly in front of the device, but beyond that the darkness obscured everything.

She waited until she could see enough to get her bearings and then moved quietly along the hallway. From one room, she heard voices, and she slowed her pace.

A loud voice was the first that she could pick out clearly. "Yeah, we got the woman. But there was someone else with her."

"So we have two prisoners?" The voice was high pitched, and Svetlana thought for a moment that it was a woman.

There was a sound of someone clearing his throat, and then the loud voice came again. "Uh, no. Didn't think to grab her."

The high pitch turned into a sigh. "Very well. I will be sure to note your failing to my superior. Get us out of this airspace."

"Aye, Cap'n."

Svetlana ducked into a shadowy alcove and tucked her knife away. A man stomped past her, and Svetlana recognized him as the one who had grabbed her arm.

As he reached the end of the hallway, he paused and sniffed at the air.

Looking back over his shoulder, he frowned. Svetlana held her breath until he continued away from where she was hidden.

Svetlana moved down the hallway, plastering herself to the wall opposite the room where the voices had come from. A faint light shone through an open doorway. Though she couldn't see the end of the hallway in the gloom, she was certain that Vertiline had gone through the very last window on the port side. The scientist was either in the room with the light, or farther down the hallway.

Moving to the side of the doorway, Svetlana braced herself against the wall. The positioning of the room meant that her bad eye was nearest the doorway. She would have to poke most of her head into the room if she were to see anything.

A mirror would make this so much easier, she thought. Then she smiled and undid the straps holding her monocular in place. She polished the front lens on her sleeve, and held it in front of the door. The image was upside down, but a lone man was seated at a desk or table, piled high with books and papers. He wore his hair in a formal curled style that Svetlana had seen in old paintings, what little she saw of his clothing was similarly dated. But, most importantly, he was engrossed in the materials in front of him.

She moved back to the far side of the hallway and slipped past the occupied room. Her breathing slowed as well, and she took a moment to regard the man in the room. Seen directly, he looked familiar. But she did not wish to linger. She committed his face to memory and continued onward.

Once past the occupied room, Svetlana saw a sliver of moonlight at ground level. She crouched and placed her hand in front of it. A cold breeze washed across her hand. She rose and tested the doorknob, which turned freely. Hesitating, she listened for any sounds beyond the door. She heard only the wind rushing past an open window, and continued pushing the door open.

The slumped form of Vertiline was tethered to the wall with glowing silvery chains, each link made from metal as thick as Svetlana's thumbs. Svetlana rushed to Vertiline and examined the cuffs that enclosed the woman's slender wrists. Made from the same metal and just as thick, she could not find a place where the cuffs could release. Similar shackles were wrapped around Vertiline's ankles, waist, and neck. This close to the scientist, Svetlana was finally able to place the scent she wore—lilac—but there was something beneath it, too, a woody dark scent like the one Lar wore.

Vertiline's eyes fluttered open. "What are you doing here?"

"Trying to effect a daring rescue. How about yourself?"

Vertiline laughed softly, then sighed in resignation. "It's no use. The chains are enchanted. The men who locked me up said something about it keeping me with the ship when it vanishes."

"Vanishes? Thank the Skyfather that you had parachutes available."

"Parachutes? Are there others with you?"

Svetlana nodded. She continued to examine the shackles for a way to get Vertiline out of them. "Jo and Athos." She grimaced. "They, ah, used one of your bedrooms. It may have been the guest room, but I make no promises."

"It is there for guests, I suppose. Now, I didn't expect to be restrained here. My hope was that my rescuers might bring me a parachute as well, and we could escape any ship that might have taken me. So there are things that I need to tell you, quick, in case the ship does vanish." Vertiline's voice was low and pleading. "Tomorrow night, you must attend a party that an old friend is throwing in Heliopolis. His name is Lord Algernon Boughorppington the Third. Ask around about the Cranglimmering, and you should be able to find the person I hoped to talk to there."

Svetlana frowned. "You were going to Heliopolis?"

"Yes, I was hoping to catch a ride with you."

"Any other time, I'd be happy to oblige. Who is the person you hoped to talk to?"

"I don't know his name. Or her name. It could be a woman. I received a cryptic airwave from Heliopolis about this party moments before you arrived. But Chickie—Lord Boughorppington, that is—is an old friend. Just tell the doorman that I sent you, and you'll be admitted."

"Doorman? This does not sound like my kind of party."

"You can fit in; I'm sure of it."

Svetlana shook her head. "I haven't a thing to wear to that sort of party and no time to have something made."

"Talk to Drassilis. He'll find you something from my wardrobe. I'll be in touch with you if I can figure out how to get out of here."

Svetlana fumbled for Vertiline's wrist. "Let me try to unlock it?"

Vertiline shook her head. "I assure you, it's no use. I've tried every trick I know. There is no keyhole." She sighed. "Promise me you'll go to the party?"

Svetlana sighed. "Yes, I'll go."

Vertiline nodded and opened her mouth. Before a sound could escape, she, and the entire ship around her, vanished.

Svetlana hovered in the air for but an instant before she began plummeting toward the sea, thousands of feet below.

Looking around for Jo and Athos, she grabbed for the cord that would release her parachute. She found them off to the side, slightly above her. "Chutes! Now!" she shouted.

As she pulled on her own cord, she watched Athos yank Jo's cord and then shove away from her as her parachute opened. Once he had fallen a bit farther, he pulled his own cord. Soon the three of them were drifting on the breezes.

"Anyone know how to steer one of these?" Svetlana called out. "We seem to be ocean bound at the moment."

"They didn't teach you that at your beloved Academy?" Jo asked, laughing. "It's all tugging and leaning." She demonstrated, tugging at the ropes to her right to steer herself farther away from Athos.

Svetlana pulled gingerly on the ropes to her left and leaned a bit into it, hoping to rotate into a position that allowed her to see land. Her efforts were rewarded when she caught a glimpse of her ship in the distance.

"Great, how do we get there?" she asked, pointing.

Jo released an exaggerated sigh. "Follow me, do what I do."

CHAPTER TWELVE

SVETLANA HAD NEVER liked wearing dresses. Now, as she tried in vain to adjust the ridiculous peacock feather bustle that Annette had insisted she wear, she hated them even more. The dress itself was the simplest thing she could find in Vertiline's extensive wardrobe—a velvet dress, in blues and purples that set off Svetlana's pale skin and dark hair to good effect.

But first, the borrowed dress had been too snug. Athos had insisted that a woman needed a proper hourglass figure like Vertiline's to get away with such a dress. So Svetlana had begrudgingly allowed Annette and Jo to put her into an exaggerated corset. Then they had tried to layer her with three more skirts and a bustle beneath the narrow skirt of the dress, which again made the dress too snug. They finally agreed that Svetlana could wear the dress without the extra layers. But she still needed some sort of bustle, and the peacock atrocity was the only thing that either Jo or Annette could come up with. Somehow, the bustle also necessitated wearing another corset-like belt over the dress.

Svetlana had put her foot down about the heels they wanted to strap her into, and she was extra glad of it now, as she walked from the end of the docks where *The Silent Monsoon* was moored to the private docks where Lord

Boughorppington kept his ship. She took shallow breaths, as the two corsets allowed her nothing more. As she neared her destination, she looked up to catch a glimpse of it. Her hat, the final indignity, blocked not only her blind eye, but also her good eye with its garish peacock feathers and fussy veil. Svetlana snarled and reached up to snatch it from her head. Just in time, she recalled the number of pins that held it in place, and returned her hand to her side.

"See?" she muttered to herself. "I can be a lady if need be."

Ahead, a large red-lit airship, three times the size of *The Silent Monsoon*, loomed. Svetlana moved the netting and feathers out of the way of her good eye. The massive ship had only a single balloon, and she saw no fires burning beneath that balloon. But as she looked more closely, she saw the trick of it. Within the large balloon were a dozen small balloons, each inflated by their own flame. The large exterior balloon was purely decorative, using the excess heated air from the other balloons to remain aloft, but providing no actual lift of its own.

Svetlana shook her head in a mix between wonder and disgust. The innovation was spectacular, but she felt certain that Lord Boughorppington wasn't as interested in technology as he was in impressing his guests. And, arguably, it had worked.

Approaching the gang plank, Svetlana was not surprised to see an automaton as the doorman. Compared to Drassilis, this one looked downright clunky. But the smooth metal face was less disconcerting than Drassilis's filigree, and Svetlana suspected she wouldn't spy any signs of a living being behind this one's eyes.

"Might I have your name?" the doorman intoned.

"Captain Svetlana Tereshchenko. I come on Doctor Vertiline Dowhty's behalf, in her absence."

The automaton paused for a moment, but then gestured for her to enter. "Welcome, Captain Tereshchenko."

Svetlana nodded, impressed by its pronunciation skills. "Could you point me in the direction of the host? I should like to give him Doctor Dowhty's regrets."

"Lord Boughorppington wears a green smoking jacket this evening."

"Thank you," Svetlana replied. As she passed through the entryway, Svetlana was struck with two thoughts. The first was that, despite her best intentions, her crew had done a fantastic job of making sure she fit in with the upper crust of Heliopolis. The second was that she had selected the perfect dress from Vertiline's closet, as the narrow skirt allowed her to move through the room without having to wait for a gap two to three times her size to open. She spotted the man in the green smoking jacket and made a beeline toward him.

Lord Boughorppington was surrounded by a gaggle of admirers, but conversation trailed off as Svetlana joined them. She managed a passable curtsey, and then realized her mistake—she had waltzed into the presence of a social better and knew no one who could introduce her to him. She struggled to keep from making a rude face in light of her realization.

Fingers pressed Svetlana's bare left elbow. She jumped and then managed to incline her head so as to look in that direction. She blinked twice before her brain registered the person behind the calloused fingers. "Mirage?" she whispered. The airship captain had cleaned up in to a much more presentable version of himself than she had last seen. Then again, having bathed in the past week would have been a better version than the ether-abusing, sleep-deprived wreck of a man she had met with at The Flying Fist.

"Lord Boughorppington, please allow me to present my dear friend, Captain Svetlana Tereshchenko, of *The Silent Monsoon*."

Lord Boughorppington took Svetlana's hand and pressed his lips to her knuckles. "Milady, a pleasure." A smile spread across his face as he righted himself. "And here I thought that all of the airship captains had adorable names like Mirage."

The gathered group tittered, and Svetlana held her tongue as they did. "Alas, not all of us are so fortunate as Mirage."

Lord Boughorppington laughed outright at that, and his gaggle burst into laughter a moment later. "You, my dear, must call me Chickie. I would allow nothing else." He peered at her. "How is it that I cannot recall having met you previously?"

"I don't believe that you have," she replied. "I come on behalf of Doctor Vertiline Dowhty. She sends her regrets."

"Oh, Vertiline. She is simply the best, sending me such a charming new guest. Well, my dear Captain, do make yourself at home. If you require anything at all, you must but ask."

"Thank you, I—" Svetlana trailed off as she spotted another familiar face in the crowd. Larson Kavisoli looked to be attempting to extricate himself from conversation with an elderly society matron. His thick hair was bound with a silvery-grey ribbon that matched his eyes. Svetlana caught herself staring, trying to catch his gaze. "Pardon me, L ... Chickie. I would be delighted to speak with you further. But I feel as though I know so few in attendance, that I should get out and mingle."

"Oh, yes, you simply must," Lord Boughorppington said. "Ta!"

Before Svetlana could head in Lar's direction, she felt Mirage's fingers gripping her elbow tighter. "We need to talk," he murmured.

Svetlana looked up at him. His eyes looked unmarred by strong drink or ether, so she nodded. As she scanned the room for a more private spot for a conversation, Mirage tugged her along by the arm. Lar glanced up, directly at Svetlana, and raised an eyebrow. But she shook her head and turned away to face the direction Mirage was dragging her in.

Several dark spaces extended off of the main parlor, and Mirage poked his head into several before finding one that suited him. Judging by the gasps that Svetlana heard when Mirage stepped into several of the nooks, they were popular places for trysts.

"Mirage, if you're trying to get cozy with me, stop now."

The other captain scoffed. "I have information you need. About the cask. Are you familiar with Lady Elinor de Whittvy?"

Svetlana glanced back at the party. She could no longer see any one in attendance, and she had the impression that no one could see her or Mirage either. "I don't know, which one is she? The one Lar was speaking with?"

"No. She's not in attendance. She must be otherwise occupied, or I'm certain she would be here."

"Yes, of course. Mirage, what is it that you want?"

He bit his lip and hesitated before answering. "There are some who say that Lady de Whittvy is behind some of the biggest heists of the past ten years. She's never been implicated, but she seems to always wind up with interesting new curios after the police release word of a heist. Say your favorite pearl necklace went missing? Next week, she'd show up with one that could almost be the genuine article. Only hers wouldn't be cream colored, it'd be lavender. Or some such."

"I've heard that's what some of the wealthy women do after a heist." Svetlana shrugged. "They try to find something like what was stolen in the hopes of attracting a copy cat thief."

Mirage shook his head. "No, it's not like that. Say, would you like a drink?"

Svetlana arched an eyebrow. "Did we just take an unanticipated left turn, or are you still getting ether?"

Mirage frowned at her and remained quiet.

"Sorry, didn't mean to bring up past habits. I just ... I'm having trouble keeping up, Mirage. Can we hit all the stops, please?"

"Chickie is serving a drink tonight that is allegedly a re-creation of Cranglimmering. I think it could be the genuine article. And it stands to reason that Lady de Whittvy is the one who stole the Bartram Cask."

"And she uncasked it for a random party?" Svetlana shook her head. "No, that's ridiculous. Besides which, I don't think her absence tonight, assuming she's not in attendance, implicates her as the thief. Like I said, you need to slow down, because it's not making any sense to me."

Mirage shrugged. "I'm not saying it's reasonable. Have you met these people?"

"Actually, now that you mention it, I haven't, Mirage. Because I flounced in to meet the host, which was poorly thought out on my part, but you rescued me, for which I'm grateful, and then you dragged me off to assignation alley here. So tell you what. I'll go mingle, try the maybe-Cranglimmering, and we can meet up tomorrow night at the Fist. Deal?"

Mirage stared at Svetlana for a long time. "I'm just trying to help. After that ... you know, debacle with the bomb and all, I owe you."

"Let's call ourselves even then. You owed me for the bomb and repaid me by introducing me to Chickie. Alright?"

"Yes, okay," Mirage said. "And we'll talk tomorrow in a less suspect location." Svetlana snorted at the idea of the Fist being less suspect than a high society party, but Mirage ignored her and continued. "And perhaps we can recover the Cranglimmering."

"If the Cranglimmering's been uncasked, I'm not going to be able to sell it to my original buyer or my second buyer." *Better not to tell Mirage about the third buyer, the one who only wants the cask itself,* she thought.

"This goes deeper than that." Mirage's eyes had begun to gloss over.

"Sure it does. Tomorrow night, after Lift? The Fist?"

"If you like."

Svetlana nodded before she spun on her heel and headed back to the party. This conversation had started off better than the last one she'd had with Mirage, but now she just wanted a stiff drink. She pasted a smile across her face and strolled out of the hallway and straight to the bar.

Nearly every group between her and the bar had at least one person holding up a glass of amber liquid and staring intently at it. She caught snippets of conversation as she passed.

"—might just be the real thing!"

"Bartram's Cask is rumored to have gone missing, after all."

"—and it's only half aged!"

Svetlana smiled at the bartender when she reached the bar. "I'm not sure what it is that everyone's raving about—"

"You'll be wanting this, ma'am." The young man held out a squat glass with an inch of liquid at the bottom. It sloshed a bit up the side clinging to the glass as it slid down. The air wafting across the top brought an acrid aroma of alcohol to Svetlana's nose. "How do you take it?"

"Ah ... I ... well," Svetlana stammered.

"Neat," came a voice behind her. She turned to the side and saw Lar. He winked. "And another neat for me as well."

The bartender handed two glasses across the bar, and Lar accepted both then handed one to Svetlana.

Svetlana sniffed at the contents of the glass. It smelled a bit like the peat fire they used to cook onboard *The Silent Monsoon*, and she grimaced.

"Don't smell it first," Lar whispered, lips inches from her ear. "Come with me." He reached down and took her hand, dwarfing her slender one in his. Caressing her fingers, he led her toward one of the hallways.

Svetlana tugged at Lar's hand. "Hey, I've been down that road already this evening."

He stopped and turned toward her, eyebrow arched. "Really? My, Captain Tereshchenko, I didn't realize."

She shook her head. "That's not—" Leveling her gaze at him, she asked, "Is that your intent? Get me into a darkened hallway?"

"Actually, I was planning to take you to my room." Lar grinned.

Svetlana laughed. "Oh, that's much more dignified."

He leaned close to her. "It's about the drink."

"Real, or not real?"

Lar hesitated. "Complicated."

"Isn't it always?" She sighed. "Well, lead on."

Lar raised his glass and clinked it against Svetlana's. "I was hoping you'd say that."

Svetlana collapsed on Lar's bed the moment he closed the door. "Oh, sweet Skyfather, get me out of this dress!"

"Hmm, I was not expecting to hear those words, but as it turns out, I suppose I was hoping you'd say that as well."

Svetlana raised an eyebrow and shook her head at Lar. "Ever worn a corset?"

"Can't say that I have."

"I've got two. Please, would you mind helping me out of one and loosening the other so that I can breathe?"

Lar approached Svetlana, glass still in hand. "Don't you want to try the Cranglimmering?"

"Depends. You said it's complicated." She set her glass on the dressing chair and turned her back to him. "And, for the record, I am sincere in requesting your assistance with this devilry that my crew insisted I wear."

Lar set his glass down beside hers, and encircled her waist with his hands. Svetlana knew that she was imagining that they reached all the way around her waist, but warmth burned through all of her layers of clothing. She no longer detected the strange woody scent that he and Vertiline both wore—today he smelled like astringent soap and shaving powder.

His voice was a low rumble. "For the record, your crew did well. You look stunning."

Svetlana felt the warmth spread to her face. "Thank you," she whispered hoarsely.

"Now then, the complicated," Lar said, his fingers moving on either side of Svetlana's bustle, remaining above her waist. "The liquid in those glasses is a synthetic. It's an attempt to reproduce Cranglimmering on a larger scale than it was previously available."

"Who made it?"

Lar laughed as his fingers found the elaborate knot that attached the bustle to the corset. "I did."

Svetlana tried to turn to face him, but Lar had the ribbons to the bustle in hand and stopped her. "You?"

"My people, if you'd like to be technical about it."

"Why?"

Lar tossed the feathered bustle onto his bed. "To see if we could. If we're successful, it would be quite lucrative."

"But won't that devalue the remaining casks?"

"Of course. I have no stake in any of those casks, but if they are hoarded or if they are all consumed before we learn their secrets, then I am affected."

Svetlana's next breath came easier, as she felt Lar's fingers slackening the lacing of her outer corset. "You're a hedonist."

He leaned in close, so that she felt his breath on her ear before she heard his next words. "My home is a pleasure platform. How could I be anything but?" He paused, and withdrew slightly. "How much of this would you like taken off?"

"Ah ... I'd like ... well, I think ... It would be nice to be able to breathe freely," Svetlana stammered. She paused to compose herself. "So, not real Cranglimmering. Any thoughts on where the real cask went? The cask itself, not the contents."

"I thought you were after the contents."

"They're a little less consequential than I thought." She cursed herself mentally as she realized that she was letting her guard slip in Lar's presence. "Especially with your people synthesizing it."

"They haven't been successful yet," he replied. "What about this hat?"

Svetlana shook her head, the feathers and veil dancing before her good eye. "Jo and Annette used half a roll of hair pins on it, I think. It's probably stuck to my head forever."

Lar chuckled. "Very well, then. Lift your arms. And tell me, is there something consequential about the cask itself?"

Svetlana put hands to the sky as he bade, and took the moment as he slid the corset up and over her head without jostling her hat to collect her thoughts. The reasons she could think of to trust him were next to none, while there were plenty of reasons not to trust him. It was the same problem that her crew had pointed out with her trusting Vertiline. But they weren't here to remind her of that, and she suspected that Lar could be an even better ally than the scientist. "The staves are part of a map. Ever heard of the Last Emperor's Hoard?"

"The greatest treasure in all the world? Of course." He hesitated. "Captain, if I'm to continue helping you out of your clothing, you'll have to turn to face me. This dress appears to button down the front."

"Oh," Svetlana said, turning slowly. "Isn't there a way to loosen the corset and keep the dress on?"

Lar shook his head, smiling. "I'm afraid not." He gestured at his wardrobe. "Perhaps you could slip one of my shirts on over the dress?"

Svetlana considered his offer. He alternated between playing the cad and being a perfect gentleman, and she was beginning to suspect that the latter was closer to the truth. She shook her head. "No, it's fine. As you say, your home is a pleasure platform. I suspect you've seen a woman naked before."

"That I have. But it is rare that I have seen one as singular as you, Captain."

"Sveta," she murmured, looking down to watch his hands unfasten her buttons.

She could hear his smile when he spoke again. "Sveta. Lovely. So, a map to find the Last Emperor's Hoard?"

"In pieces. Split between the seven casks. I ... I know who has ...," she stammered, partly at a loss for how to explain Vertiline's probability engine, and partly as Lar's hands slipped her arms out of the cap sleeves of her dress. She was acutely aware of just how tight Annette and Jo had pulled the corset, and just how much of her breasts were exposed.

"You'll need to turn around again," Lar prompted her.

Svetlana nodded and turned around, hoping that her flushed skin would be less noticeable from the back. "So the map is only partly recovered. There's a scientist working on predicting the rest." Her words tumbled out, coming more easily as Lar undid the knots keeping the corset tight around her ribcage.

"Tell me when to tie it back off."

"Oh, ah, I suppose it's good there."

Lar tugged at the laces as he knotted them. "There you are. Would you like my assistance getting your arms back into those sleeves?"

Svetlana shook her head and fumbled for the upper half of her dress. Her arms did not want to follow the commands that her brain was issuing them. After a moment, she sighed. "Never mind. I'll worry about it when we go back out."

"I must say, Sveta. You surprise me at every turn."

Svetlana arched her eyebrow. "How so?"

"Well, I've taken half of your clothing off, and I didn't find a single weapon."

"Am I going to need a weapon?" Svetlana asked, tensing.

"I doubt it. But the tales I've heard of Captain Svetlana Tereshchenko are of a woman who never goes anywhere unarmed."

Svetlana smiled. "Ah, but you assume I'm unarmed. There's half of my body you haven't checked."

Lar smiled back. "Is that an invitation?"

Svetlana moved closer to him, feeling a return of some control over the situation, now that she wasn't confined by the double layer of corsetry. "You'd like that, wouldn't you?"

"I would, but—" He trailed off and took half a step back. "Is this what you would like?"

Perfect gentleman, she concluded. "I'll be sure to let you know if we're headed in a direction I don't like the looks of."

"Of course." He kept his distance still and looked at her. "But before that, you were telling me something about a possible map for a hidden treasure trove that may or may not exist."

Svetlana laughed. "Shut up and kiss me. I'll tell you more afterward."

Lar wrapped his arms around her and obliged.

CHAPTER THIRTEEN

POUNDING FISTS ON the door shattered the moment before it had time to begin. "Open, in the name of the Republic!"

Svetlana pulled away from Lar. "Those shirts you were mentioning. Wardrobe?"

Lar nodded and hurried to the bed. He yanked back the blanket, covering the rest of Svetlana's discarded clothes. "Hide in the wardrobe. If they're looking for you, I'll tell them they have the wrong room, and we can get back to—" He trailed off and smiled. "Well, we can continue."

Svetlana opened the wardrobe and snatched a shirt before she pulled the door closed behind her. Dust and moth balls assaulted her nose as she tried to maneuver in the small space. She kept the wardrobe door open just a crack, and found that it afforded her a good view of the door to the room. Lar tugged off his shirt and tossed it on the floor, and Svetlana admired his muscular back, wishing that she could see it up close rather than having to hide from whomever was at his door. He paused, looked in her direction, and nodded before answering the door.

Svetlana craned her neck to try to get a view of the group at the door. She was certain that anyone knocking that heavily had come looking for her. She also knew it would be Air Fleet, but who they sent would tell her more about what was going on. Unfortunately, Lar's body blocked her ability to see who was in the hallway.

"Yes?" he asked.

"Mayor Larson Kavisoli? You are wanted for questioning in the theft of Mayor Ambrose Bartram's Cask of Cranglimmering." The voice was feminine, and it tugged at Svetlana's memory—she knew this woman, but the distance muffled the sound so that she couldn't place it.

"I'm sorry, what?" Lar asked. "You think that I stole the Bartram Cask?"

The voice replied, louder than before. "You're just wanted for questioning, Mayor."

Svetlana's memory clicked into place, and she gasped. She covered her mouth too late, and the sound escaped her hiding place. Lar turned to glance at the wardrobe, his eyes widening.

"Is there someone else here?"

Svetlana shoved the wardrobe door open and clambered out. Lar's gaze pleaded with her, but Svetlana could already see Captain Narcissa March beyond him. "Hi, Narci."

Lar stepped back, frowning. "You two know each other?"

Svetlana looked at Narcissa. She knew why the Air Fleet had sent Narcissa—to put her off her guard in every possible way. Her former lover looked much the same as she had all those years ago, though the stress of time showed on her face. Her hair was a little longer, in stubby dark brown dreadlocks shot through with silver where once there had been gold.

Narcissa stiffened and said nothing in response to Lar's question.

Svetlana nodded. "Yeah, we go back."

"Svetlana Tereshchenko—" Narcissa began.

"Captain Tereshchenko, if you don't mind. I might not be Air Fleet, but I still own a ship."

Narcissa frowned. "We heard rumors that your ship went down in the Southern Sea."

"It did, but—" Svetlana trailed off and took a few steps closer to Narcissa and Lar. "Now that's interesting, where'd you hear that?"

"It's not relevant," Narcissa said, waving her hand. "Svetlana Tereshchenko, I've been asked to request that you accompany me to Air Fleet headquarters. Admiral Beauregard has some questions for you in relation to ... well, I suppose you heard it already."

"Really?" Svetlana crossed her arms over her chest, hoping the gesture didn't look completely ridiculous in the too-long sleeves of Lar's shirt. "Bobby told you to come for me, and you did, even though you thought my ship had gone down?"

"Standing orders." Narcissa shrugged. "From before we heard anything about your whereabouts."

Svetlana threw her hands up, but before she could respond, Lar interposed himself fully between the women again.

"Wait, I'm to be brought in for questioning, and she gets a polite request?" Lar growled.

"That's correct, Mayor," Narcissa said.

"Well, I do hope you'll allow me to get dressed before we go?" His words were clipped.

Narcissa seemed to notice that Lar was shirtless, and that Svetlana wore a man's shirt over her dress, for the first time. Pink colored the soft brown of her cheeks, popping her darker brown freckles into sharp relief. "Of course, Mayor. And if Svetlana needs a moment as well—"

"She's dressed just fine for her audience with the Admiral, I'm sure." His voice was nearly a snarl. "She might want the rest of her effects, though." In one fluid motion, he bent forward to scoop his shirt off the floor and remove the blanket covering Svetlana's outer corset and peacock bustle.

Svetlana glanced at him, trying to draw his gaze, but his eyes had gone steely, and he did not look at her as he buttoned his shirt. She collected her outerwear and bundled the pieces together, trying to prevent the peacock feathers from being crushed.

Narcissa lingered in the doorway, but her attention was turned toward the hallway.

"Narci," Svetlana said quietly. "I may have information that clears Mayor Kavisoli."

"Save it for Bobby," Narcissa replied without looking at Svetlana. "Save all of it for Bobby, Sveta."

Svetlana was grateful to see that the Air Fleet had sent carriages to transport them back to Headquarters. But as she tried to follow Narcissa to one of the carriages, the Air Fleet officer stopped her. "You ride with him."

"Can't we talk?" Svetlana reached for Narcissa's arm.

Narcissa took a step away from Svetlana. "Not now."

"Later, then?"

Narcissa frowned, her eyes growing dark. "We'll see about that. But right now, you're a civilian, and I'm an officer. You ride with the other civilian."

Svetlana nodded stiffly and headed to the carriage where Lar waited.

He laughed as she entered the carriage, and she looked up at him with a tentative smile. "I should have known."

"Known? Known what?"

"You're an Air Fleet lapdog."

Svetlana laughed in response. "No, not really. I left because I didn't want to be their lapdog."

"Oh? Then what is it between you and her? Something a little beyond chummy, I think."

"Like I said, we go back," Svetlana said quietly. "Narcissa and I attended the Academy together. We—"

"You love her."

Svetlana hesitated before she answered, and she shook her head as she did. "Loved. Our paths took us different directions. She hates what I've become."

"Ah, yes, I remember the stories. The Butcher of Barkovia." Lar had returned to his clipped pattern of speech.

"Don't," Svetlana pleaded. It was one thing to have a random Air Fleet Academy graduate recognize her for her past. Hearing it come out of Lar's mouth crushed her.

"I always thought it was strange. A woman captain, about to receive the highest decorations of the Air Fleet, resigns her commission and becomes a pirate." He spat out the last word.

"No." She shook her head. "I'm not a pirate. I'm in the shipping industry. We do legitimate work."

Lar arched his eyebrow. "From where I'm standing, there's not much of a difference between the two, Captain. You play whichever side garners you the most benefit at the moment—good little lapdog for the Air Fleet one moment, a scoundrel consorting with a crime lord the next, if it suits your needs at the time."

"Don't call me their lapdog," she said, her voice suddenly low. She felt a flush rising in her cheeks, and she bit at the inside of her mouth to keep her temper in check.

"No? Why shouldn't I tell it as it is?"

Svetlana took a deep breath before she spoke again. "Because you don't know the half of it. You ... you don't know me."

"You're right, I don't," he replied, his voice quiet. "Which means I've no reason to trust you. Was anything you told me the truth, or are you just grasping at straws to get my attention?"

"Skyfather knows why, but I told you the truth. If you don't want to trust me, that's your choice. But I know you didn't steal the cask. I'll talk to Bobby —"

"Bobby," he said flatly. "Don't you mean Admiral Beauregard?"

Svetlana clenched her teeth. "I'll talk to Admiral Beauregard. I'll tell him what I know, and he'll have no reason to keep you."

Lar frowned. "Give me one gods-be-cursed reason why I should trust you,

Tereshchenko."

"I saved your life."

Lar sat up straight and looked away. "Fine. Know this. Before our conversation was interrupted by your attempt to seduce me—"

"*My* attempt?" she sputtered.

Lar held up a hand to silence her. "I was preparing to share some additional information about the cask with you. Get me out of Air Fleet custody, and I'll give you the information."

Svetlana tried to read Lar's face, to tell whether he was bluffing or not, but with his refusal to meet her gaze, she had no way of determining. Since his gentlemanly behavior had disappeared as soon as his liberty was threatened, she suspected that he might be scrambling just as much as she would be in dealing with Bobby. She sighed. "You realize that any information you have might help me get you released more quickly."

Lar barked out a laugh. "You sound just like one of them. Work your magic on them, not me, woman."

"Suit yourself. I'll do all I can. But if you've got the missing piece, I hope you enjoy cold floors and hard beds. The Air Fleet's got plenty of both."

The carriage stopped, and Svetlana threw open the door before Lar could respond. She turned to the first person she saw. "Take me to Admiral Beauregard now. He's expecting me."

Svetlana marched into Bobby's office. The lingering smell of his cigars almost put her at ease, but she forced herself to stay sharp. "You've got the wrong person."

"Svetlana?" Bobby rose from his desk. "You're ... we heard your ship had gone down." He walked around the side of his desk and embraced her warmly. "I'm glad to see you whole and well."

She leaned into the embrace, as much as she could with her hands full of her discarded clothing, and sighed. "Yes, it's good to see you too, Bobby. But I didn't think it would be like this. Why have you ordered Mayor Kavisoli brought in?"

Bobby returned to his seat, and spread his hands wide as he sat. "Confidential information, Sveta. Tell me what happened to your ship."

"It's not relevant, Bobby," she said, shaking her head. "I need you to let Kavisoli go. I'm getting close to finding out about the bomb on Rrusadon and the missing Cranglimmering."

Bobby frowned. "Sveta, I'm worried about you. Are you ... how long was your ship in the water?"

"We didn't hit the water. We hit—" Svetlana trailed off, unsure about how much she wanted to say about Bonebriar. Bobby had ignored every request she had made for him to release Lar and responded by asking about what had happened to her and *The Silent Monsoon*. On another day, she would not have thought much of his concern for her. But it felt false. Finally, she shrugged. "We hit some sort of land mass. A glorified sandbar, I suppose."

"I see. So what made the ship go down?"

Svetlana hesitated again. Vertiline had not told her anything about the device they had found on the bridge of *The Silent Monsoon*. "I don't know, exactly. Our instruments went wild. If I had to make an educated guess, I'd assume magnetic interference. There's a reason so few of the islands in the Southern Sea are inhabited."

Bobby frowned. "So what in the name of the Skyfather were *you* doing so far out?" He let out a deep sigh. "Sveta, I've had alarming reports about some new trend among the shipping captains. Something about widespread recreational usage of ether?"

Svetlana shook her head. "No, that's just Mirage. Well, it might be others as well but not me. You know Annette would never allow me to do something so idiotic."

"I'm just looking at what I see, Sveta. And right now, I see a promising young woman who appears to be wearing a ridiculous hat and a ball gown, covered by a man's shirt, who just returned from a crash landing on a sandbar in the Southern Sea. I'm worried about you."

Svetlana watched Bobby as he expressed his concern. His brow didn't wrinkle in the way it had when she was at the Academy, though the lines there were deeper etched than they had been all those years ago. Had she been less exhausted, she might have tried to steer the conversation herself and learn what he was after, but she could barely muster the energy to stand. She was more than ready to call it a night. "Bobby, I'm fine. I'm tired is all. I was at Chickie's ... uh, Lord Boughorppington's party."

"With Mayor Kavisoli?"

"I showed up on my own. We were just talking."

Bobby arched an eyebrow at Svetlana and smirked, though he said nothing.

That was the Bobby she remembered from the Academy, and it brought a smile to her face. "I feel like I'm coming back late from a date, and my father is grilling me." Svetlana shook her head. "Really, Bobby, I'm fine. I know what I'm doing."

Bobby rose from his desk. "Of course, Sveta. I'm sorry." He walked over to the large map on the wall of his office. "Whereabouts was this sandbar?"

Svetlana left her extra clothing on a spare chair. She scanned the map to see if Bonebriar appeared on an official Air Fleet map. But there was no island where she expected it to be. Squinting, she tried to determine if it had been painted over. Finally, she waved her hand in an area that was more than a hundred miles north and west of where she thought the island was. "Somewhere around here, maybe? Our instruments were no use, and there was nothing out there to take a bearing from."

Bobby nodded and patted Svetlana on the shoulder. "Well, if any of our ships happen to be in the area, we'll try to get some information for you on what made your ship act up."

"Thank you, Bobby." She paused. "Now, about Kavisoli?"

Bobby sighed. "I'm sorry, Sveta. We're going to hold him until he answers our questions."

"Great. I'm sure he'll be here a while then. Would it help if I told you that I've heard that the Bartram Cask was taken by Lady Elinor de Whittvy?"

Bobby shook his head, his lips pressed together. "I'm afraid not. We had heard the same information. But no one has been able to find her. We received intelligence earlier this evening that she and Kavisoli were once close. She may have helped him start his fortune."

Svetlana frowned. She hadn't mentioned the lady thief's name to Lar. Could that be the information he had? Was she struggling to get him released so that he could tell her something she already knew? And would he still be angry with her if she did get him out? "If he answers your questions, will you let him go?"

"Assuming his answers don't implicate him, we won't have much reason to hold him."

Svetlana nodded. "Can I see him?"

"Not at the moment. I'm sorry."

"Okay, what about a note? I'd like to encourage him to help you out on this, Bobby."

Bobby laughed. "Sveta, have patience. Go back to your ship, have a nice cup of tea, and get out of that ridiculous outfit. I'm sure Mayor Kavisoli will give us the information we need and be back in his lovely city in no time."

CHAPTER FOURTEEN

SVETLANA STEWED FOR the duration of her cab ride back to *The Silent Monsoon* from Air Fleet headquarters. Lar would not be pleased with the delay in his release. It was likely to convince him even more of her duplicity. Bobby had seemed less concerned about the fact that the Air Fleet had taken a suspect into custody, and more concerned about the location of Svetlana's crash. If he had simply been concerned about the crash, she might not have thought much of it. Perhaps all of the layers were just making her paranoid. She rubbed her eye and yawned. Perhaps, too, a lack of sleep was getting in the way of her good judgment.

When the cab rolled to a stop, Svetlana stumbled out. She half expected to be blinded by the sunrise, but it was still night, not even false dawn yet. Every light on *The Silent Monsoon* looked to be burning, and Annette was pacing on the bridge. Self-consciously, Svetlana straightened out the peacock bustle still clutched in her hand, and headed for the bridge.

Annette threw her hands into the air at the sight of Svetlana. "Where have you been? We heard that Air Fleet raided the party!"

"They did. But it wasn't for me," Svetlana quickly added. "They came after Lar."

"Kavisoli?" Annette frowned. "Why?"

Svetlana shrugged. "I guess they're claiming that he stole the Cranglimmering. Or at least they want to question him about it."

The door to the bridge flew open behind Svetlana. "Welcome ... hey, you're half dressed," Jo said.

"Ah, yeah." Handing Jo her discarded clothing, Svetlana started pacing as she pieced together her various conversations over the night. The details were already slipping away. "Where's Athos?"

"Sleeping," Jo replied. "Should I wake him?"

"No need," Athos mumbled as he slipped through the back door onto the bridge. "Annette, you sound like my nan did when I used to come in late. Woke me straight away."

Annette rolled her eyes. "Lovely, I remind him of his dear, old nan."

"Could be worse," Svetlana murmured. She took a deep breath as she decided where to begin. "The Kavisolis have synthesized Cranglimmering. I'm not sure how. We didn't quite get that far into the explanation."

Annette arched her eyebrow. "So maybe the Air Fleet does have something on him?"

"Maybe." Svetlana rubbed at her eye. "Also, Mirage was at this party. And he says the thief was Lady Elinor de Whittvy."

Athos laughed. "Lady de Whittvy? Oh, I very much doubt ... hmm, wait, no, I could see that." He frowned. "Don't know about the why, though."

"You know her?" Svetlana asked.

"Only by reputation. I don't believe we're acquainted. She's rumored to primarily go after the wealthy and vain, which I suppose Mayor Bartram counts as. But the Cranglimmering seems a bit too high profile compared to her usual marks. It'd be tough for her to claim it was anything but that."

"Is it possible she could have done the job with a specific buyer in mind?" Svetlana asked. "Maybe the Kavisolis?"

Athos shrugged. "Anything's possible, I suppose. I'm just not sure she would see the point in it."

"Well, she's Mirage's suspect. He seems like he's slightly more sane, for what that's worth. I'm supposed to meet him tomorrow ... or today ... in the evening. Gods, I need sleep."

"So did you find the person Vertiline sent you to find?" Annette asked.

Svetlana sighed. "I have no idea. Mirage introduced me to Chickie and then dragged me off to talk. When I came back from that conversation, Lar wanted to talk. And then there was the Air Fleet raid, and I wound up talking to Bobby at Headquarters."

"Did Bobby have anything to contribute?" Athos asked.

"No, unfortunately. He had heard that our ship had gone down, though, and I think he was genuinely surprised to see me. But—" Trailing off, Svetlana shook her head. "He was behaving strangely. He was more concerned about where the ship had gone down than any of the information I tried to give him to clear Lar's name."

"It wasn't just that he was worried about you? And maybe me and Athos?" Annette asked.

Svetlana swallowed hard. As much as she hated to admit it to her crew, her suspicion about Bobby's motivations still lingered. "No, I could tell. It wasn't like he used to be with me. He wanted to know where we crashed. He feigned a little bit of concern over me being half dressed and I guess not entirely coherent, but ... something's changed, and I don't know what it is."

Annette hugged Svetlana. "I'm sorry, Captain," the doctor murmured.

Jo snapped her fingers, drawing their attention. "You don't suppose Vertiline's contact was Mirage, do you?" Jo asked.

Frowning and shaking her head, Svetlana pulled out of Annette's embrace. "That would be an odd coincidence. Vertiline said she had no idea who the person was either. For all I know, it was Lady de Whittvy who sent Vertiline the message. I'm beginning to think this whole party was a wash, much like every other bit of investigating we've been doing. All I learned is that the Kavisolis have chemists or something working on recreating

Cranglimmering because Lar wants to spread joy all around the world."

"You seem awfully familiar with him," Athos said, tugging at the collar of the shirt Svetlana had borrowed from Lar's closet.

Svetlana cleared her throat. "It's not what you think, and it doesn't matter now. He's convinced I set him up. Narci was leading the Air Fleet raid."

Athos inhaled deeply and choked back a laugh. "I would have paid good money to see that. You told him that you and Narci go back, didn't you?" He shook his head.

"Athos, I 'go back' with just about anyone who's been in the Fleet for longer than the past ten years."

"Yeah, but you and Narci, that's a little bit different," Athos said. "And it's not like it's not apparent when you two see each other."

Svetlana shrugged. Athos was right, but she didn't want to dwell on Narcissa's expression when she had seen Svetlana in Lar's room. "Look, it'll all be fine. I just need to figure out how to get the Air Fleet to release Lar, and he promised me information."

"What kind of information?" Annette asked.

"Something related to the cask is what he said. He could have been bluffing, but I don't know."

"Do we have a plan?" Jo asked. "I'm getting kind of tired of this running around in circles for no profit thing. You want me to go get Lar out?"

Svetlana laughed. "From Air Fleet? No, Jo, I don't think so. And no, we don't have much of a plan. We still need more information. Something that makes sense would be nice. I'm thinking I want to talk to Chickie. Vertiline said he was an old friend of hers, and he would be the most likely person to know everyone at that party. Maybe he'll have some idea who she was supposed to talk to and can point me in the right direction."

"You want any of us with you on that?" Jo chewed at the inside of her cheek as she spoke and shot a couple of glances at Athos. Her unwillingness to go was plain as day.

"No, I think this is one I can handle best alone," Svetlana said. "But if you and Athos want to help out, you could ask around about Lady de Whittvy and see if you can confirm what Mirage told me."

"Worth a shot," Athos said.

"Is that enough of a plan for now, Jo?" Annette asked.

Jo shrugged. "Sure, can we go in the morning?"

Svetlana nodded. "I'm not going anywhere till I've slept. Possibly half the day. Go when you're ready. We can compare notes once we're all done."

Lord Algernon Boughorppington the Third was prominently listed in the Heliopolis city directory, but Svetlana was having trouble locating his townhouse. Most of Heliopolis had neatly laid out streets, but some of the wealthier parts of town were labyrinthine, filled with gently curving paths and decorative hedgerows that obscured both homes and addresses. Not that the addresses mattered much—it seemed that each individual homeowner had determined the number they most wanted to apply to their house, and then did so, with no rhyme or reason in regards to their neighbors. At one point, Svetlana had even found two houses, both numbered 13, side by side.

Absent, too, were the crowds of urchins who could be hired in the other portions of the city to lead you to an address. The few people who were out and about were society matrons, taking a midday stroll. Most of these spotted Svetlana at some distance and changed their route so as to avoid her. Svetlana had worn clean clothing and even combed out the rats' nest from falling asleep with the peacock-feathered hat still pinned to her hair. But she did look too rakish for society ladies in her blouse, trousers, and boots.

Svetlana spotted a cluster of street signs affixed to a white wooden pole. Two men stood nearby, chatting with one another, but they paid her no mind as she approached. As she read through the street names, she couldn't help but overhear their conversation.

"I heard news that a ghost ship was spotted over Bluesummer last evening. Your sister's there, isn't she?"

"No, no, they were there for a year, but my brother-in-law got a promotion. They're back up at Aldfort now."

Svetlana chewed on her lip, debating whether she should interrupt the men to learn more details. Bluesummer was in one of the interior valleys on a large landmass to the south of Heliopolis, which meant that the ghost ship could be nearby. And if it wasn't the one that Vertiline was onboard, the crew of whatever ghost ship she found might be "persuaded" to give her information on the ship that had the scientist. She considered trying to find her way back out of Chickie's neighborhood, so she could get back to *The Silent Monsoon* and go after the ghost ship, but at that exact moment, she spotted the sign for Chickie's street, Brightmaple. Besides, she told herself, even if a ghost ship had been at Bluesummer last night, it could be anywhere by now.

As she set out toward Brightmaple, she spotted signs that she had missed the last time she passed this way. The shrubbery along the side of the street bore no relation to any maple tree Svetlana had ever seen in drawings or old photographs, but each walkway was flanked by a small green metal sign, nearly the same color as the foliage, in the shape of a maple leaf, giving the number of the houses beyond.

Svetlana approached Chickie's townhouse tentatively. His address was just one part of a larger structure, with several entryways on the ground level, and stairs clinging to all the sides of the building she could see, leading to higher entrances. Chickie's entry was off to the left of the building, shaded by a trellis entwined with flowers. Svetlana frowned at the last detail—some of the flowers had been torn from their stems, their delicate petals crushed on the path below.

As she neared the door, her frown grew deeper. The door stood barely ajar—so nearly closed that it was only obvious from the small brick porch. Svetlana glanced over each of her shoulders in turn and rapped gently on the door. "Chickie?" she called out.

No response followed, so she nudged the door with the toe of her boot. It swung open to reveal an entryway that looked like a storm had blown through it. She moved inside quietly and pushed the door nearly shut before continuing.

Making her way through the rooms on the first floor, Svetlana found each one in a similar state of disarray. Paintings and mirrors had been pulled from the walls, the latter smashed into glittering shards that crunched beneath her feet. Where there were pieces of furniture with drawers, every drawer had been removed and the contents spilled atop the discarded décor.

The strangest thing was not the mess that had been made but the obvious valuables that had been left behind. While Svetlana was not a collector of art, she recognized the signatures on some of the paintings, several of which were small enough that they could have been removed by whomever had ransacked the townhouse. A row of delicate figurines on the mantle had survived the upheaval, and those, too, struck her as collectible pieces.

As she moved closer to examine one of the figurines, a creaking sound above drew Svetlana's attention. She had seen but one staircase, which she ran up. At the top, a landing with five closed doors awaited. Svetlana moved to the first on the left. Behind her, she heard another creak, this time of an opening door. Before she could turn to investigate, she felt something cold and cylindrical brush against the back of her neck.

"Raise your hands, but make no other movement," said a whispery voice.

Svetlana did as she was bidden, but glanced down at the doorknob. The polished brass did a fine job of reflecting, but right now, she stood between the doorknob and whoever was behind her.

After a long silence, the voice spoke again. "Captain Tereshchenko?"

"Yes," she said, frowning. "You know me?"

"Acquainted, yes. What are you doing here?"

"Looking for Chickie."

"And you had to ransack the whole place just to make sure you had looked everywhere?"

Svetlana tilted her head to the side, recognizing something in the voice. "Chickie?"

The man sighed. "Yes, darling, it's me. I suppose you can turn around."

Svetlana turned to face Chickie. Gone was his over-the-top wardrobe of the previous evening; today he was dressed almost identical to Svetlana. His hair was pulled back into a braid, tied with a bright green ribbon that was his only concession to fashion.

"I didn't ransack your house."

"Oh, I know. But I had to ask to be sure, of course. Shall we adjourn downstairs? I can't offer you tea, but we might be able to find a couple of pieces of furniture that haven't been upended." Without waiting to see if she followed, Chickie brushed past Svetlana's shoulder and headed down the steps. She followed him down.

"Why, exactly, would someone ransack your house?" she asked.

"Well, I assume that they were looking for something. But I haven't the slightest idea what they thought they might find here."

Svetlana paused long enough to right a chair opposite the piano bench that Chickie perched on. She considered her options in terms of how to broach the topic she had come to ask Chickie about. In the end, she settled on the most direct route. "How much do you know about the Bartram Cask?"

Chickie laughed. "Oh, are people still on about that? The Kavisolis are working on a new blend. I'm sure it'll be much better than the stuff they served at my party."

"You know that Lar was taken into custody by the Air Fleet last night, don't you?"

"Yes, indeed. There is nothing that goes on in the confines of my ship that I don't know about when it happens or learn about soon after. Speaking of—" He pulled something small and glittering from his breast pocket. "I believe Lar will want this returned. I suspect you'll see him again before I do."

Svetlana accepted the offered item, a jeweled cuff link. "Maybe, maybe not. He got a bit cross with me after the Air Fleet hauled us out of there."

"Well, that is a bother. Still, keep it for now." Chickie looked at her for a moment. "So, the Bartram Cask."

Svetlana shook her head. "I'm actually here about Vertiline."

"Yes, dear Doctor Dowhty. You said she sent you to the party in her stead. But whatever for?"

"Lord Boughorppington—"

He wagged his finger at her. "I told you to call me Chickie."

"Yes, of course. The matters I am currently dealing with are of a potentially sensitive nature. I'm not certain how much I should share publicly."

Chickie smiled. "My dear Captain. Sharing with me is hardly the definition of sharing something publicly. I have considerable discretion. I can assure you that while I know what happens on my airship, that information does not spread. The same goes for my home. Whatever you wish to discuss with me will remain in the strictest of confidences. On my honor as a member of the nobility."

The final phrase solidified Svetlana's assurances that Chickie was being honest with her. Had he said "as a politician," she would have had every reason to distrust him. But after the nobility had been phased out of politics by the Republican Senate, they prided themselves on their honor. The oath he had given was not one to be treated lightly.

"It's all tied up with the Bartram Cask," she said. "Hell, even a nobody like Corporal Richards at Port Authority has got his fingers in the pie somehow. As of this moment, though," she held up a hand, counting off information on her fingers, "the Air Fleet thinks Lar stole it, Mirage told me it was Lady Elinor de Whittvy, and Vertiline wanted me to talk to someone at the party about it."

Chickie arched one perfectly groomed eyebrow at Svetlana, a sly smile playing across his lips. "That is quite a stew, isn't it? If you don't mind my asking, how is it, exactly, that an airship captain based out of Heliopolis knows Vertiline? It's been ages since she lived here."

After Bobby's interest in where *The Silent Monsoon* had crash landed, Svetlana hesitated to throw around the name of Vertiline's home willy-nilly. "I met her in the Southern Sea."

"Oh, Bonebriar? Is that where she's camped out these days?" Chickie shuddered. "Dreadful place. The humidity just destroys my hairstyles in an instant."

Svetlana smiled and nodded. "I suppose those of us without hairstyles to speak of might find it a bit more charming." She looked at Chickie for a moment, noticing that his hair color matched Vertiline's. "Are you and she related?"

Chickie laughed loudly, his eyes sparkling. "Oh, goodness no. Simply old friends." He winked. "And no, before you go getting ideas, not like you and Lar are friends."

Svetlana opened her mouth to speak, but Chickie hushed her immediately. "Now, darling, don't get offended by what I say. I play the fool so as to hide my true cunning. So, I must know. What kept Vertiline from the party?"

Svetlana frowned. "You won't believe me if I tell you."

"Try me."

"Ghostly pirates on a ghost ship."

He chuckled. "Oh now, is that so?"

Svetlana stared at Chickie. "You don't seem surprised by that."

"I have seen many inexplicable things, darling; I'm not much of a skeptic. Drives my scientific friends absolutely mad. Speaking of, what was it she sent you to my party for?"

"She told me that someone had contacted her anonymously about the whereabouts of the Bartram Cask. I'm looking for what's inside, and ... well, she has interests in the same."

"Hmmm." Chickie's brow creased slightly as he drummed his fingertips across his lips. "Well, I'm afraid that I don't know who she hoped to speak with. I'd be happy to share my guest list with you, but I suspect you won't want to pay all of them social calls of a vague nature."

"Was there anyone else at the party who took a special notice of the synthetic Cranglimmering, perhaps?"

"We all did, darling. It's not every day that you get to sample something that may resemble a nearly priceless liquor. I'm afraid that won't get you any closer."

Svetlana sighed. "I was hoping this might get easier if I spoke to you about it. It's been one dead end after another, ever since we found out the Bartram

Cask was missing."

Chickie rose. "Well, my dear, I think you've got the gumption to get to the bottom of this. But at this point, I'd say you either need to find that ghost ship and rescue Vertiline, or talk to Lady de Whittvy. But I must say, I think finding Ellie might be just as difficult as retrieving Vertiline."

"Why is that?" Svetlana asked.

"Oh, Ellie's elusive. It's part of her charm," Chickie replied with a shrug and a smile. "And though I haven't any experience with ghost ships, I suspect they fall within the elusive category as well."

Svetlana nodded. "If you do hear anything more or think of anything else, could you send a message to *The Silent Monsoon*?"

"But of course, my dear. Now, then, if you need me again, you can find the place?"

Svetlana winced. "I doubt that."

"I'll give you a little secret. As you leave, turn left at the end of the street, left on the second street, and then keep turning left at the second street all the way out."

"Wouldn't that just put me back where I started?"

"Some places, maybe, but not here, darling. Ta!"

CHAPTER FIFTEEN

SVETLANA CAUGHT A cab at the entrance to Chickie's neighborhood to give herself some time to try to put together the pieces she had. If what Mirage said was true, then Lady de Whittvy was the key to finding the Cranglimmering. If what Bobby believed was accurate, then maybe it was the Kavisolis she ought to be looking at. Either way, she didn't see an easy path to the riches promised by locating the cask.

By the time the cab stopped at the docks, she had no better sense of a next step than she had prior to returning to Heliopolis. She walked across the space to *The Silent Monsoon*, still deep in thought. It wasn't until she got there that she realized something was amiss. The ship was still docked where she had left it, but the gangplank was up.

"Athos?" she shouted. "Annette?"

"Just a minute, Captain," Annette replied, her face appearing over the bulkhead. "We'll get the gangplank back out."

"Why is it up in the first place?"

Annette smiled. "Because someone brought us a present."

Svetlana wanted to ask her more, but Annette disappeared again. A moment later, the winches began to run out the gangplank. Svetlana leapt from the ground to the end of it as soon as it drew near and ran the rest of the way onto the boat.

In the center of the deck, Athos and Jo stood beside Corporal Richards, who was seated on one of the mess chairs and gagged. Nearby, Indigo tinkered with something that looked like a pair of small rockets. Annette strolled up beside Svetlana, carrying a coiled rope. "Look what the cat dragged in. And by cat, I mean ... okay, just look who showed up."

"Showed up?"

"Yep. Flew on board with that rocket pack. Wanted to talk to you. Athos decided that maybe a little payback was in order first."

Svetlana spun toward Athos. "How is that a good idea? You're just going to make him mad!"

"Don't think it matters this time, Captain. Notice anything different about Richards?"

Svetlana paused and scrutinized Richards. Stubble darkened his cheeks, and his eyes looked a bit sunken. She gasped. "No uniform?"

"No uniform," Athos confirmed. "Seems our friend *Mister* Richards is no longer a corporal with the Port Authority. Meaning he has no authority. So payback."

Svetlana smiled. "Well then, why is he here?"

"He said his information was for no one but you. So we gagged him before we tied him up, just to make sure that juicy gossip didn't get to anyone else first."

Svetlana took the rope from Annette and sauntered up to Richards. "You know one of the things that we learn in the Air Fleet? Knots. Lots and lots of knots."

Richards mumbled something unintelligible through the gag.

"Sorry, didn't catch that?" Svetlana drawled.

"... don't have to tie ..." Richards said, a bit louder this time.

"Oh, I don't?" Svetlana frowned. "But I want to." She unwound a length of the coiled rope and began wrapping the rest around Richards, starting at the level of his armpits.

"Make it good and tight, Cap'n," Jo said. For once, she wasn't hiding below decks, and she seemed as enthusiastic about finally having Richards at their mercy as Svetlana was.

"Can't make it too tight on his torso, Jo," Annette said. "He needs to breathe a little bit to be able to talk."

Svetlana shifted the wrapping pattern to hold the tops of Richards legs to the seat of the chair, but did not linger long there. Winding the rope around his legs and the lower uprights of the chair, she tied a constrictor knot around his ankles, then rose and made a matching knot at the top. She stood on his toes as she untied the gag. "So."

Richards sighed. "So. I've got information you want. What're you offering for it?"

"Mmmm, that we don't cast off right now, and then drop you when we're done?" Jo suggested.

Svetlana hushed Jo. "I don't have much to offer you, Richards. I'm just a humble ship captain, looking for something that'll fetch me a mighty pretty penny. Till I've got that, all I can offer you is the warm hospitality of my ship. And a promise that I won't call Air Fleet and tell them that you're trespassing on said ship."

He paled. "Don't call Air Fleet. Please."

Svetlana looked at Richards. The man trembled beneath her gaze, but she suspected it wasn't her that was making him nervous. "Why not?"

Richards bit his lip. "Air Fleet was behind Kavisoli's inauguration being disrupted."

"Really? Why?"

Richards shrugged, as much as he could with his arms bound behind him. "They didn't tell me that. Officially, they didn't tell me anything. But I know they're involved. The bomb plans, the dismissal from the Port Authority, all of it goes back to Air Fleet."

"Bomb plans? You're trying to tell me that the Air Fleet, who had an inordinate number of high ranking officers at Kavisoli's inauguration, wanted you to *bomb* it?"

"I got the bomb plans from someone ... unaffiliated with the Air Fleet. But I recognized the way the blueprints were drawn. Had to be Air Fleet."

"Uh-huh. Had to be. Who gave you the plans?"

"This urchin lordling. Goes by the name of The Crow Man."

Svetlana glanced at Athos and Jo, who both stood behind Richards. Athos was barely stifling a laugh, while Jo's eyes went wide. Indigo turned his attention to Richards for a moment, and Svetlana gave him a quick warning glance. He nodded and went back to poking at the rocket pack. "What did this 'Crow Man' look like?" Svetlana asked.

"Tall. Real tall. Thin as a rail. Wears a top hat, and this whole suit made from crow's feathers. His hair even looks like it's made from feathers."

"Okay, so this 'Crow Man' gives you these bomb plans, you make the bomb, you give it to Mirage to take to Rrusadon, and then what? You just figured it'd blow and ruin Kavisoli's life, and ... I'm at a loss here, Richards."

"I made sure you'd hear that Kavisoli was getting the Cranglimmering, so you'd go look into it. Two birds, one stone, and all that."

"Okay, that part I'll buy," Svetlana said. "But the rest of it doesn't make any sense. A lot of people could draw up bomb plans that look like they're Air Fleet." She shrugged. "C'mon, if Athos or I drew them, you'd probably think they were official Air Fleet. If either of us were an engineer, at least."

"What about a rogue element within the Air Fleet? I'm thinking this Crow Man was only in with one part of the Air Fleet, because the rest of 'em got upset about the bomb. When I got hauled in for my dismissal, I could've sworn the staff sergeant had something on Air Fleet stationery."

Svetlana nodded, lips drawn tight. "Sure, that makes sense. Richards, do you have any proof of any of this? Or should I have Annette check you for signs of a head injury?"

"No." Richards sighed. "No proof. I was keeping the plans at my apartment, but when I got home after getting the boot, they were gone."

"Oh, that's convenient," Jo said with a smirk.

Svetlana agreed with Jo, but she didn't say as much out loud. She decided to try a different angle. "Have you ever met Admiral Beauregard?"

Richards frowned and shook his head.

"See, here's the thing. When I cut my ties with Air Fleet, there was one person there who didn't want me to go. And that was Admiral Beauregard. He and I have a pretty good relationship, at least most days. If what you say is true, then I should be marching into his office and confronting him about this bomb. Only that wouldn't make a lick of sense. Because had your stupid bomb gone off, you'd have killed him too. I'm not buying it, Richards. Gonna give me the real story?"

"Look, all I know is what I saw. The blueprints looked like they came from Air Fleet. I guess they could've come from somewhere else."

"Like the Crow Man?" Svetlana asked.

"Are we about done?" Richards snapped. "I can't feel my feet."

"If you'd stop trying to get loose, you wouldn't have that problem," Svetlana snarled. "Okay, so let's say that I buy even half of your story. What do you get out of siccing us on the Air Fleet?"

"Look, I just figured—" Richards trailed off. When he spoke again, his voice was softer, barely loud enough for Svetlana to hear without leaning closer. "I've got nowhere else to go. Tom and Henry wouldn't even look me in the eye when they escorted me out."

Svetlana sighed. *The last refuge of a desperate man. Yeah, that sounds like us.* She still didn't trust him, but he'd given her the first inkling of information that she could use. She pulled out her knife and slashed through the upper constrictor knot. "Go home, Richards," she said, reaching down and cutting the other knot, leaving him in a coil of rope. "You stay out of our way, and we'll be sure to stay out of yours." A smile twisted her lips as she nodded to the rocket pack. "You'll be leaving that. Indy's not done playing with it yet."

Richards shrugged his way out of the coiled rope and shook his head as he walked toward the gangplank. "Don't come crying to me when I'm right, Tereshchenko."

"Don't worry. I won't ever have to," she snapped back.

As soon as Richards was away from the ship, Svetlana looked around at her crew. "Well, that was an entertaining little farce."

Jo nodded. "Crow Man's an urchin lordling now?"

"Well, to be fair, he does employ a higher than average number of children who live on the streets," Athos said.

"Yep," Svetlana agreed. "Indy, put that thing away. You can play with it later. We need to go find your friends."

Indigo lagged behind Svetlana as they walked. Each time she noticed he was not beside her, she turned to find him looking in a shop window at some fancy gadget. She also noticed that he was looking at her sidelong.

"What's going on, Indy?"

"Nothin'."

Svetlana sighed. "Here's the deal. Tell me what's bothering you. We're not going to go until you do. And until we've talked to the Crow Man, we can't go back to the ship either. Which means no more tinkering on the rocket pack till we're done."

Indigo pressed his lips together in a tight line. "I don't like the Crow Man," he finally responded.

"Why not?"

"He's scary. Tells people he'll have their eyes and feed them to his birds."

"Hmmm. Ever seen anyone who lost their eyes to the Crow Man?"

"No."

"Then do you suppose maybe he doesn't actually have anyone's eyes out?"

"There's an eyeball on top of his walking stick."

Svetlana balled her hand up into a fist and held it out in front of her. "Indy, that eyeball's this big. I don't think it came from a person. Anyway, he only says he'll take the eyes of people who speak out of turn. If you keep quiet, he won't threaten you."

Indigo nodded slowly. "I can stay quiet."

"Good. But I need your help to find Deliah."

"Oh, her?" Indigo pointed at a dilapidated building beside the store whose window had caught his attention most recently. "She's been following us this whole time."

Svetlana peered into the gloom of the building's doorway. The setting sun made little progress through the dirt-caked windows but still caused enough of a glare that she had a hard time distinguishing details. All she could see was blackness, none of Deliah's bright colored hair or clothing.

"Deliah?" she called, taking a step toward the building. The door jerked open about half a foot, though she still couldn't see any inhabitants. Indigo's hand brushed against hers for a moment, and then he gave the door a push, swinging it wide open.

"May we come in?" he asked, his voice wavering.

"Yes." The single word sounded ominous as it echoed out from the darkness.

Indigo pulled his goggles from around his neck and slid them up. He giggled as he focused them, and Svetlana saw traces of the blue light that had surrounded the lenses when Annette had used the x-ray setting. "Bones," he murmured.

"Indigo, you are one creepy boy," she muttered. "Worried about getting your eyes taken out, and then laughing about skeletons?" Svetlana shuddered, but followed him into the building.

Under her feet, something crunched. The sound was such that she could have thought of it as leaves or other debris if Indigo hadn't already told her that there were bones. Now she imagined the entire building was carpeted with them, and there was nowhere to step where she wouldn't disturb some poor soul's final resting place. She moved as slowly as she could while still feeling Indigo's presence nearby.

Svetlana's eye adjusted to the darkness once she was surrounded by it, but it was still difficult for her to see much beyond the ghostly glow of Indigo's goggles. She again considered handing over her monocular to the boy to add new settings, but in addition to Indigo's stack of successful projects, he also had an enormous pile of those he had discarded as boring. Few things that wound up in that category ever found their way out of Indigo's workshop, and she was unwilling to lose her monocular permanently.

Deliah's face was the first thing Svetlana could make out. Indigo stood near enough to her that his goggles lit her skin, eerily pale in the blue light. "Hello, Captain," she said. "Thank you for bringing Indy to visit."

"I'm sorry that it can't be a very long visit, Deliah. We need to speak with the Crow Man."

Deliah frowned but nodded solemnly. "He knows."

Before Svetlana could ask <u>how</u> he knew, a rush of cold air surrounded her, and the sound of flapping wings echoed throughout the dark space. Deliah's face vanished back into the gloom, and Indigo's hands clutched at Svetlana's trousers. She found his hands and held them, but then his legs began to kick, as though he was trying to run. Wrapping her arms around his shoulders, she pulled him close. "Shh. Just be quiet, Indy."

A sphere, glowing purple, rolled across the floor and stopped a few feet in front of her. Deliah's small hand covered the top of the ball, and the girl giggled, ghostly in the darkness. Svetlana had enough presence of mind to tug the goggles away from Indigo's eyes and shield her own good eye. A quick popping sound, and the room was lit by a whiter light, still tinged with purple around the edges.

As soon as Svetlana took in what there was to see, she almost wished the room had stayed dark. A dozen young men and women dressed in black had surrounded her, Indigo, and Deliah. All of the sullen gazes, framed by gaunt faces, were fixed on Svetlana.

One of the girls, wearing a threadbare cloak that had been patched with stray feathers, spoke. "You wish to see the Crow Man?" Though her cloak was not impressive, she had more feathers on it than any other person in the room. Svetlana knew it marked her as a leader among this group of Crow's Children.

"That's correct."

"We can make that happen." The girl smiled. A wickedly curved silver blade slid from her sleeve into her hand. The tip, which looked more like a scoop than a point, caught Svetlana's attention, and she swallowed.

"I'm requesting audience."

Several of the assembled Crow's Children drew back at her statement. The girl pursed her lips before growling, "His Grace does not accept requests from no ones. Who do you think are you, to ask for him to see you?"

"Captain Svetlana Tereshchenko, of *The Silent Monsoon*. More importantly, I'm the one who's heard disparaging comments about the Crow Man's involvement with an officer of the Port Authority, and perhaps the Air Fleet." She paused, letting her words sink in. More of the Children drew back, and there were whispers as well. "I'd like to give him the opportunity to address those comments, and if his answers are satisfactory, I'm prepared to give him the name of his accuser."

The girl frowned, gaze darting to one of the other girls in the group. "You ... you would come willingly to share this information?"

"To be sure, there's going to be some exchanging of information. Tit for tat. But yes. I have information for the Crow Man. Take me to him." She glanced down at Indigo, who had gone rigid in her arms. "Myself and the boy. Neither of us to be harmed. And this girl, Deliah, she is under my protection as well."

"Deliah is already under the Crow Man's protection." The leader of the Crow's Children sighed, and plucked one of the feathers from her cloak. She handed it to Deliah and nodded solemnly. "The boy and yourself. We will take you to see the Crow Man."

The room that the Crow's Children took Svetlana and Indigo to was far more civilized than the run-down building where they had spoken with his messengers. Though she and Indigo had been blindfolded as they made their way across the city, Svetlana had a good sense of where they had been taken.

The uphill hike and fresh air, untainted by garbage or sulphur, put them in one of the best neighborhoods of Heliopolis.

The décor in the room led Svetlana to the same conclusion. Overstuffed chairs, plush carpets, and what appeared to be real wood paneling surrounded them. Sunlight filtered through the windows and caught dust motes swirling in the air, but the room itself was tidy, despite the shelves being burdened with an overabundance of small, shiny knickknacks.

Svetlana heard a muffled click from behind her. Indigo spun to look in that direction. Svetlana sighed and put a hand on his shoulder. Looking him in the eyes, she mouthed, "Stay quiet."

"Captain Tereshchenko." The voice was that of a man, inflected with the sing-song quality that many of the street urchins used. "My Children tell me you have witnessed aspersions against my character."

"Indeed." Svetlana rose from the overstuffed chair she had perched on the edge of and turned to face the Crow Man. The man fit Richards' description— tall and gaunt, with black hair like feathers brushing across his cheeks and trailing over the shoulders of his feather-covered suit.

"Speak of them, then. Do not keep me waiting."

Though Svetlana had told the Crow's Children that she would only share her information when the Crow Man answered her questions, she opened with what she had, suspecting it would make him more amenable to sharing information with her. "Corporal Richards. Or, rather, Adrian Richards, seeing as he's been released from his commission at the Port Authority. He claims you gave him the plans to build a bomb."

The Crow Man chuckled, though it sounded more like the cawing of his namesake bird. "And if I did?"

"That bomb was taken to Rrusadon and could have put a big dent in Larson Kavisoli's inauguration. Now, I'll admit that Lar and I aren't seeing eye to eye at the moment, but I believe that if I tell him you were behind this, he will send someone after you."

The Crow Man cackled at that. "Captain Tereshchenko, I believe you know my reputation. One does not simply find the Crow Man."

"Yes, that's true, we had to be brought here by your most gracious Children. But there is something you're forgetting."

"Oh?" He cocked his head to the side and stared at Svetlana with dark glittering eyes.

"It becomes much easier to find you if someone knows your other name, Lord Corwin."

He stiffened and glared at her. "How dare you suggest—"

"Please," Svetlana said, shaking her head. "It's one of the worst kept secrets in Heliopolis. Sure, the guys at Port Authority might not have caught on just yet, but every low life scum in this city knows who you are."

"I see. And you count yourself among Heliopolis's scum?"

"I do." Though *The Silent Monsoon* was her true home, if she had to pick anywhere else to live, it would be Heliopolis.

He took a step forward, his face placid, but his eyes sparkling. "And what is to stop me from taking your good eye and making an example of you?"

"Your carpet." Svetlana gestured at it when she spoke.

"What?" he sputtered, breaking the stoniness of his expression.

"Rather, the carpet in this room. If you're not Lord Corwin, then whomever does own this house will be mightily upset if you get my blood all over his carpet. And if you are Lord Corwin, why would you want to ruin your own parlor just to get one measly eye?" She kept her gaze locked with the Crow Man's, not wanting him to threaten or even look at Indigo. The boy had remained calm thus far, and she didn't want to jeopardize the negotiations with him panicking.

The Crow Man frowned, lowering his chin as though he was considering the carpet. His gaze darted up to Svetlana occasionally, but several minutes passed quietly. Svetlana remained standing, ready to move into action if needed. But Indigo seemed to relax in the silence, and settled himself into one of the parlor chairs.

"What is it you want?" The voice, though still that of the Crow Man, had taken on a gravelly rumble and careful articulation of each word.

"Richards claimed that the plans for the bomb came from you, but he also told me that they looked like Air Fleet plans. I need to confirm or disprove that."

He cocked his head to one side and regarded her. "You are not Air Fleet."

"No, I haven't been for a while. But I have an old friend there, and if someone in his chain of command has been handing out bomb plans, I need to let him know that."

"It is not the Air Fleet," Lord Corwin replied. "At least, to the best of my knowledge, which, I am certain you will agree, is quite extensive." He hesitated. "The plans for the explosive device came from a higher source."

"Higher source? What, like the Skyfather?" Svetlana scoffed.

"Hardly. You were Air Fleet once, Captain Tereshchenko. Tell me, to whom does the Air Fleet answer?"

Svetlana shrugged. "The High Council, and the High General himself."

Lord Corwin inclined his head, a barely perceptible motion.

A shiver rippled down Svetlana's spine. "But only the High Council communicates with the High General."

"Indeed. And, despite my authority within the Heliopolis City Council, I am not a member of the High Council by any stretch of the imagination. Our beloved Mayor Bartram has a better chance of catching the High General's ear than I do."

Svetlana stared at Lord Corwin as she tried to make sense of what he told her. If the High Council was involved, then this might be their move to consolidate the missing casks. She needed to find the remaining casks and spirit them away as Lady de Whittvy had allegedly done with the Bartram Cask. But then another thought occurred to her. "Did you suggest Rrusadon as the target, or did the High Council?"

"Captain Tereshchenko, consider my words carefully. I have named no names."

She clenched her jaw. The shift from threats to political speak was not an improvement in this conversation. She spoke slowly. "I need to know. Did your source for the plans choose the target?"

Lord Corwin shrugged. "News of Rrusadon's acceptance into the Republic has been in all of the newspapers for the past month. So too have certain advertisements. When taken together, the advertisements could be interpreted into a shape. Plans, if you will." He crossed the room and picked up a newspaper from the table. Without a word, he turned to one of the last pages and presented it to Svetlana.

It took a moment before she could make sense of what she was looking at. It was, as he said, an advertisement, for washing powder. But the lines of the illustration looked off. She lowered the newspaper and showed the advertisement to Indigo.

"Circuits," Indigo replied immediately.

Svetlana blinked. "Really?"

The boy nodded.

"Circuits for what?"

"Dunno. Need more pieces." He took the paper from her and began rustling through the pages.

Svetlana returned her attention to Lord Corwin. "Blueprints, in the newspaper. With articles about Rrusadon placed strategically along the margins." She shook her head. "And you just pointed out the pieces?"

"I played my role, Captain Tereshchenko. In the end, that's all that any of us can do. Play the role we're given. You'd do well to remember that. Those in authority don't appreciate it when we overstep our bounds." He bowed curtly. "I believe we are done here. My Children will see you out."

CHAPTER SIXTEEN

THE REST OF the crew of *The Silent Monsoon* was waiting on deck when Svetlana and Indigo returned from their meeting with the Crow Man. Svetlana didn't bother with words, instead she headed straight to the mess. When she arrived, she took a key from a pocket in her trousers and unlocked a high cabinet. The door squeaked with disuse. She reached in and pulled out a delicately cut glass bottle, topped with a cork and sealed with wax.

Annette gasped when she saw the bottle. "Is that—" she asked, using the hushed tones of reverence people generally reserved for the holiest of occasions.

Svetlana nodded, but then she decided to elaborate. "Indy did well with the Crow Man. So first drink of the hundred-year rum's for him. But you're all going to need a sip, I think."

She carried the rum to the table. Gripping the top and cracking the wax, she pulled the cork out. Indigo's eyes grew wide as he looked at the bottle, but he accepted it when Svetlana pushed it in his direction. He took a small swig, and then coughed at least half of it back out onto the table.

"And that's not even Cranglimmering," Jo murmured. Turning to Svetlana, she spoke louder. "So, that bad?"

Svetlana took a quick pull from the bottle and then set it down on the table, her hand not straying from the neck. "Lord Corwin can't say it in so many words, being a politician and all, but he implied that the High Council arranged for the bomb on Rrusadon. I don't want to dig too deep to figure out if that was their idea or the High General's, because the long and the short of it is the same either way—someone doesn't want the Kavisolis getting a vote in the Republican Senate."

"Then why'd they let them join in the first place?" Jo asked.

"Money, if I had to take a guess. The Kavisolis have that in abundance, and the Republic is expensive to keep running. Again, just guessing here, but I'd say there was a loan somewhere, and that loan wouldn't need to be repaid if there were no Kavisolis to repay it to."

"Should we go to Lar with this?" Athos asked, his tone solemn.

"Not yet. Because there's more to it. Vertiline saw the staves from the first three casks of Cranglimmering in the High Council's chambers. So it seems reasonable to assume they'd be after the rest of those staves as well. Which makes this the second time the High Council's come up in relation to the Cranglimmering."

"Third," Athos said, frowning.

"Come again?" Annette replied. "The bomb and the staves. That's only two."

"It didn't ... it just now clicked. Hortence Bartram. Daughter and sole heir of Mayor Ambrose Bartram and his late wife. Not known for beauty, talent, or extraordinary wealth. That engagement party that my aunties told me about, that was for her to be presented as the betrothed of Robert Swaisbrook, Junior."

"Swaisbrook? That sounds familiar," Annette muttered.

"That's because the Senior, Junior's daddy, is on the High Council. Now I thought to myself, 'That's a bit odd, a Mayor's daughter marrying a High

Councilor's son.' But I figured my aunties just had the story wrong—that the betrothal was to someone else." Athos shook his head. "I'm thinking they were right."

"Why didn't you mention that earlier, Athos?" Svetlana growled.

"It wasn't relevant at the time! Jo didn't want to hear any more of my idle gossip, remember?" Athos sighed. "Besides which, that's all it was, then. It's only significant when you put together with the other pieces. It means that the engagement party was going to be the occasion when the Bartram Cask was opened, to celebrate the betrothal. And then once it's open, I'm sure that Robert Swaisbrook, Senior, made a deal with the Mayor to take the cask itself off his hands. If so, the High Council would have another set of staves. Four out of seven. What're the odds those new pieces have what they need to find the Last Emperor's Hoard?"

"One in four, I'd guess. But they don't have Vertiline's machine. She—" Svetlana stopped and frowned. Now that she thought about it, she was certain that the map on the wall at Vertiline's house was well over halfway completed. But Vertiline had said herself that she had only seen the staves from the three opened casks. "Vertiline must have predicted where the staves from the Bartram Cask should go. Or perhaps her probability engine is that good at its job."

Jo frowned. "Wait, you're telling me that Vertiline already has better than three sets of staves worth of the map?"

"I can't be entirely sure. I didn't count the pieces, or anything like that. And then there was the whole ghost ship attack. But I have to admit, it's beginning to look that way," Svetlana said.

"Hmmmm, okay, bear with me on this one," Jo said. "Athos, what does Lady de Whittvy look like?"

Athos shrugged. "I haven't had the pleasure of meeting her. They say she's quite lovely, though."

"Lovely," Jo scoffed. "Do you suppose they'd say that about a fair-skinned ginger?"

Svetlana shook her head. "Jo, I see where you're going, but no. Vertiline couldn't possibly be Lady de Whittvy. I mean, Lady de Whittvy lives here, and Vertiline lives a day away by airship. She can't be two places at once."

"Then what, Lady de Whittvy stole the cask and sold the staves to Vertiline?" Jo suggested.

Svetlana shrugged. "Sure, that's possible."

"Don't you think Vertiline would have mentioned it if that were the case?" Annette asked. "Especially since the two of you were talking about the casks before she disappeared? Hate to disagree with you Captain, but Jo's wild theory is sounding pretty good."

Svetlana looked at Athos, hopeful that he had some piece of information that could prove that Vertiline wasn't Lady de Whittvy. If they were the same woman, and Vertiline already had the staves, then sending Svetlana to Chickie's party no longer made any sense. It was just another part of the wild goose chase that they'd been on since Richards arrested Athos.

Athos shrugged. "It might hold hot air, Cap'n. I suppose we could go ask around, find someone who knows Lady de Whittvy personally?"

"Chickie knows both of them," Svetlana said. "Or at least he led me to believe they're not one and the same. But let's just try this on for size. Would the Mayor know her?"

"If Lady de Whittvy's the one who took the cask, then absolutely," Athos replied. "She's said to pay cordial social visits to her victims before she steals from them. Something about knowing her enemies."

"Perfect. Can you get us in to see him?"

Tensing his shoulders, Athos hesitated. He shot a quick glance at Jo, but her gaze was fixed on the bottle of rum. He nodded and said, "I can try."

"Then let's go to the source."

Svetlana hung back as Athos started toward the gatehouse at the Bartram Estate. "Why don't you just go and see if he's in and then holler if you need me?"

Athos looked up at the house then back at Svetlana. "He's in. What's wrong? You suggested this. I'm the one who's been arrested recently."

"I'm just not good at this respectable thing. Mayors are—" Svetlana shuddered.

"Larson Kavisoli's a mayor, and you have one of his shirts in your room as we speak."

Svetlana blushed. "Fine. Let's just do this. 'Hi, Mayor Bartram. Can you tell us if the woman who stole your prized family possession was a cute little ginger, about three inches taller than me?'"

"Right. Let me do the talking?"

"You've got it." She fell into step behind Athos, trying to match his stride so that she could fade out of sight behind him.

The guard at the gatehouse stared straight at Svetlana. "Don't I know you?"

Svetlana looked at the guard and recognized him as the one she and Jo had dealt with the first time they came to check out the Bartram Estate. "Um, no, I don't think that you do." She turned to Athos and whispered, "Should we give him money or something?"

Athos gave her a withering look before turning back to the guard. "Don't mind her. I'm here to speak with Mayor Bartram about a business opportunity. Refinished wood products."

"D'ya have an appointment?" the guard asked.

"Appointment. Ah. My assistant was supposed to arrange that." Athos' gaze darted around until it fixed on a closed black ledger book, which he gestured to. "It should be in there."

"Under what name, sir?"

Athos drew in a deep breath. "Are you trying to tell me you don't know who I am?"

"Can't say that I do, sir. And I'll need your name to look you up in the appointment ledger."

Athos huffed loudly. "Lord de Whittvy."

The guard arched one eyebrow. "Lord de Whittvy?"

"Very good, you heard me."

"Beggin' your pardon sir, unless the Lady de Whittvy's gone off and gotten married since she was last in attendance, there ain't no Lord de Whittvy." He paused and narrowed his eyes. "Besides which, I don't believe I've seen her name or yours in the ledger for this evening."

Svetlana tried not to chuckle, particularly when Athos turned his venomous attitude in her direction. "Well, I suppose I will have to see my assistant beaten for her insolence." He grabbed the back of Svetlana's collar, spun her around, and marched away from the gatehouse. She stumbled along, playing the role of the bumbling assistant that she knew Athos was going for.

Once they were a few blocks away, she shrugged out of Athos' loose grip on her collar. "Well, that may qualify as one of the worst plans you've ever had," she said.

"Yes and no," Athos said, a grin spreading across his face. "I verified that Lady de Whittvy paid them a visit recently, which means that she could very well have taken the Cranglimmering."

"Still don't understand how," Svetlana said, craning her neck to look back at the tall house at the center of the estate. "Jo and I went over it. There's no good place to get something that big out of there, other than up."

"Well that's true. But that gives me an even better idea." His eyes sparkled. "You can't get much of any substantial size out of there, but smaller things, things like you and me? Those I can get in."

"Past the guard?"

"Circumventing the guard entirely." Athos removed his hat and jacket and tucked them into a nearby rain barrel. With no rain in weeks, it would be dry, but Svetlana still listened for a splash. "Come along."

Svetlana followed Athos back up to the top of the hill, and along the right-hand side of the estate, the same side she had walked a week earlier. "There's no entrance over here," she whispered. "I've been over it already."

"Nothing formal, no." Athos paused at an ivy-covered trellis between two tall bushes. Fumbling at one side of it, he then rolled back several of the poles of the trellis. The trellis was, in reality, a large painted piece of canvas, rendered in exquisite detail and offering the illusion of depth. Only on close examination could Svetlana tell it was not real. At the side that Athos had drawn back, a short length of rope hung down, and on the other side of the gap, an ornate green ivy leaf jutted out from an iron post.

"And why didn't you think to tell me or Jo about this when we were headed this way before?"

Athos shrugged. "I may have been suffering from having been punched a bit. I also didn't anticipate you wanting to just go barging in."

"This is a secret entrance. It's not barging in."

"Come now, you really think that you and Jo would have snuck in quietly?" He shook his head. "I know you both too well. Anyway, you couldn't have gotten in to the house this way."

"Why not?"

"Because you don't have friends and relations all over the city."

Svetlana smirked. "Oh, who is it here?"

"She's just a chambermaid, but she aspires to the opera. A distant cousin, I believe."

Athos and Svetlana made their way across the manicured lawn. As they moved, Svetlana noticed that it looked little like the painting that hid the lawn from prying eyes. But she supposed that most who walked past would never notice the illusion.

Athos stopped at a low window and tapped. A moment later, a young woman came to the window and looked out. Her eyes brightened when she saw Athos, and she opened the window. "Athos? You ... who's she?"

"Maddie, darling, this is my friend Sveta. We go way back. Nothing serious, I assure you. Old school chums. Is the lady of the house in?"

"She's in her suite." Maddie pouted. "Whadd'ya want with her, anyway?"

"It's my friend that wants with her," Athos whispered, still loud enough for Svetlana to hear. She smirked, but let him continue. "I just need to go along to make sure no one spots them together. You understand. I'll come back and visit you another time, eh?"

Maddie nodded, her smile spreading back across her face. She ducked out of sight for a moment and returned with a rope ladder, which she lowered over the windowsill. Athos scampered up it, and Svetlana followed him through the window.

Svetlana glanced around the room. It was small, but more importantly, it had a staircase leading up. When she turned back to Maddie, the girl was giggling under her breath. "Doesn't that just top all? Miss Hortence has a lady friend."

"Keep it quiet, if it's all the same to you, Maddie," Svetlana whispered conspiratorially. "Miss Hortence needs to keep up appearances for her father."

Maddie nodded solemnly. "You been here before, then, Miss?"

Svetlana shook her head. "I'm afraid not. And this is a bit of a surprise visit." She gestured toward the stairs with her chin. "Up, I suppose?"

Maddie nodded again. "First on the right."

Svetlana nodded in reply and hurried up the stairs, Athos close behind her.

"Will you never grow tired of pairing me up with women?" she whispered as they surveyed the long upstairs hallway.

"You started it with Narci. And Laurlei. And what was the other one's name?"

"Not important."

"All I'm saying is that you like women just as much as you like men, Cap'n. And it still shocks enough people to find out that someone they know prefers the same sex. So I use that to my advantage."

Svetlana chuckled. "I don't know that it's a shock if they've spent any time with the upper class. I saw plenty of people pairing up with whomever they pleased at Chickie's little party." She shrugged. "Anyway, I suppose it works out when your cousin seems hurt that you'd come to see the lady of the house."

"What can I say? I have jealous family members."

"Of course you do. Come on."

Svetlana walked to the designated door and tried the knob. It turned freely. Grabbing Athos' sleeve, she tugged him into the suite behind her.

Before she could survey the room, Svetlana felt something narrow and pointed against her right cheek. She released Athos' sleeve and raised her hands slowly. "I don't want any trouble."

"Well, you're in for a world of it," a female voice whispered.

The pressure dropped from Svetlana's cheek. She turned, hands still raised. Before her stood a pale-skinned younger woman, perhaps in her twenties, dressed in a fitted military uniform that Svetlana did not recognize. In her right hand, the woman held a slender rapier with no handguard visible. The blade quivered, but that was a result of the flexibility of the blade, not a wavering on the part of the wielder. The young woman's face was unremarkable. Her eyes matched her dark brown hair, and she would have blended into any crowd if her gaze was not filled with fiery determination.

"Who are you?" the young woman asked.

"Captain Svetlana Tereshchenko. You must be Miss Hortence Bartram?"

The young woman nodded.

"Miss Bartram, we are in need of some information."

"So you sneak into my room in the middle of the night?"

"It's just now evening," Svetlana said, lowering her hands.

Hortence stepped closer to Svetlana, raising her sword to Svetlana's good eye.

"As you say, in the middle of the night," Svetlana said. "It is most improper of us, but we are desperate for the information we seek."

The young woman arched her eyebrow. "Ask, then."

"We understand that you are engaged to marry Robert Swaisbrook, Junior."

Hortence wrinkled her nose. "So they say. I haven't made up my mind yet."

"Haven't made up your mind?"

"I've never met him. I told my father that I won't have anything to do with a man I've never met."

Svetlana kept her face still but wanted nothing more than to smile and encourage the girl. "And your father?"

Hortence shrugged. "He insists that I will come around."

"There was to be a celebration—" Athos began.

"I'm speaking with her," Hortence said, swinging the point of her blade toward Athos for a moment before returning it to threaten Svetlana's eyesight.

"My friend does bring up the next question I had for you," Svetlana said. "The celebration, to announce your betrothal?"

"Well, it was cancelled. And I'm glad of it."

"Glad simply because it was cancelled?"

"Glad because Mother ensured it was cancelled."

Svetlana frowned. "Miss Bartram, forgive me. I was given to understand that your mother departed this world some years ago."

"So I believed as well. But then just last week, she returned. In secret, of course. She couldn't stay long. She just came back to take what was rightfully hers."

"And that was?"

"*Her* Cask of Cranglimmering. Father took Mother's name when they wed, as she had the station and the finances. She brought the cask as well."

Svetlana pursed her lips and turned to Athos. He mouthed "de Whittvy" with a slight nod.

"How can you be certain that this woman was your mother?"

"How can you imply that I would not know my own mother? It may have been some twenty years, but I could never forget her." Hortence sighed. "She still smelled the same."

"Of what did she smell?" Svetlana asked, already knowing the answer.

"Lilac."

A clatter from below interrupted anything else she might say. "Father!" Hortence gasped. She removed a brass hoop from inside her jacket and slid the point of the rapier into a narrow gap in the hoop. The blade curved into the hollow space within the hoop, and soon looked to be nothing more than a fancy oversized bangle. "You must go. I must change my clothes."

Svetlana nodded and reached for the doorknob.

"Not that way!" Hortence hissed. Svetlana turned back to the young woman, who gestured at the window.

Athos grabbed Svetlana's hand and pulled her in that direction. He threw open the window and looked down. "Roses. Of course."

Svetlana turned back to Hortence. "Thank you, Miss Bartram. You've been more help than you might imagine. Best of luck with your betrothal. Or with your own arrangements."

Hortence's lips twitched up into a half-smile. "Best of luck with the roses."

CHAPTER SEVENTEEN

THE NEXT MORNING, Svetlana was still finding rose thorns in her boots as she and Annette walked across the city. It was early and the streets were quiet. Seeing no traffic, wheeled or pedestrian, Svetlana asked Annette to stop for a moment. She sat down on the sidewalk and removed her boot. Several small thorns clung to her woolen sock. She sighed and stripped it off then felt around the inside of her boot for any additional thorns.

"So what do you plan to tell Bobby?" Annette asked, seating herself beside Svetlana.

"I've got the information I need to get Lar out. The guard at the Bartram Estate confirmed that Lady de Whittvy had visited their estate. Hortence told me that a woman claiming to be her mother took the cask. They're one and the same, I'm certain of it."

"What about the lilac part?"

"I suppose that makes Jo's theory plausible. Vertiline might be Lady de Whittvy. But I don't have to share that part with Bobby. Chickie said that Lady de Whittvy would be as difficult to find as ... oh."

"What?"

"Chickie said it would be just as hard to find Lady de Whittvy as it would be to find Vertiline, when I told him about Vertiline being kidnapped. I suppose if they are the same person, that would be true."

"Which means, in effect, that you'd be selling out Vertiline to the Air Fleet in order to get Lar out of jail."

"Yeah." Svetlana considered the options. Vertiline had been nothing but cordial and helpful to her and her crew. Lar had appreciated her saving his life but otherwise just left her confused, and his quick shift in personality when he believed Svetlana had sold him out was troublesome. "You're right. Maybe I shouldn't tell Bobby after all."

"Then we don't need to go back to headquarters?" Annette rose to head back to *The Silent Monsoon*.

Before Svetlana could answer, she spotted a young boy heading in their direction, lugging a sack filled with copies of the morning newspaper. As he drew nearer, he began crying out the headlines. "Phantom ship strikes Starryglass! Ten missing!"

Svetlana fished a small coin from her pocket and flipped it to the boy. He handed her the paper. "Starryglass," she muttered as she scanned the article. "Why does that sound familiar?"

Annette leaned over her shoulder and looked at the article. "Home of Lord Mayor Silver. That's where one of the casks is."

"Is there a cask at Bluesummer too?"

Annette scratched her head. "Could be. Bluesummer could be someone's summer retreat. That might be the sort of place you'd store your valuable whiskey, especially if you can afford to keep the place staffed year round."

"So it's plausible, then? A ghost ship going after the other casks?"

"Sure, I suppose." Annette scanned the article. "There's nothing here about the Silver Cask."

"But Lord Mayor Silver and his family are among the missing. They might have taken them to wherever he's keeping his cask."

"A ghost ship never came here, though."

Svetlana tensed. "It may have. The night when Richards had you in lockup, I thought I saw something. I dismissed it as just the moon on the clouds. Anyway, the cask would have already been gone from here—" Svetlana trailed off as it hit her. "—that's it! That's how you could get the cask out of the Bartram Estate! On a ship that can vanish at will!"

"So we definitely don't need to go to headquarters. We just need to find the ghost ship. Which seems somehow both more and less difficult."

"No, we should still go to headquarters. If anyone would know about a phantom ship, it'd be Bobby."

"And you think he'll tell you all about it today?"

Svetlana chewed on the inside of her cheek. Annette had a point. Bobby hadn't been forthcoming with information recently. Normally, the two of them had an easy rapport. But now, Svetlana wondered if telling Bobby about the ghost ship would gain her any information or favors. She wanted to believe that it would, but the memory of her last interaction with Bobby told her otherwise. "I think we should try," she said finally, though her voice was quiet.

"I was afraid you were going to say that," Annette said, shaking her head. "I assume you have a plan to get in to see him?"

Svetlana shrugged. "I don't think we need a plan. I tell the desk clerk I've got information on the cask, and I think they'll show me right in. You can just smile and look pretty."

Half an hour later, Svetlana stomped out of the lobby at headquarters, fuming. The desk clerk had refused to let her in to see Bobby. Annette had stayed behind. She and Svetlana had entered separately, giving Annette the opportunity to start in on her sob story about being a military widow after Svetlana stormed out. Svetlana put an ear up to the door and could hear Annette's voice, an octave higher than usual, begging the desk clerk to let her speak to someone about her dead husband's pension. Svetlana frowned. Annette hated to bring up Jack, but the story worked every time.

Seizing the opportunity created by Annette's histrionics, Svetlana found an open window just off the main entrance and clambered inside. The classroom was vacant, though she knew the cadets would start filling the room soon enough. She tugged one side of her shirt from her trousers and mussed her hair. And then she ran out into the hall, looking as frantic and disheveled as she could manage.

Under her breath, she muttered, "Crap, I'm late," over and over again. Most of the cadets in the hallways cleared out of her way as she ran, and few of them paid her much more mind than that required. One, however, stopped moving directly in front of her.

She stepped to the side to evade him. The young man stepped a moment after she did, continuing to block her path.

Svetlana looked up into hardened eyes, not the sort you typically saw on a cadet. A moment later, her brain caught up with the officer's insignia she had seen, and she snapped a hand up to give a perfect salute.

"You're out of uniform, Cadet," the officer said.

"Yes, sir. Sorry, sir."

"Well, don't you think that you should remedy that before you rush off to wherever it is that you're going in such a hurry?"

"That is exactly what I was intending, sir." Svetlana was acutely aware of the gazes of a number of the cadets she had bowled past now fixed on her.

"Really? I find that hard to believe, Cadet."

Svetlana frowned. "And why is that, sir?"

"Because you're running away from the direction of the dormitories."

"Ah, yes, sir. You see, my jacket, I, uh, left it in the commandant's office."

"Did you now?"

"Well, I believe so, sir," Svetlana said. She hoped beyond hope that she hadn't misread his insignia. If this was the commandant, whatever remained of her cover was blown. The assembled cadets began shifting away from the conversation between Svetlana and the officer, tension filling the air.

"Then you must have spent some time out of uniform, Cadet. The commandant has been away from this office for the past week."

"My apologies, sir, I wasn't clear," Svetlana said, allowing just a hint of a smile to cross her lips. "I took my jacket off while I was cleaning the commandant's office, in preparation for—" Svetlana allowed herself a moment of hesitation. The officer had not specified the gender of the commandant, and Svetlana wasn't familiar enough with the Academy right now to know the commandant. She decided to go with the most likely scenario. "—his return."

The officer regarded her for a long moment, his eyes narrowed. "I see. Carry on, Cadet."

She saluted again and picked up her pace toward the wing where the officers and instructors kept their offices. As soon as she was out of earshot, she let out a long, shuddering breath. While the Air Fleet might claim that all were equal in the defense of the Republic, Svetlana's time had taught her that it was still an old boys' club of sorts. The commandant had never, to her knowledge, been a woman, and it seemed that still held true.

She slowed as she neared Bobby's office. It had not moved in all the years she had known him, still in a smaller space than the admiral was entitled to. Svetlana tried the doorknob and was not surprised to find it unlocked. Listening at the door for a moment, she heard no sound beyond. She nudged the door with her toe and slipped in.

The room was dim, the curtains drawn over the tall windows. A stale aroma of cigar smoke lingered, but it was at least a couple of days old. Svetlana thought about when she had last been here and was surprised that it had been just a bit longer than a day ago. All of the days had blurred together since they had begun to pursue the cask.

She walked over to Bobby's desk, looking for anything that might suggest where he was. With Lar in custody, she doubted that Bobby would go far, but a tidy stack of maps and gazetteers on his desk suggested otherwise. Several of the books were older, but a new map near the top of the stack showed her the likely subject of Bobby's study.

The map was marked with a circle around Heliopolis, giving the date when the cask was taken from the Bartram Estate. Another carefully drawn mark encircled Bluesummer. Stars and a handful of numbers marked the cities of Starryglass, Merrowbarrow, Esterbridge, and Orwall. Svetlana could not be certain, but she had an inkling that the Somerset and Gyrfalcon families lived in one of those locations. He was either tracking ghost ships already or was making the rounds to ensure the security of the remaining casks. Either way, he was on the same path as she was.

The numbers were curious. They didn't look like dates or coordinates, but they had to mean something to someone. Perhaps between her and Athos, they could puzzle out the meaning. She folded the map up and tucked it into her jacket. Athos would also know which families lived in which cities far better than she did.

Svetlana paused, considering whether she should leave Bobby a note asking him to contact her about Lar's imprisonment. But for her to have been here while he was out would heighten his suspicion of her motivations. Better to get out of here quickly and speak with him about all of this later.

Svetlana found Annette waiting outside of the gates of Air Fleet headquarters. "How'd it go?" she asked the doctor.

Annette shrugged. "No one from pensions was available. But I carried on for a good long while. Did you find Bobby?"

"No, he was out. But I found a map. I'll show you when we're back on the ship. I think ghost ships are going after the remaining casks, and I think the Air Fleet might be looking for the ghost ships."

"Well, they've got better resources for covering a wide area."

Svetlana nodded. "It would have been nice if Bobby had mentioned it to me, though. We could have helped."

"You know he has no reason to share that information with you. You left the Fleet."

"Yes, I know. But sometimes independent contractors work with the

Fleet."

"We're the only independent contractors I've ever seen working with the Fleet, Svetlana."

Svetlana sighed and turned away from Annette, looking down the side of the hill to the docks. A large black carriage was parked near the *Monsoon*. She frowned and broke into a sprint. Annette yelped something about not wanting to go for a run, but Svetlana heard the doctor's pace quicken soon after.

Svetlana was breathing hard when she reached the ship, despite having run downhill. Slowing to catch her breath, she surveyed the scene. Three men stood near the carriage, all dressed in dull browns and greens. A dozen more men, similarly dressed, stood along the gangplank while a man in a suit stood on the deck. His hands were folded in front of him, and his gaze followed Svetlana as she approached.

"You are Captain Svetlana Tereshchenko?"

"I am. And you are?"

"Alejandro Kavisoli. I come on behalf of my cousin."

Svetlana cursed under her breath but walked through the gauntlet of men that guarded the gangplank. Each of them towered at least a head taller than her, and their arms were thicker than her thighs. "What can I do for you, Mr. Kavisoli?"

"Mayor Kavisoli has informed me that you are responsible for his imprisonment, and that you made him a promise that you would get him freed. He has now been in prison for more than seven Lift cycles. It seems that you have backed out of your promise."

"Whoa, whoa," Svetlana said, waving her hands as she joined Alejandro on deck. "I told him I would *try* to get him released. My contact within the Fleet was unwilling to listen to reason. And now he's not available. I'm still working on it, but I need time."

Alejandro shook his head. "You gave Mayor Kavisoli reason to believe that he would be released *quickly*. But it seems that you have insufficient motivation."

"Are you here to offer me more motivation?"

"We are."

Annette joined Svetlana on deck. Her gaze shot up to the balloons above them, and Svetlana glanced up as well. All of the balloons were at full inflation, and she could feel the thrum of the propellers beneath her feet. She turned to look at the bridge. The light reflected off the glass so that she was unable to see who was on the bridge, but she shook her head, hoping that Jo or Athos would follow her orders. If the ship moved right now, the bravos on the gangplank might not make it on board. But their weight on the gangplank might also slow the ship enough that they could scurry up it and board. It was a risky maneuver, and Svetlana was not ready to execute it.

"Are you planning to elaborate?" Svetlana asked Alejandro.

Alejandro chewed at his lip. "We'll take this one." He gestured at Annette.

"Excuse me?" Annette sputtered.

"I think not," Svetlana said at the same time, interposing herself between Annette and all of Kavisoli's people.

"I'm here to take a hostage, to ensure that you keep up your end of the bargain, Captain Tereshchenko." Two of the bravos from the gangplank came on board the ship.

"You're not taking her. You're not taking any of my crew." Svetlana moved closer to Alejandro. Though all of his rowdies were quite tall, he was just inches taller than Svetlana. She stood toe to toe with him and glared. Her voice remained steady but increased in volume as she continued. "You're going to tell Larson Kavisoli that if he wants me to get him out of Air Fleet custody, he needs to back off and not try to threaten me. I work on my own terms, and he'd best learn that if he thinks he wants to involve me in his nonsense."

To his credit, Alejandro didn't flinch while Svetlana yelled at him. "Oh, I see why he likes you," he whispered, only loud enough for Svetlana to hear.

Svetlana took a quick step back. "Get off my boat. Now."

Alejandro shook his head. "I can't do that. I need something better than your word that you'll do what needs to be done."

Svetlana noticed movement in the distance and flicked her gaze toward it.

Narcissa's calm stride led a unit of Air Fleet troops. Svetlana grimaced. *As if things weren't bad enough.*

Alejandro noticed the change in Svetlana's expression. His shoulders tensed when he spotted the new arrivals. "I see. Your friends are here to arrest me now?"

Svetlana sighed. "No ... maybe, I don't know. They're not my friends."

"So you say." Alejandro's gaze flickered back to Annette. "Fine. No hostage. But Mayor Kavisoli will not be pleased when I tell him that you still have no results."

"I think he'll be a bit more upset about your lack of results, Al. Now, do you think you can take your boys out of here without getting into a row with the Air Fleet?"

Alejandro bristled and turned back to his men. He shouted a few terse orders, and the rowdies filed down the gangplank. He climbed into the carriage, and it began to roll before the door was closed. He shot one last venomous look at Svetlana before tugging on the door. The bravos surrounded the carriage and moved at the same speed.

Svetlana spun toward Annette. "Start the winches. We need to go."

Annette nodded and switched on the machinery that would pull up the gangplank. Svetlana rushed onto the bridge, leaving the door wide open in her wake. Jo stood at the controls. "How about we go now, Captain?"

"I don't want the gangplank banging against the side of the ship all day."

"Really, is that a priority right now?"

Svetlana frowned. The gangplank was replaceable, and the ship's hull was stronger than it. Taking off before it was up would allow them to avoid Narcissa entirely. But before she could give Jo the order to take off, she heard Narcissa.

"Sveta? We need to talk."

Chapter Eighteen

Narcissa's words tugged at Svetlana's memories. "Wait for my signal," she muttered to Jo as she turned back.

Narcissa stood on *The Silent Monsoon*'s deck, Annette watching her from beside the winch mechanism, which was silent now. Narcissa's unit waited at the bottom of the gangplank, save for two of her men who were marching up.

Svetlana glanced at Annette, who retreated a few steps away. She tried to keep a hard edge to her voice. "What do you want?"

"Lieutenant Francis at the front desk said you were just in asking to see Bobby. I thought I'd come by on his behalf."

"That's kind of you. So where is he?"

Narcissa shrugged. "He doesn't keep me apprised of all his comings and goings. I assume he's taking care of Fleet business elsewhere."

"He's got Mayor Kavisoli in custody, and he just jets off?"

"He is the Admiral, Sveta. He goes where he's needed, regardless of local matters."

"It's not a local matter. Mayor Kavisoli should be returned to Rrusadon. If he's as dangerous as you all are letting on, send a unit with him."

"If it has to do with an incident that took place here on Heliopolis, he stays at Headquarters until it's resolved."

Svetlana shook her head. "You're still fixated on Lar ... Mayor Kavisoli being the thief. I think you're wrong. Has anyone looked into Lady de Whittvy like I suggested?"

"No one's found her as of yet."

"I doubt you will, either," Svetlana muttered. "Look, we were just getting ready to leave. Let Bobby know that I'd like to speak with him when he's available."

"I can't let you leave," Narcissa said, biting her lip. "After you were turned away, you went into headquarters anyway, didn't you?"

"What makes you think that?"

"A map is missing from Bobby's office."

"So I'm the immediate suspect?"

"You were spotted, Sveta. Running down the hall, climbing out the window. You're not subtle, and you're known around headquarters."

Svetlana frowned. "You want the map back?" She reached into her jacket, silently repeating the litany of the cities she had seen marked on it. Even if she couldn't recall the random numbers, the names of the starred cities stayed with her. She removed the map and held it out toward Narcissa.

"Captain Svetlana Tereshchenko," Narcissa sighed. "You're under arrest for theft of Air Fleet property." The two men who had followed Narcissa up approached her, and three others began to walk up the gangplank.

"Jo, now would be great!" Svetlana called out. She felt the deck shift beneath her feet, and the gangplank scraped along the edge of the dock.

The three on the gangplank, two women and a man, quickened their pace as the ship began to move away from the dock. They leapt onboard just before the gangplank slammed against the side of the ship. Narcissa and the first two men bent their knees as the ship began to move, edging away from the gap in the bulkhead where the gangplank hung vertically now.

Svetlana drew her pistol and waved it at them. "You're on my ship now. All of you, over there."

The five lower ranking Air Fleet personnel raised their hands and moved where Svetlana directed them. Narcissa stood her ground.

"Sveta," Narcissa pleaded. "Don't make this difficult."

"Difficult? Narci, I'm giving you the map back. I don't want any trouble. I'm just trying to find Bobby."

Narcissa shook her head. "I'm beginning to think he brought me in on this assignment just to keep you off his back."

"Wait, what? Bobby brought you in?"

"Yes, Sveta. You might have noticed that I left this cesspool as soon as we graduated. I've done everything in my power to stay away from Heliopolis. Bobby brought me back here on special assignment." Narcissa grimaced and looked away from Svetlana.

"Special assignment?" Svetlana narrowed her eye.

"It's classified."

"Of course it is." Svetlana stepped closer to Narcissa and brought her pistol up toward Narcissa's face. "Still classified?"

Narcissa looked back at Svetlana, her eyes the only part of her face that betrayed any emotion. Tears hovered just above her lower lashes. "Don't," she whispered. "Don't make me choose between you and the Fleet."

"You chose the Fleet a long time ago, Narci. Don't try to make me believe you'd change that decision now."

"I chose the Fleet because you wouldn't let me drag you out of here. I never stopped caring about you."

"Don't—" Svetlana trailed off. She set her jaw before she looked into Narcissa's eyes. The tears had begun to flow, and part of her wanted nothing more than to wrap her arms around Narcissa and comfort her. But too many secrets tickled at Svetlana's brain, and Narcissa wouldn't help her solve any of them. "Get off my ship," she whispered, her voice husky. She looked away from Narcissa as she tucked the map back into her jacket.

"I ... we're airborne, Captain Tereshchenko," Narcissa replied.

"Then let me show you the way off." She grabbed Narcissa's arm and hauled her to the opening in the bulkhead. Jo had swung over the city, and Svetlana spotted a bike messenger below, pedaling through the lower altitudes above Heliopolis. She pointed at the large basket towed behind the bike, and nudged Narcissa forward. "Leave me alone, Narci. I can't take this right now."

Narcissa looked at Svetlana, the steel returned to her gaze. "Fine." She leapt off the side of the ship before Svetlana could unclench her hand from her sleeve. Narcissa's downward momentum pulled Svetlana off her feet, and she found herself scrambling at the edge of the deck to avoid falling behind Narcissa.

Svetlana lay on her stomach, watching Narcissa's descent, until she saw her former lover land in the basket behind the bike messenger.

When Annette's boots approached, Svetlana rolled to her back and squinted up at her, silhouetted against the bright blue sky.

"Did you just throw Narcissa March off your ship?"

"Technically, she jumped," Svetlana paused, "but I was about to, yes."

Annette extended her hand down to Svetlana. She took it and allowed Annette to pull her to her feet. Keeping Svetlana's hand in hers, Annette pulled Svetlana close. "I'm saying this once. It is a very bad idea to piss off the Fleet."

"I'm aware." Svetlana pulled her hand back out of Annette's grasp and turned to the remainder of Narcissa's people. "Tell Jo to fly as low as we can over Bobby's house. We'll drop these fine folks off over there."

One of the men who had come on board with Narcissa opened his mouth as if to speak, but the other one elbowed him in the stomach. "I'm Lieutenant Gregory, ma'am. We'd be pleased if you'd drop us off at Admiral Beauregard's house."

Svetlana nodded then turned to enter the bridge. Athos hung in the rigging above it. He shook his head when she looked up at him. "Special assignment? Bobby asked for her? What in the abyss is going on, Sveta?"

"I don't know. I aim to get out of here and have a sit down with all of you as soon as we've deposited the rest of Narcissa's leavings." She turned back to the assembled group of Air Fleet personnel. "Any of you care to shed light on what Captain Marsh wasn't telling me?"

"Rear Admiral," Lieutenant Gregory said, his voice soft.

"Rear Admiral?" Svetlana's eye widened as she realized that Narcissa's insignia had changed. On anyone else, it would have been the first thing she noticed, but she had let her emotions distract her from checking Narcissa's rank. "She got a promotion? When?"

"Last week, ma'am. Just before we came out here."

Svetlana shook her head and looked back up at Athos. "And I didn't think to send flowers." Turning back to Lieutenant Gregory, she asked, "I don't suppose you happen to know where the Admiral's gone?"

He shook his head, "No, ma'am, I'm afraid not. As Rear Admiral Marsh said, he is the Admiral. He travels at the whim of the High General."

The mention of the High General made Svetlana wince, but she seized on that information. "Do you know if he's been in contact with the High General recently?"

"I suspect that he has, ma'am. My understanding is that they are in regular communication. Heliopolis is a bit of a—" He hesitated, glancing away from Svetlana before he finished speaking. "—hotbed of trouble."

"Well, at least you didn't call it a cesspool," Svetlana said, smiling.

The Silent Monsoon swooped to the side, and Svetlana grabbed hold of the nearest piece of the ship. Below, she could see the flat roofs of some of the affordable housing in Heliopolis, and she poked her head into the bridge long enough to remind Jo of the color of Bobby's house. Jo nodded, focused on maneuvering the ship in such close quarters.

Athos came down from the rigging, bringing one of the long rope ladders down with him. "Figure even Jo can't land us on a roof."

Svetlana nodded and helped him fasten the top of the ladder to the deck, near the gangplank. The ship slowed as it neared Bobby's house, and Svetlana gestured to the Air Fleet officers. Four of them clambered down the ladder, but she stopped Lieutenant Gregory before he left. "In case my other message gets neglected, please tell Admiral Beauregard that it is of the utmost importance that I speak to him as soon as possible, on neutral ground. Tell him to look for us at Orwall."

Svetlana leaned against the control console on the bridge and looked around at her assembled crew. "Sorry you all had to witness that. I've had it about up to here with people on my boat that I didn't invite. I'll be certain to give my apologies to Rear Admiral March the next time I see her."

"Oh, you mean she didn't fall to the streets?" Jo said. "Pity. She's a grouch."

"She's got issues," Annette said simply.

Svetlana pulled the folded map from Bobby's office back out of her jacket and spread it out in front of her. "This is what I found at headquarters. I'm beginning to suspect that the ghost ship that took Vertiline is at the heart of the matter. This map's got circles where ships like it have been spotted, and these numbers that I can't make sense of near cities where I don't think it's been. Yet."

"It was spotted in Heliopolis?" Jo asked.

"If you had to sneak a ship into Mayor Bartram's yard, how would you want to do it?"

"Out of Aetherwhere!" Jo gasped. "That's where it goes, just in and out of holes or something?"

"Something like that, I'd say. The chains they had on Vertiline must be how they keep the living with them when they slip in and out. Which is why we fell and she didn't. Any rate, the map also has these starred cities and numbers. Annette, do any of these match up with where the Somersets or the Gyrfalcons might live or store their whiskey?"

Annette nodded. "Merrowbarrow has been the home of the Somersets for generations, and I think the Gyrfalcons have houses at all the rest."

"So the Air Fleet is tracking down the rest of the Cranglimmering all of a sudden. Probably because the ghost ships are too. Must have been that they kidnapped Vertiline because she knows where the other casks were located."

"Why is the Air Fleet involved, though?" Jo asked. "They just keep popping up everywhere."

Svetlana shook her head. "No, this is the first time—"

Jo shook her head in response. "No, not the first time. First, there were Air Fleet crawling all over Kavisoli's inauguration. How many ships, half a dozen? What's protocol, one?"

Svetlana and Athos both nodded.

"Then, we've got some piece of tech on the ship that messes with our instruments or something. Now granted, we never learned for certain where that came from, but there aren't a whole lot of people who have the technology to make something that unnoticeable that causes that much havoc. I'd guess Vertiline could, but we hadn't met her at that point. The other folks I'd look to? Air Fleet."

"Okay, maybe," Svetlana said.

"I'm not done yet." Jo held up a third finger. "We get back from Bonebriar, and suddenly Narcissa March is at the same party as you, arresting you and your ... arresting you and Mayor Kavisoli. And taking you to see Bobby. Who then grills you, not on 'oh, how did the ship crash?' but 'oh, where did you end up?'" She paused to take a breath. "Am I the only one seeing all of this?"

Svetlana opened her mouth but closed it again. Though she hadn't put the pieces together quite in the same way, they were beginning to fall into a similar order for her. "Bobby requested Narci for Special Assignment in Heliopolis. Not just anyone, Bobby in particular. If I had to take a guess, he probably requested her to confirm my death. I mean, if all of us were dead, I suppose he and she are the only two other living people who were close to me at one point in my life. But he's kept her here, and he knows that I'm fine. Which means he's got her working on something else."

"Well, what's Narci good at?" Annette asked.

"Plenty of things," Svetlana said. "She's die-hard loyal to the Fleet, because they ... oh, sweet Skyfather, that's it. The Air Fleet saved her when she was a little girl. Her village was under attack by a phantom ship. She was one of maybe a dozen survivors, and most of the others were far older. Aside from us, she's one of the few living eyewitnesses to a ship like that."

"Do you think it's the same ship?" Athos asked. "That seems ... improbable."

"It might not matter if it is or isn't. Athos, remember that lab in the basement of headquarters? The one that all the older cadets always tried to get the first years to sneak into?"

"Yeah," Athos said. "Great place to take dates. Very secluded. Lots of nooks and crannies in the darkness."

"You made it in there?" Svetlana gasped.

Athos winced. "'In there' is a strong term. I made it near there."

"Narci used to be a part of some sort of special program. She's the only cadet I knew while I was at the Academy who ever went in there. But I met a guy a few years back who said he had worked there for a while. He was living on the streets when I met him. A bit on the loony side of things. He said he knew about Aetherwhere." Svetlana paused. "If that was an Aetherwhere lab, and they've been working with Narci for years, getting her to tell them about the ghost ship—"

"And so they brought her in to help them track ghost ships that seem to be popping up in all of the places where the casks are located," Annette said.

"Exactly."

"Will she realize that we've put this together, do you think?" Athos asked.

"She might."

"And now she's going to be mightily pissed at you, Sveta."

"So we don't go back to Heliopolis for a while."

"No, we don't," Athos said. "But we've got friends there. And Lar. You know Narci. She's likely to start rounding them all up to see who might be able to give her a hint to where you're going next. She's going to try to stop us."

Svetlana frowned. Heading back to Heliopolis would be dangerous for her and now for all of her crew, too. But Athos was right. It was also dangerous for Lar and any number of people who had helped the crew of *The Silent Monsoon* recently. She wasn't willing to let her friends suffer on her behalf. "Jo?"

Jo sighed. "Back to Heliopolis after all?"

"'Fraid so."

CHAPTER NINETEEN

SVETLANA AND INDIGO had been searching for Deliah for hours in the portions of Heliopolis she was known to frequent but had turned up no sign of the girl.

"Do you think the ghosts got her?" Indigo asked, barely louder than a whisper, as they turned down another street.

Svetlana reached over and slung an arm around Indigo's thin shoulders, pulling him close. "If anyone could deal with the ghosts, Deliah could." She shook her head. "But no, I don't think the ghosts got her. I think maybe Narci found her."

"I think it was the ghosts."

Svetlana cocked her head to the side. She could have sworn that the words she heard were in Indigo's voice, but the sound came from above her by several feet. As she turned and looked up, a small face with bright green eyes pulled back from a window.

Indigo looked up as well, and the face returned. The child's face was a patchwork of light and dark, and his close-cropped hair showed that the pattern continued across his scalp. One dark hand and one light hand gripped the windowsill, and Svetlana suspected that the boy's entire body was mottled in a similar fashion.

"Who's that?" she asked Indigo quietly.

"Spot." Indigo waved at the boy, beckoning him down to street level.

"Can't," Spot said. "No more stairs."

Svetlana looked at the building. It had seen better days, but it did not look so dilapidated that she would expect it to have lost its staircase. "Shall we go see for ourselves?" she asked Indigo.

Indigo nodded and hurried into the building. Once inside, they saw the truth of the matter. The back half of the building was shattered, including the narrow staircase that had once connected the upper story of the building to the lower. Spot dangled his arms over the bannister that ran along an upstairs hallway. "See?"

"Would you like help getting down?" Svetlana asked.

Spot nodded, bells jingling as he did. A row of fine silver colored bells ran along the inside of one of his sleeves.

"What's with the bells?" she asked Indigo.

"Spot's a sneaker. Someone's punishing him."

Svetlana frowned but made her way to the ruins of the staircase. "Alright, Spot. Get as low as you can, then jump down. I'll catch you."

Spot shook his head. "I think I'll wait for the ship to come back."

"Ship?" Svetlana asked. "What ship?"

"The one that appears from nowhere and disappears to the same place."

Now she understood. "You saw a ghost ship?"

Spot nodded.

"Did you see a ghost ship take Deliah?"

Spot nodded again then shook his head then nodded once more. "The ship came. But the ghosts didn't take Deliah. A lady did."

"A lady on the ghost ship?"

"She's not really on it," Spot said, nodding solemnly. "It's more like a spiderweb."

Though puzzled, Svetlana still felt like she was getting further talking to this urchin than she had with large portions of their investigation so far. "Why did the lady take Deliah?"

Spot shrugged. "Maybe she was lonely."

Svetlana frowned. "What did the lady look like?"

"Pretty," Spot replied.

"What color was her hair?" Svetlana prompted the child.

Spot shrugged again. "I didn't see her. But her voice was pretty. She called Deliah's name, and it sounded like a song."

Svetlana realized then that she had hoped that Spot was going to describe red hair surrounding a pink face. Sighing, she rubbed her hand over her face. "Okay. Did anyone other than you see the ghost ship or perhaps the lady?"

"No. It wasn't here, and then we didn't have a wall or stairs, and then Deliah went on the ship, and then it was gone."

"Wait, she went on it, or the lady took her?"

"Don't know." Spot looked down at the floor. "If you find some pillows for me to jump on, I'll come down."

Svetlana sighed but nodded. Searching around the lower part of the house, she and Indigo found as many mildewed cushions and other soft items as they could. Occasionally, Spot pelted them with a pillow or sheet from above. Once they had collected a sizable pile, the boy bounded over the bannister and landed in the center of the pile.

He rolled out of the pile, eyes aglow and laughing. "I want to do it again!"

Svetlana laughed. "Well, then you'll just have to find another house where a ghost ship comes." She fished in her pocket for a small coin to hand to the boy. "If you see the ship again or if you see Deliah, run to dock 37, and look for *The Silent Monsoon*." She paused, fumbling for a better explanation for a child who might not be literate. "Blue and black balloons, with one red one."

Spot nodded. "Where Indy goes." He giggled. "Indy goes. Indigo."

"Indy, you have the most charming friends," Svetlana muttered under her breath as she hurried him out of the crumbling house.

Svetlana had an easier time navigating Chickie's neighborhood on her second visit, though she had difficulty getting Indigo to keep up with her. He stopped to peek through the bushes in front of every other house. When the sun dipped down past the horizon and the streets lit up with gas lamps, his oohing and aahing echoed through the quiet streets.

"Indy, I don't think the people here will take too kindly to us gawking at their houses. They live in this sort of neighborhood for a reason."

"But their houses are pretty. Why wouldn't they want people to look at them?"

"Alright, they don't want people like us looking at their houses. They only want people with similar houses to look at their houses."

Indigo frowned but nodded. "Ours is nicer."

Svetlana bit back a laugh. "You think so?"

"Of course. Our house can live wherever we want it to. That's the best kind of house."

A wry smile crossed Svetlana's face. She hadn't thought of it that way before, but Indigo had a good point. The crew of *The Silent Monsoon* could wake to a different vista every morning and could watch the sunset from another place each evening. It was nicer than this stagnant neighborhood. "Well, we're nearly there. Let's look at their houses on our way back out, okay?"

Indigo nodded and quickened his pace to match Svetlana's.

No lights shone from Chickie's windows, but Svetlana approached nonetheless. She frowned when she saw that the door was still ajar, and her frown deepened when she noticed that one of the windows on the door had been smashed. "Chickie?" she called out.

From within, footsteps sounded across the floor. Before Svetlana could move away, the door swung open. A small hand grabbed her wrist, and Svetlana grabbed Indigo's wrist in turn, allowing them both to be pulled in.

Once inside, Svetlana released Indigo and touched the fingers still clenching her arm. It was far too small a hand to be Chickie but too large to be that of a child.

The other hand pulled free of Svetlana's grasp. Svetlana peered into the darkness, trying to locate the person who had grabbed her. "Who's there?" she finally asked.

"Give me a moment to light a lamp," a woman's voice hissed.

A small golden light flickered and then grew into a respectable flame. It dimmed as the woman lowered the shade on the lamp then the warm glow illuminated the room.

Svetlana looked at the young woman. She seemed familiar, but Svetlana couldn't quite place her. Even with no distinguishing traits, Svetlana knew that she had seen, and perhaps even spoken to, this woman recently. "I'm afraid you have us at a disadvantage, Miss—"

"Call me Madeline," she said, her voice perfectly cultured. "Or Maddie," she continued, her voice slipping into a lower class accent.

At that, Svetlana recognized her. She was the chambermaid who had helped Athos and Svetlana into Mayor Bartram's house. But even at that realization, Svetlana knew that she had also seen the woman at Chickie's party, gracing their host's arm when Mirage had introduced Svetlana to Chickie. "You are—"

"I'm both. And more. I'm whoever Chickie needs me to be at the moment. And, for the moment, I suppose that means I'm his assistant. How can I help you, Captain Tereshchenko?"

"Well, I'm looking for Chickie."

"Ah. That, I'm afraid, I cannot help you with today. I assure you that he is both safe and sound, but he is not in residence."

"Do you know where I might find him?"

"In this case, he felt it best to get out of the city without telling me his whereabouts. I shall be departing soon myself, and I would advise you to do the same. We have no idea who keeps ransacking this house, but it does not seem wise to linger here for very long."

Svetlana breathed a sigh of relief. "Not here. Alright. Good. If I had to guess who's been breaking in, I'd say it was Air Fleet goons. They may be looking for Chickie at this point."

"Well, they've certainly looked at everything else here," Madeline said with a sigh. "It's going to take so much work to get this place tidied up when we come back."

"Surely, a Lord can afford a team of cleaners," Svetlana said.

"I know," Madeline replied. "It's more the principle of the thing. Honestly, Chickie doesn't keep anything secret here. This place is an open book." Her voice grew louder as she spoke, to the point where Svetlana wondered if she was trying to convince anyone who might be casing the townhouse to give it up.

"Of course," Svetlana replied, keeping her voice soft.
"You are right, though, we should be going. If you do see Chickie, please tell him that I said thank you. And that it would be wise to avoid any sort of entanglement with the Republic, or any of its branches."

Madeline nodded. "Understood. He has, I trust, told you how to find your way back out?"

"He has."

"Best of luck, Captain Tereshchenko."

"Likewise," Svetlana murmured as she led Indigo out of Chickie's townhouse.

Svetlana breathed easier when *The Silent Monsoon* came into view. No carriages or troops surrounded it, and she and Indigo had made their way across the city without being arrested or killed. She had one more stop to make before they could leave, but she wasn't about to take Indigo with her to Air Fleet headquarters, especially not when she was unsure what it would take to get Lar out of Air Fleet custody.

Indigo ran ahead of her up the gangplank but stopped short when he reached the top. Svetlana quickened her pace. Standing just far enough on board to be invisible from the dock, was Alejandro Kavisoli. He glanced from Indigo to Svetlana as she came into his line of sight.

"Captain."

Svetlana's gaze darted around for the remainder of her crew. The bridge was dark and likely empty. From the boards of the deck, she could feel the faint thrum of music. Alejandro had probably boarded without anyone even noticing. She forced a smile. "Mr. Kavisoli. How can I help you this evening?"

"I'm looking for my cousin." Gone was the bluster of that morning. She noticed how young Alejandro looked—he couldn't be more than a few years older than Indigo, and the latter was barely a teenager.

"Sorry, I don't have him," Svetlana said with a shrug. "I was just stopping by to drop off the boy before going to go see about getting him out." She gestured to where Indigo had been standing, but the mechanic was already gone.

Alejandro shook his head. "No, it's too late for that. They've moved him somewhere else." He barked out a short laugh. "First I hoped you had gotten him out and hidden him for his safety. Then I hoped you had information on where they'd moved him to. But it looks like we're both at a loss here, Captain."

Svetlana nodded. "What I can tell you is that there are no other facilities on Heliopolis, that I'm aware of at least, where they might hold him here." She thought for a moment. "But I did suggest to an Air Fleet officer earlier that he should be moved to Rrusadon."

Alejandro shook his head again. "No, I've been in contact with the family there. Unless he's still en route, he's not on Rrusadon either. We've had people watching Air Fleet headquarters all day long, and no one saw him moved. We've got a few people inside as well, and he's not there."

"Did you have anyone watching the docks below headquarters?" Svetlana asked. She wasn't certain how many people knew about the Air Fleet docks' location, but anyone who had flown past Heliopolis could not have failed to see the gleaming ships of the Air Fleet, with their matching sails and balloons.

"Yes, but not as consistently as we'd hoped." He sighed. "Those docks are heavily patrolled."

"That's probably where they took him out." She hesitated as she considered the possibilities. "If you can find out what ship Cap ... I mean, Rear Admiral Narcissa March is commanding, that'd be a good place to start looking for him. Meanwhile, keep in contact with Rrusadon. She ... Rear Admiral March, that is, might just surprise me."

"Alright." Alejandro nodded. "Can I trust that you'll continue to look for him as well?"

Svetlana ran her hand through her hair. Before she could answer, she heard a newspaper crier off in the distance. "Air Fleet deploys to Southern Sea."

Svetlana felt the blood drain from her face, and she gasped for air. Words tumbled out of her. "Oh, sweet Skyfather. Mr. Kavisoli, we need to be going right now."

"Going?" He frowned. "Where?"

She took little heed of what he said and continued trying to make polite goodbyes. "You're welcome to join us if you like, but I don't think we're going to find your cousin at in the Southern Sea. We'll be back to looking for him just as soon as we make sure—" She paused to take a deep breath and compose herself. "Sorry, we have to go now."

Alejandro, raised his hands and opened his mouth, but whatever he saw in Svetlana's panicked expression seemed to make him change his mind. Nodding, he hurried off the ship while Svetlana started the winches to bring in the gangplank. Not caring who was around to hear it at this point, she screamed, "Josephine Dean! Time to fly!"

CHAPTER TWENTY

THE GLOW ON the horizon was apparent when they were still miles from Bonebriar. The night sky around them was dark, and Svetlana was certain it wasn't the sunrise. "Is that—" she muttered.

Athos stirred from the chair he had fallen asleep in, unwilling to leave the bridge as long as Svetlana and Jo insisted on staying there. "It looks like they're burning a funeral pyre." He shifted, trying to find a more comfortable position on the hard wooden seat, and then shot bolt upright. "They're burning the whole damn island?"

Jo nodded stiffly, her knuckles showing white. "At least we've got something to navigate by, if the sensors go weird again."

Svetlana sighed. "We've been over the bridge seven times, Jo. There's no hidden device this time."

"You're still assuming that device was what made the sensors go screwy. I'm taking all the precautions I can." She paused. "I bet that tree squid doesn't like fire much, though."

"Well, at least we've got that going for us. All the same, let's skirt the south side, so we can dock at the city." Svetlana grimaced and amended her orders. "Assuming there's still a city to dock at."

Annette and Indigo joined them on the bridge as *The Silent Monsoon* flew along the length of the island. It looked as though every tree on the island was in flames. Overhead, their designations were shadowed despite the light of the fire, more than a dozen Air Fleet ships rained blasts from their flamethrowers down to the island.

Svetlana spotted a lone ship, hanging in the sky farther west than the rest of the Fleet's ships, and pointed it out to the crew. The line of fire stopped where the ship sprayed liquid onto the jungle below. "I think they're keeping the city from burning."

"The underground parts didn't have much wood anyway," Athos said.

"No, but there was enough on the far side of the island. It's like they're actually protecting the people here."

"Sure, while they destroy their means of sustenance," Jo said. "Captain, there's about zero chance that we can get in there without being spotted."

Svetlana nodded. "If we see any of their ships break off from their attack, then we'll just keep flying. But I think they're going to be far more interested in their burn everything orders than they are in one little ship docking."

"Your damned rose balloon's going to be the death of us, Cap'n," Athos said, shaking his head. He pointed up. "That's the *Himmelgnade*."

Svetlana peered at the ship again, trying to read its designation. Then she widened her focus and took in the whole of the ship. Athos was right. The shape was the stocky design that had been in favor when the *Himmelgnade* was commissioned.

Athos continued. "That means Bobby's here. He's going to spot your rose, and he's going to know it's you. What do you suspect the odds are that he won't send someone after us?"

"He hasn't sent anyone yet. All we need to do is land, get to Vertiline's house, and—" Svetlana sighed. "Trash her map room. She's going to be mad as the abyss at me."

202

Indigo's head whipped around to look out the windows at the back of the bridge. "Gh-ghost," he stammered, eyes going wide.

Svetlana and the rest of the crew turned. Behind them, gaining quickly, were the blue-white sails of a ghost ship. "One thing after another," Svetlana muttered under her breath. She turned back to the crew. "Athos, go below with your gun. Annette, stay up here. Both of you, don't fire unless they do. I'm not sure we can hurt that ship. Indy, see if you can't coax a bit more speed out? Jo, you want me on main or altitude?"

"Altitude."

Svetlana nodded and took up the secondary pilot position. "Anyone who's not flying this boat, keep your eyes on that one. I want to know if it so much as wiggles its course."

"Aye, Cap'n," Athos and Annette both replied.

Svetlana immediately dropped the ship's elevation by more than a hundred feet, and Annette gasped. "Sorry, didn't mean to drop us so fast," Svetlana said.

"Not that, Captain. They just did the exact same. And they're moving alongside. Uh, port side."

Jo swung the wheel to the right, creating a larger gap between the two ships. Annette clutched the brass railing beneath the windows on the bridge as she watched the other ship.

"They've ... they're ..." she stammered.

"Annette, now is not the time to lose your words!"

"You need to see this, Captain."

Svetlana locked the altitude controls in place and looked over at where Annette was standing. Beyond her, on the deck of the ghost ship, she saw two bright spots of color—one orange and pink, and the other golden yellow and green. Both were moving rapidly, and as Svetlana focused on them, she saw that they were waving. "Is that—"

"Vertiline and Deliah, I think so, yes," Annette said.

"Jo, get us closer," Svetlana said.

"Why? So that the ghost crew can board and kidnap us as well?" Jo asked.

"Just do it." Svetlana ran from the bridge to the port bulkhead. The wind whipped past, tangling her hair, but she felt *The Silent Monsoon* shift its path and move closer to the ghost ship.

Soon, Vertiline and Deliah's faces were clear, and Svetlana could see both of their smiles. "We've made some new friends," Vertiline called out.

"You've made friends with the ghosts?"

Vertiline nodded. "Deliah did, really. She is quite charming. She tells me she knows you and your crew."

"That she does." Svetlana sighed. "So now what?"

"Come aboard over here. We can land this ship in the city without being noticed. We need to get to the probability engine before the Fleet does."

Svetlana hesitated, unsure about trusting Vertiline—who had likely stolen the Bartram Cask—but the scientist was right. They couldn't allow the Air Fleet to reach the map. Nodding, she conceded. "Alright. We'll swap. Me for Deliah."

Vertiline looked down at the girl and wrapped her arm around her. "Would you like that, sweetie?"

Deliah nodded, though her eyes were wary. "I can go home?"

Svetlana sighed. "I'm not sure that home will be safe right now, Deliah. But you'll be with Indy and the rest of my crew. It'll be like home for now."

"Okay," Deliah said.

Vertiline nodded. "Ask Jo to slow your ship a bit. It will be much easier if we are not whipping through the air at such a speed."

Svetlana smiled. She stomped twice on the deck, signaling Athos to return to the bridge.

"Slow her down, Jo. I need to go over there."

Jo opened her mouth as if to protest, but when Svetlana shook her head, Jo released the speed throttle, and *The Silent Monsoon* slowed.

Athos shoved the bridge door open. "What's going on?"

"Athos, the ship is yours. I'm going with Vertiline into the city, and Deliah's going to come over here."

"You're going with her?" Athos asked.

"We need to make sure that the Fleet doesn't get to Vertiline's probability engine."

"Right. Be careful. Remember who she might be."

Svetlana nodded. "Trust me, I won't forget. Maybe I can get some answers out of her too."

"So what's the plan for us then?"

"That's the whole plan. Just Vertiline and I are going in. I want you to take the *Monsoon* and get out of here. Lay low for a while. Maybe go back to the village where we found Indy." She shook her head. "It's going to get worse before it gets better, and being outside the reach of the Republic might be a good idea."

Athos shook his head. "No. No way. At least take me with you. Fleet might have troops on the ground, Sveta."

"Which is why two of us is a good number. We'll attract less attention. Vertiline's been here for years. She'll know how to get past prying eyes."

"At the risk of actually agreeing with another member of this crew, Captain," Jo paused, looking at Athos, "he's right. It's a suicide mission."

"If it is, I don't want to take any of the rest of you down with me," Svetlana replied. "Annette, you got anything you want to add?"

The doctor looked at Svetlana for a long moment before she said, "Be careful."

Svetlana did a double take, having expected the most opposition from Annette. "What?"

Annette shrugged. "You're right. It's going to be easier for two of you to sneak. If the Fleet is keeping one part of the island safe, they're not doing it for humanitarian reasons. Much as I'd like to stay and help evacuate the people, I don't know that there's time for that, and we'd only have enough space for a handful of them anyway." Annette looked at Athos and Jo. "I'm going to choose to trust our Captain to do what's needed. And I'm going to go where she sends me."

Svetlana blinked back unexpected tears and hugged Annette tightly. Athos and Jo embraced her in turn. "Keep the kids safe, alright? No letting

Indy blow anything up back home." Svetlana looked at each of her officers. "Take good care of my boat, guys."

All three of them nodded, and Svetlana turned away before they could see the tears spill from her eye. She came back on deck to find Deliah crossing an unconvincing rope bridge that had been rigged up between the two ships. It swayed unpredictably even under Deliah's weight.

"It's not too hard," the girl said after she had leapt down to the deck. "Just don't look down."

Vertiline led Svetlana through a narrow tunnel that extended from the lower docks and wound upward. She had warned Svetlana that the lighting would be poor, so Svetlana had borrowed Indigo's goggles from him. They hung around her neck now, glowing faintly. Wearing them properly made her eyes cross, as she still couldn't see out of her blind eye. At least their light was helping her keep track of Vertiline.

"I realize that now is probably not the time for small talk, but I have to ask," Svetlana said. "Did you steal the Bartram Cask?"

"Oh, that's rather to the point," Vertiline said with a soft chuckle. "But no, I did not have that honor."

"So are you Lady Elinor de Whittvy?"

"That is a name that I have used, yes."

Svetlana frowned. "So you are her, but you didn't take the cask. You know everyone thinks she—you—did, though?"

"Captain, I appreciate your concern in this matter. But I can say, with some certainty, that at the moment, none of this information matters. We are here to prevent the Air Fleet from unlocking the secrets of my probability machine, because I am certain that if they do so, they will find their way to the Last Emperor's Horde and claim the Gem of the Seas as their own. We are in accord that they must be stopped, are we not?"

"We are," Svetlana said with a sigh. "But when this is all said and done, we're going to have a long talk about what's really going on. Fair?"

"Quite. Shall we, then?"

Svetlana nodded, though she remained on edge. Vertiline—or Lady Elinor—still kept some secrets close to her chest. But Svetlana also agreed that now was not the time to question the scientist. She could do little more than be wary.

As they continued through the tunnel, they encountered no one else, though they saw a few of the underground homes from time to time. "Where is everyone?" Svetlana asked.

"They will have moved to the lowest levels of the cavern."

"Won't that cause problems if everything above them collapses?"

"They would be better off under the rubble, with the possibility of digging their way out, than they would be if they fell hundreds of feet. There is not much soft to land on down here."

Svetlana nodded, trying not to look down into the underground city when they passed gaps in the tunnel. They were reaching a dizzying height, and this passageway was not as well maintained as the main path through the city.

Vertiline stopped, and Svetlana noticed a moment before she ran into the other woman, her lilac perfume having grown stronger. The scientist slid a small wooden block aside, and a blast of cool air rushed past them. Svetlana saw the outline of a door surrounding the rectangular aperture through which Vertiline looked.

"There are troops on the ground. We can get out here, but there will be much ground to cover before we reach my home."

"Is there anywhere closer that we could come out?"

Vertiline nodded. "It is a bit of a steep climb." She pointed at an even more narrow path, little more than foot and hand holds farther up. From this angle, it looked like the curve of the wall led into the ceiling of the cave, and a portion of the wall hung over the vast space beneath.

"That's a bit more than a steep climb!"

"I have seen it done, once or twice."

"You've never done it yourself?"

Vertiline cast her gaze downward. "No."

"I may have been able to scurry up something like that ten years ago, but I'm much better at sneaking." As she switched off Indigo's goggles, Svetlana pulled a dark colored bandana from her pocket and handed it to Vertiline. "Tuck that over your blouse, pull your hands into your sleeves, and keep your head down as much as you can."

Vertiline nodded and did as instructed, then opened the door slowly. Svetlana stepped out, grateful to be on level ground again. To the east, the glow of the burning jungle was brighter than the sunrise would have been, though sunrise was still hours off. In the dark of night, the fire gave them plenty of light.

Svetlana spotted one group of Air Fleet personnel, four strong, all walking along the path that Vertiline had pointed out. Holding a hand out until the airmen had gone past, Svetlana then turned to Vertiline. "Which way?"

"Straight on for about 500 or 600 meters. Then you should see the stairs up to the next level."

"You're coming with me, right?"

"Of course, Captain. But I think you should lead the way. You are far more likely than I to spot the patrols."

Svetlana nodded and looked both ways, listening for the clack of boots on the rock-paved path. Hearing none, she beckoned Vertiline forward and ran to the path. Plant life grew close to one side of the path, and Svetlana stayed close to that side, brushing up against overhanging leaves. She tried to keep her eye on the edge of the path, looking for the gap that would indicate the stairs, but did not see it. Vertiline stopped her by grabbing her hand, and tugging her toward the stairs.

After climbing the stairs, Svetlana recognized where they were. The wide alley onto which many of the houses outside of the cavern backed was empty. Svetlana frowned. "You'd think they'd have patrols out here."

Vertiline's gaze was fixed on one of the houses, and she started when Svetlana spoke. "Ah, what? Yes, you would think."

"What's wrong?"

"There are lights on in my house."

Svetlana turned her attention back to where Vertiline was looking. Only one house had lights on inside, and she spotted someone walking past one of the windows, outside the house. Another figure followed, and both stopped near the back door.

"Is there another way in?" Svetlana asked.

Vertiline nodded and led Svetlana to the nearest house. An oversized well dominated the back yard. The aroma of sulphur wafted out of it. Vertiline lifted her skirts and sat on the brick wall surrounding the well then swung her legs over. Svetlana heard a splash then Vertiline's boots struck something wooden. "It will be a tight squeeze at first, but it opens up soon enough." Vertiline walked along the interior edge of the well, slowly decreasing in height.

Svetlana looked into the well, and Vertiline smiled up at her. Though it looked like it was full to the brim, Vertiline had no issues walking down a spiral staircase set into the wall of the well. Svetlana chuckled and followed the scientist down.

After turning in tight circles for long enough to make her dizzy, the path straightened. Still the smell of sulphur hung in the air. "Are we underwater?"

"No. The smell is from the spring beneath this portion of the city. It gave me an excuse to put a well in my neighbor's yard, and give myself another way in and out of my house."

"You have to do this often?"

"More than you might think, Captain." Vertiline pointed to a door ahead. "Fortunately, we installed an automated dumbwaiter at our end."

Svetlana and Vertiline rode up to the surface in silence. When they reached it, Vertiline slid a narrow horizontal panel aside and checked the hallway. "Either Drassilis failed to turn off the probability engine in my absence, or the Air Fleet has found the means to turn it back on."

Svetlana nodded and drew her pistol. "What do we need to do, then?"

"I will see about turning it off. Can you cause a diversion?"

"Oh, I excel at that," Svetlana said, grinning.

The two women exited the dumbwaiter. Svetlana glanced up and down the hallway, and then strode toward the door to the probability engine room, which stood open.

Inside the room, the gas lamps lit the edges of the space, while the crackling purple light of the probability engine gave the center of the room an eerie atmosphere. Scientists wearing Air Fleet insignia surrounded the machine, while a small cluster stood at the end of the room with the map. Most of them held notepads and pens, while a few held measuring tools. Their conversations were a low murmur throughout the room, competing with the hum of the probability engine.

Svetlana smelled cigar smoke before she spotted her former mentor. He leaned against the back wall of the room, well out of the way of the scientists and the machine but watching all of it with a seasoned eye. Svetlana tucked her pistol back into its holster and marched over to him. "Bobby?"

Surprise registered on his face as he looked at her. "Svetlana! What are you doing here?"

"I could ask you the same, Admiral."

He gestured at the probability engine. "For the good of the Republic. This device is a bit of a conundrum, but I'm given to understand that we need it."

"Do they even bother to tell *you* why they give you the orders they do?"

Bobby looked at Svetlana, his gaze calm. "Would it make you feel better if I told you that they do?"

"No, it wouldn't. Because that means that you've known all along. About the cask, about the Gem of the Seas, all of it."

Bobby nodded, his gaze flickering back to the work of the scientists.

"Why didn't you tell me?" she asked.

"Because you're no longer a part of my chain of command, Sveta. Had you stayed with the Air Fleet, you and I would be on the same page, working together. Instead, you left. You are your own chain of command now."

"You could have at least warned me," Svetlana said quietly. "You could have told me to back off from this one."

Bobby laughed. "Yes, I suppose I could have. But I know you. That would only have drawn you deeper in."

Svetlana pressed her lips together, knowing he was right. "Fine. So now what?"

"Just as soon as these gentlemen determine how to remove the data from this machine, we'll move on."

"And when you say move on, you mean you'll pull the *Himmelgnade* out of position and the rest of the island will burn. You are aware that there are thousands of people living here, beneath this city?"

Bobby sighed. "Not according to the Republic, there aren't."

Svetlana felt all of the blood rush from her face. She was nauseated, like a person experiencing Lift for the first time. Finally she stammered, "What?"

"Bonebriar left the Republic. There are no Republican citizens here, aside from my men. Oh, and yourself, I suppose."

Svetlana's head whirled. She'd heard such a position stated by other Air Fleet officers but never from Bobby. Then it dawned on her. "Is that why I was given my orders at Barkovia?"

Bobby turned to look at her, confusion creasing his brow. "Barkovia ... ah." He shrugged. "Similar situation, yes."

Svetlana shook her head. "What happened to the Bobby I looked up to?"

"He's right here," Bobby replied. "Nothing changed about me, Sveta. Only you."

Svetlana looked at the map at the end of the room, fighting back the tears that threatened to spring from her eye. "Bobby, these people have done nothing. They just happen to be citizens of a place that decided to leave the Republic years ago."

"They've been harboring a criminal."

"A criminal?"

"The person responsible for the theft of the Bartram Cask makes her home here."

"She didn't—" Svetlana trailed off. "What if Lady de Whittvy didn't actually take the cask?"

"That particular crime is just one of many of which she stands accused. I take it by your question that you admit that she lives here."

"So they all have to die for it?"

He shrugged. "Some may survive. It happens. The Republic cannot crush all of its enemies in one fell swoop or there'd be no need for the Fleet."

"That's not the Fleet I joined."

"Perhaps not, but it's the way of things now."

Svetlana shook her head. "Bobby, I'm begging you. Put out the fires. Leave this place alone. I don't care if you take the information. Just spare the people."

"I can't do that, Sveta. My orders stand." His voice was steely, the same voice that she had respected for so many years. Now it sounded hard and brittle, not powerful and commanding.

Svetlana took a deep breath. "Then don't expect me to jump to follow your orders when you've got something you need done through my sort of channels. We're through." She let her breath out in a shudder as she stomped out of the probability engine room.

Vertiline stood cloaked in the shadows near the doorway. She grasped both of Svetlana's hands and pulled her away until they had moved far enough that Svetlana could no longer see into the room. "I have reconfigured the probability engine. It will stun everyone in the room." She held up a small device, not unlike the one that they had found on *The Silent Monsoon* and smiled. "I reconfigured one of their own tools to do it."

Svetlana glanced back toward the room. Her first thoughts went to Bobby, and she wanted to run back and warn him to get out. But she shook her head and set her jaw. "Do it."

Vertiline wrapped her fingers around the device, and the humming sound from within the probability engine room increased in volume and rose in pitch. The purple lighting arced through the walls of the room, though it did not reach to where she and Vertiline stood. A series of thumps followed, and the smell of singed hair reached her even at this distance.

Vertiline sighed. "All that work. Gone."

Svetlana spun and faced Vertiline. "What happened to it? Did you just zap all of the information away?"

212

Choking back laughter, Vertiline said, "Oh no, no. I was speaking of the probability device itself. It took me quite some time to perfect it. The information it had gathered is quite safe. But we should leave. That little light show is certain to have drawn some attention."

"Mother?" A feeble voice called out.

Vertiline looked around. "Drassilis? Where are you?"

"Down." His voice slurred before he could say anything more.

Both women ran toward the ramp that led down to the first floor. Below, Drassilis lay on the floor, his torso separated from his lower half.

"Drassilis, what happened?" Vertiline cried.

"I can't feel my wheels, Mother."

Vertiline glanced at Svetlana, her lips drawn tight. "I'm afraid there has been an accident, Drassilis."

"Another?" the automaton asked.

"Yes. I am going to have to put you to sleep for a little while. When you wake up again, you will be right as rain."

"Just like before?"

"Just like." Vertiline lifted Drassilis's filigree mask from his face, and Svetlana caught a glimpse of a young man's face, reddened where the metal of the mask had been pressed to his skin. The metal plates of Drassilis's eyelids were fused with the man's face, and the same fusion appeared behind his ears and at his collar. Vertiline slid her hand around behind his left ear, and Drassilis's eyelids slid down with a faint clink.

Vertiline looked up at Svetlana, who was still on the ramp. "We need to take him with us."

"How much of him?" Svetlana asked.

Vertiline surveyed the wreckage of his body and tugged at one of the bolts on the side of his neck. "I need my tools." She rose just as the entire building began to shake.

Svetlana clutched at the railing on the spiral ramp, but fell and slid down. As Svetlana righted herself, she saw Vertiline crouched over Drassilis's frame, covering his head with the bulk of her body. The building had stopped shaking, but now the back portion of the house opened to the sky and the sea beyond. Nearer, just outside of the rubble of the rear wall, stood Narcissa and her unit.

Narcissa's gaze caught Svetlana's, and the officer shook her head. "I should have known."

"Narci, please. I don't want to fight with you right now. Just let us go."

"I can't do that, Sveta. You know that."

"Yeah." Svetlana sighed and drew her pistol. "Vertiline, get what you need."

"My tools are upstairs."

Svetlana looked at Drassilis. "Do you think I can carry him?"

"Not if you intend to fight your way out of here." Vertiline's voice was flat with exhaustion.

The front door opened behind them, and Svetlana spun to face it. She didn't recognize the officer standing there, but a field of blue uniforms stood behind him.

"We've got you surrounded, Captain Tereshchenko," Narcissa said. "Surrender."

Svetlana looked down at Vertiline and Drassilis.

"If we do, Drassilis won't survive," Vertiline said quietly. "I can bring him back if I do it quickly. It might already be too late."

"I'm sorry," Svetlana said. "This might be our only way out of this." A low whine tugged at the edge of her hearing, and she frowned. She turned back to Narcissa, scanning the sky beyond her.

Five ships hovered in the distance. The blue and black stripes of *The Silent Monsoon*, with the rose balloon bobbing in the center, caught her gaze first. Flanking it, the green and black of *Calypso's Price* and the giant red outer balloon of Chickie's airship brought a smile to her face. Almost dwarfed by Chickie's ship was the ghost ship, shimmering blue-white in the darkness. The fifth ship was one she had never seen before, bearing silvery white balloons and flying alongside the other four.

"Vertiline, go fetch your tools," Svetlana said, smirking as she pointed at the ships behind Narcissa.

Narcissa turned as Vertiline rose from her crouched position. A shot rang out, and Svetlana looked around frantically. She patted her torso but felt no indication that the bullet had hit her. Narcissa spun back around, eyes growing wide as she fixed her gaze on a point to Svetlana's right before she snarled.

Svetlana turned slowly. Vertiline was on her blind side, and by the time her gaze reached the scientist, she was crumpled to the floor, again covering Drassilis's frame with her body. Svetlana could see the bullet hole through the back of Vertiline's jacket.

Facing the officer behind them, Svetlana leveled her pistol. Another shot rang out, and the officer staggered backward. Svetlana's thumb still hovered above the hammer.

Narcissa rushed past Svetlana, her pistol smoking. "Look after your scientist. I'll take care of him."

Svetlana dropped to her knees beside Vertiline. Vertiline's breathing was shallow. Lifting her off of Drassilis, Svetlana leaned her up against the wall.

Vertiline took a ragged breath. "Damn."

Svetlana undid the buttons on Vertiline's jacket and looked at her blouse. No blood had stained it. Svetlana frowned. "Are you hurt?"

"My corset is holding back the blood, I suspect." Vertiline tried to lift her arm, but it flopped back beside her. "There is a film between my corset and my blouse. Can you get it?"

Svetlana's fingers fumbled with the tiny pearl buttons on Vertiline's blouse, and as each came undone, she caught glimpses of a shiny black sheet of film, wrapped around Vertiline's torso.

"Take it," Vertiline said. "It—" She coughed and grew still.

Svetlana extracted the sheet of film and rolled it up. Brushing her hand across Vertiline's face, she closed the scientist's eyes. Then she picked up Drassilis's torso.

"Sveta?" Narcissa called out.

"Am I free to go?" Svetlana asked, her voice husky.

A moment passed, and Narcissa said, "Yes."

Svetlana nodded stiffly and made her way across the demolished back half of Vertiline's house, her gaze on the ships standing watch.

CHAPTER TWENTY-ONE

NO ONE ON *The Silent Monsoon* had managed to get any sleep after they landed at Bonebriar to retrieve Svetlana and Drassilis. Too many comings and goings between the ships had kept everyone awake. The ghost ship had departed soon after Svetlana was back on board her own ship, but *The Silent Monsoon*, *Calypso's Price*, and Chickie's aptly named *Rose Garden* remained docked at the edge of Bonebriar. The final ship, a Kavisoli ship called the *Dove*, was out ensuring that the remaining fires in the jungle were dwindling in the early morning rainstorm. Though Svetlana had not spoken to any of the Air Fleet officers after leaving Vertiline's house, all of their ships had left the area after retrieving their troops on the ground.

Across from Svetlana, Deliah and Chickie pored over the film that Vertiline had hidden in her blouse. Indigo had commandeered the corner nearest to her and was working to get Drassilis' systems restarted.

Svetlana had not seen Annette slip into the mess, but the smell of the cook stove drew her attention. Annette held the pot for tea and had already set out mugs on the counter. Svetlana gave her a warm smile then rose to look at the film.

Chickie shook his head. "It's just like Ellie to put as much as she could on here."

"You knew all along, didn't you," Svetlana asked him.

"But of course, darling. I just didn't realize how deeply involved she was in all of this. I mean, look at this film. We've got the map, we've got blueprints, formulas, and things I can't even identify. It's as though she made about a dozen different films and then processed them all together. We're going to have to figure out each layer separately to get it all straightened out."

Svetlana looked at the notation that Chickie had pointed out when he said "formulas." Her knowledge of chemistry was rudimentary, but what she was looking at looked more like a recipe than a formula. "What if we focus on the formula?"

Deliah nodded. "That's easy stuff." She picked up a piece of paper and started transcribing it.

Svetlana walked over to the counter, where Annette was pouring tea. She picked up a mug and breathed in the smell, tempted to take a sip despite the heat. The scent calmed her but also took the edge off of her encroaching exhaustion.

"Captain, I'm sorry about Vertiline," Annette said, placing her hand atop Svetlana's.

Svetlana nodded. "I don't know what to think about her, truth be told. There was so much more going on with her than she let on. More than anything, I'm angry that I couldn't sort her out. I feel like I can't sort anything out right now."

"Well, I take it we're off Bobby's invitation list for his next party?" Annette asked.

"Mmhmm." Svetlana sighed. "Though I may wind up on Narci's good side again. Assuming she makes it through her court martial."

Annette cocked her head to the side. "I'm sorry, what?"

"She shot the guy who murdered Vertiline. I didn't see that one coming.

Honestly, two shots fired, and neither one at me. What are the odds?"

"You must be losing your touch in your advancing age."

"Well, I'm not ready to settle down quite yet," Svetlana said.

"Speaking of, there've been a few messages sent over from the *Dove*. Lar would like to see you."

"And I'd like to see him," Svetlana muttered. "But I want what Deliah's working on before I go. Besides which, aren't they on fire suppression right now?"

Annette gestured to the window, where the brilliant silver balloons of the Kavisoli ship had just slipped into view.

Svetlana sighed. "Well, at least maybe we'll make a little money off this whole mess." She picked up the sheet of notes that Deliah had made and smiled.

Lar looked up as Svetlana walked into the Captain's office on the *Dove*. His shirt was covered in soot, and a trace of grey hung across his forehead. He looked even more dashing than he had in his formal wear at Chickie's party.

"I'm sorry," she said. "I should have let you clean up before I came over, Mayor."

He shook his head. "Not at all, Captain. My messages asked for you to come over as soon as I returned. It is I who owe you an apology."

"For what?"

"For expecting you to solve all of my problems. You owe me nothing, Captain. You have done nothing but help me, and I've repaid it with insults."

Svetlana smiled. "Well, suffice it to say that if that party happened now, we'd both be hauled in by the Fleet. I don't think I'm on Bobby's good side anymore."

"And is he still on yours?"

Clenching her jaw, she said, "Not even remotely."

Lar nodded, a smile playing across his lips. "Did you know that one of the perks of being mayor of a city-state is that you can appoint people to a small military force? Strictly for the protection of the city-state against non-Republic threats, of course."

"I've heard that's the case. It's how Heliopolis operates their Port Authority."

"Rrusadon will be opening a Port Authority on my return. I'm looking for an admiral."

Svetlana covered her mouth to suppress her gasp but shook her head. "No way. I'm not interested."

"Sveta, think about it," he said. "I can assure you that working for me, you'd still do what you're doing now. You'd just have a bit more authority and standing, without having to be tangled up in Fleet politics."

"You'll forgive me if I'm a little wary of any sort of organized military at the moment."

"Why would you be wary of a military that you would head?"

Svetlana sighed. He had a point, but she wasn't ready to commit to anything. Especially not anything related to Lar—not yet, at least. "May I think on it?"

"Of course. The position will remain open until I've had a response from you."

Svetlana nodded. "How do you ... er, how does the government of Rrusadon feel about exploration?"

"It's not something we've done much of." He shrugged. "Aside from in scientific fields."

Svetlana reached into her coat and produced Deliah's notes. "I've heard that distilling might be among those fields?"

Lar took the paper from her and skimmed it. His eyes widened as he did. "Is this—"

"I can't be certain. But it's from Vertiline—Lady de Whittvy, that is. I believe she's had at least one Cask of Cranglimmering in her possession. Though I do wish she'd bothered to tell me where she put the contents of it."

"If this is the recipe, then who cares about those contents? We can make more."

"Sure, but it won't be ready to drink for a good seventy years or so. I'd like some now."

Lar smiled. "Well, I can at least give you a bottle of our attempts. Call it a signing bonus."

Svetlana arched her eyebrow. "I haven't signed anything yet."

"Sleep on it," Lar said, winking at her. "We have plenty of beds on the *Dove*."

By nightfall, everyone had returned to their respective ships. Svetlana felt much better after resting, even if she had done little sleeping on Lar's ship. She had left Lar with a kiss and a promise that she'd visit him on Rrusadon soon with an answer of some sort.

Svetlana stood behind the wheel, with Jo managing the altitude controls. Athos stood at the windows, waving to someone on Chickie's crew, and Annette was at the door of the bridge, yelling at Deliah to get down from the bulkhead.

As the ship lifted off from Bonebriar's docks, Svetlana chose a swooping path that flew near the wreckage of Vertiline's house. She looked down at it, silently. Then she gave the ship a bit more speed and put the last rays of the setting sun to their backs.

"Heliopolis?" Jo asked.

"Just long enough to drop off Deliah and anyone else who wants to stay. At the very least, I think I ought not linger there too long. Even if I don't take Lar's offer, I'd say Rrusadon's a fine place to make our home port for a while."

"Why on earth would we want to stay in Heliopolis if you don't, Sveta?" Athos asked. "You're the glue. We couldn't run a ship for five minutes without you."

Svetlana smirked, looking at Athos as she did. His expression was serious. It was mirrored on Jo's face. Annette smiled when Svetlana looked at her. "It's true, Captain. We go where you go."

"And we assume you've got a plan for that, one way or the other," Jo said.

"Heliopolis, then Rrusadon. Then we need to figure out how much Vertiline got plugged into her machine before she blew it up." Svetlana took a deep breath. "I want to finish what she started. We'll find the other casks, and then we'll find the Gem of the Seas."

"And then?" Annette asked.

Svetlana turned her gaze to the windows, blue skies clear ahead. "Then we start setting things right."

Acknowledgments

Thanks to Christine and Alisha, who have helped me shepherd this book from "hey, this is cool," to "wow, this is really awesome," and extra thanks to Christine for the cover art. Thanks to Andi, Nate, Morgan, Anne, Amanda C., Joe, Jeremy, Craig, Scratch, Kel, and Caroline, who all gave me ideas that found their way into the book in various places. Though you may not remember the specific ideas you gave, I appreciate all of them. Thanks to Dietrich for answering my science-y questions in a way that didn't make me feel completely ignorant about how things work. Thanks to Amanda R., who read an early draft of the book, and whose kind words made me excited about working on the hard fixes. Thanks to the original crew of *The Silent Monsoon*: Andi, Ariel, Craig, Emerald, Katie, Megan, and Tori, and our fearless "leader," Jeremy. Though your characters aren't here, they helped make Svetlana into the captain she is today ... even if there are no cat-cousins for her to use as a weapon. Thanks to Mom and Dad, who always encouraged me to read and write whatever I was interested in. Though Dad can't read this, I'm sure he'd still debate the science of airships with me if he were here to do so.

And though he's already been mentioned in other places, the most thanks must go to Jeremy, for getting me into the habit of writing, for accepting the many nights when I needed to work on this book, and for being my biggest fan through the whole process. I couldn't have done it without you!

ALSO FROM RAZORGIRL PRESS

NeuTraffic by Andrew Gaines

John Graham, Thought Commuter License 178, has a simple mission: deliver a message. In a near-future, post-revolution Seattle, he and the other underground messengers are the only tenuous threads that keep the fledgling New Cascadian Order from falling back into chaos. Careful, paranoid planning and incredible luck can only take the young Nation-State so far — and now even the Thought Commuter network's secret intelligence can't save them from a devastating air raid.

His route home destroyed, John is forced on an odyssey through the bizarre new environment of his changed city. Seattle is boiling under the threat of renewed chaos, and the new society's structures are threatening to dissolve...but that's the least of John's problems. Because as John journeys through the mental landscape of his past, he's beginning to suspect that society isn't the only thing unravelling. His own sanity might be coming spectacularly undone.

School of Sight **by Alisha A. Knaff**

There is a world not everyone can see: a world of fairies and witches, shapeshifters and vampires. A world that co-exists with everyday life. When a young sibyl gets a first glimpse of that world, reality seems to crumble and everything becomes one big question mark.

The world of the supernatural proves to be deeper and wider than the young sibyl could ever have guessed as the local sybil community is threatened and the young sybil is drawn into a dangerous game between powers too old to be understood. It is more important now than ever to have friends at your back, but in a world this secret, enemies and friends look just alike.

Shifting Borders **by Jessie Kwak**

When a resurrection goes awry in a cold Seattle cemetery, mother-of-three Patricia Ramos-Waites finds herself possessed by the ghost of her sister's dead lover. God forbid her only problem be sharing her body with Dead Marco. Yesterday Patricia's only worries were her teenage son's new deadbeat friends, and putting her kids through college; today she's become the target of a Central American drug-smuggling gang who desperately want to get their hands on the ghost she's hosting.

On top of all this, Patricia is beginning to suspect that either Marco is an exceptionally powerful spirit, or she has ghost-handling abilities that haven't been seen in centuries. Will Patricia be able to stay out of the crosshairs long enough to fix this botched resurrection?

Trace **by Ian M. Smith**

Joanne Shaughnessy needs a job, and bad, which explains why in the course of 24 hours she has joined a shady medical study on the chi of amputees with a questionable physician at its helm, and agreed to buy antiques for an eccentric Chinese woman who seems to think Joanne has a supernatural affinity for it. She might just be taking advantage of two easy marks' open pocketbooks, but when she stumbles into a cache of mysterious letters, she starts to wonder if Ming is right, and if she can actually hear the voices of the dead.

To complicate matters more, she's being followed by a band of monocle wearing tech-heads desperate to harness her mysterious powers into unbelievable technological advancement.

Made in the USA
Columbia, SC
10 May 2019